Go Hard or Go Home

A Car Warriors: Autoduel Chronicles Anthology

Three Ravens Publishing
Chickamauga, GA USA

Welcome to the world of the Car Warriors: Autoduel Chronicles — Tales from the freeways of the future, where the right of way goes to the biggest guns and death sports rule the airwaves. From clandestine highway battles to prime-time arena combat, jump behind the wheel, follow the fast-paced action, and never forget to Drive Offensively!

Car Warriors Autoduel Fiction is licensed by Steve Jackson Games Incorporated and set in the *Car Wars* universe.

Go Hard or Go Home A Car Warriors: Autoduel Chronicles Anthology
Is a collective work of contributing authors and Published by Three Ravens Publishing
threeravenspublishing@gmail.com
P O Box 851, Chickamauga, GA 30707
https://www.threeravenspublishing.com
Copyright © 2024 by Steve Jackson Games

Publishers Note: This is a collective work of fiction. Names, characters, places, and incidents are a product of the author's imagination. Locales and public names are sometimes used for atmospheric purposes. Any resemblance to actual people, living or dead, or to businesses, companies, events, institutions, or locales is completely coincidental.

CHOPPY'S CODA by Larry Dixon
CROSSED FOR GOLD by Monica Valentinelli
DESERT MERENGUE By Benjamin Tyler Smith
FOURTH TIME LUCKY by David W. Hensley
GUN BUNNY BLUES by William Joseph Roberts
UNDER THE HOOD A CAR WARRIORS TALE by Christopher Woods
EXTRA, EXTRA, READ ALL ABOUT IT by Jenny E. Wren
DESERT MOUSE by Casey Moores
THE CONSCRIPT by S.M. Stirling

Ebook ISBN: 978-1-962791-57-1
Trade Paperback ISBN: 978-1-962791-58-8
Audiobook ISBN: 978-1-962791-59-5

Thank you, to all of our backers of the Car Warriors Kickstarter project!

-Jessie D. Foster
-Kevin A Davis
-David Hankins
-Alyssa Casto
-Jeffrey Riggs
-Jorge Markin
-Randal Dilday
-Julian W. Thompson
-Jeff Dodge
-Rich Neves
-Cursed Dragon Ship Publishing
-Stace Johnson
-Val Cassotta
-Jef Farnsworth
-Jeffery Sergent
-Jason Walters
-Mark Wagner
-Keith Unger
-Jonathan Hurley
-Jim Tullis
-Mark Strahm
-Karl J. Smith
-John Pieper
-Dustin "TinyMonster" Rhoades
-Jedikiah Springfield

-Larry Southard
-Jeff Johnson
-James Emil Conason
-Aaron Spriggs
-Scott Long
-Reed Snyder
-K.C. L'Roy
-Tee Stoney
-Todd DeWolfe
-Brian Thacker
-Caleb Pittman
-David A. Jepson
-Tad K
-David Glover
-Ramón Terrell
-Eric Stuyvesant
-Gavin Inglis
-Mark Stallings
-Brooks Moses
-Brian Healy
-KB Carlisle
-Andrew Franklin
-Stephen Dedman
-Rolf Laun
-Wild Card
-Marc Alan Edelheit
-Rob Kamm
-Peter J. Jansen

-Nicholas D Miller
-Danny White
-Jordan C
-Kenta Washington
-Robert Gilson
-Marcus Evenstar
-Sammy
-Kim the Troublemaker
-Jonathan Bowen
-Brian John Skillen
-Jim Davenport
-Monty Rasmussen
-Alex Rath
-Ch. N. Heinzl
-Bart Kemper
-Jim Tetrick
-Jason Lankford
-Glitz & Blam
-Eric Moorefield
-Jerry 'Archer' Schaefer
-Milton Fernandez
-Jim McLaughlin

Table of Contents

Introduction

Apocalypse Light.

That's one way to describe the setting of **Car Wars**. A lot of awful things happened in the runup to the "present day" of this future world – climate change, nuclear exchanges, the Grain Blight – but most people survived. Many nations and institutions made it, though scarred and changed. And American culture just got . . .

Well, you know how we *already* are?

We got *more* that way.

Car Wars is about an ultra-violent world in which video is everywhere and death sports are the daily fare. And the battles don't stay in the arenas . . . your daily drive might be spiced up with machine-gun fire. The world is very light cyberpunk. You can't do much to modify your own body, but you can sure trick out your car!

It's a rough world, but it's not Hell. Nobody except the very rich can enjoy "real" food, thanks to the Grain Blight. But hunger is a thing of the past; algae burgers are, frankly, more nutritious than what we get today. And the ubiquitous video screens show more than autoduels and combat football. Everyone, at least in America, can be connected if they want to be. Education is free, and a lot of people take advantage. Even death has been defeated, or at least fought to a draw. The "Gold Cross" cloning service and its many competitors can play your braintape into a young clone of your body, and . . . you're baa-ack. It's not cheap, but it's affordable if you have a risky job. (The meat-eating elites, of course, plan on living *forever* this way. It's a little early to tell how that will work out.)

Car Wars has now inspired a novel cycle, *Dead Man's Run*, about a cross-country road rally with many, many bullets. And those novels in turn spawned this collection. There are a lot of stories in the world of **Car Wars,** and some of them are short and sweet. I'm already hearing from fans who miss the fiction in the old *Autoduel Quarterly* magazine. It's baa-ack!

In the boardgame, your driver's details aren't important. It's a game, and your *car* is the character. You might spend hours designing the perfect battle buggy. The driver? Give him a name, and you can go.

But that's not how fiction works. Fiction is about people. The cars (tanks, choppers, whatever) are in the background. The stories are about *people* who make human decisions . . . sometimes, let it be said, *very bad* decisions . . . and live out their lives on the cratered roads of Autoduel America.

And I like these stories. We've got some by authors I have respected for years, right beside work by folks I never heard of. Until now. And now, I anticipate seeing more and more from these new voices.

Read and enjoy!
- Steve Jackson

Choppy's Coda
By Larry Dixon

Okay. I'll explain things as I go, because your viewers may not get the meaning of things if I don't. You can shoot B-roll in here for a while before the place gets too busy.

Choppy was Charles Chopin. Like the composer. Chuck got the handle "Choppy" after his finishing move that clinched the Southern Discomfort Autoduel Cup for him. I figure everyone's seen the footage of that one, but just in case, it went like this. Chuck was being outrun on the slope to the checkered. He ran non-lethal, back when you could do that—it got you a budget bump, or bonus points, depending on which sponsor had the top billing. Golden Rule and all that.

Anyway, Chuck couldn't catch the gal—I think it was Debbie Donahue—because of top speed on that last run. She was pulling away. All he had left was a lethal-yield rocket, the "just in case" kind. Single shot. Debbie's rear armor was chewed up and there was wind whistling between hatch panels. Easy kill. We all saw the missile pop up and fire, and nobody breathed. The shot barely missed Debbie, and we thought he blew it, but the camera tracked on the missile, and it hit a light pole. Great eye candy, big explosion. Camera cut back to Debbie at speed, and then for a moment there was just tarmac. That pole hit Debbie's ride like a meat cleaver, right behind the cockpit, and drove armor panels down into the track like cutting-brakes. Halved her speed, borked her handling. We watched

Chuck juke hard to avoid the pole he'd just felled like a tree, then just GLH. Go Like Hell—the term's from a guy named Carroll Shelby back in History. Debbie wound up second over the line by ten car lengths. He'd pulled off a clutch win.

They asked him about it on air, why did you do that? You had her! Why didn't you take the easy kill? Chuck just looked straight into the camera and said, "She has kids, people." Instant hero. The compassionate autoduellist! Marketing gold. The win plus the bonus points for non-lethality gave him the championship, and he got made into a White Hat Hero.

We all just called him "Choppy" after that. The axe-chop was an instant classic and ran on every clip show for years.

Choppy started young in combat robotics, in antweight and on up to heavies. Solid driver. He got a seat in low-CC Gas Sims, which was a feeder series of subcompact-sized combat robots, piloted from a sim chair. Cheap way to see what someone's made of, if you're a recruiter. He did some CrapCan Series stuff and had the time of his life. Those wins staked him for trying Amateur Night with a Republic Xenon, a real beater with mismatched tires. That was a hard ladder to climb, but a pink slips tourney got him a better ride. Eventually he hit the B Street Prepared rankings in that and plinked his way to the podium with the lowest kill count ever. Yeah. Marketing made that a big deal, too. Sold a lotta collectables, like you see there in the display cases. We have a bunch for sale, too.

But you know, we racer types have this saying: 'The older I get, the faster I was.' Chuck's back was broken in a B-Prepared fight in his third year, and after that, he just didn't quite have the goods to go much further. That's autoduelling. You can glue any "human side" you want to it and sell the show, but losin' is losin'. After a couple of years, they slotted him into Brand Ambassador and Celebrity Gameshows. That was where the gold-plated axe came from. Marketing, right? They had him carry a gold-plated fireman's axe at appearances. Seriously, he had to carry *a damn fire axe around* because of his corporate image. He wore it in a back sling, because the suits would dock him if he didn't have it on him in public. *We* didn't mind. We just knew him as a person, not an icon, you know? And the axe, Choppy never once pulled it in a brawl, but one time, and it was in here, right over there by the stage. Big bruiser was whompin' people left and right, and Choppy stepped up and stood ready with the axe. Everyone knew the axe from TV, so the bruiser stopped a second, dropped who he was punching, and said, "You ain't a killer." Choppy said, "I don't have to be. You won't have arms to wave goodbye with, if you don't leave now."

Choppy had the axe back in its sling before the first medics arrived, and by then the bruiser was nowhere to be seen. See, Choppy was like that. He'd help anyone get a fair break, and that bruiser was twice the size of who he was clockin'. Footage of that made the rounds, too. How he came up with a line that good on the spot, I'll never know.

Then he became a Flagger, a Track Marshal. Flaggers relay signals to the duellists in case their onboards are borked, which happened a *lot* back then, especially in the lower ranks where the gear was third or fourth hand. Flaggers were on the business side of the walls in Flag stations—little open bunkers on stilts, like now. Outside of the Pits, we were physically the closest to the competitors, and, yeah, we took stray fire doing the job. But if someone *deliberately* shot at us? Black flag, out of the match, automatically. A lot of flaggers discovered it wasn't for them after just a few events, but if you had the grit and the mindset, it was the best thing ever. We were the first there in a deadly situation, like a car overturned, on fire, stuffed into a barrier—maybe a minute before a track crew could get there, and that minute counted.

Now, back then, flaggers bought their own gear, and were mainly volunteers. Like a lot of autoduellers, Choppy felt a debt to the track marshals like us, and he started doing it himself. We had retired drivers, mechanics, fans—believe me, if you love the sport, no spectator seat can match being *in* the events. Flaggers were like knights back then. Uncorruptible. Most of us were volunteers or started that way. Some series had flag station Chiefs with a salary, and they had to be good enough to justify the money. Volunteers got a lot of stuff comped, but we had a hard code of ethics. No sponsor logos on our gear. No favoritism, no interference. Make the call, wave the flag, save the drivers, keep Control informed. Unless there's a nuke involved, the event goes on.

Well—he found his people. Autoduelling champs are intense, when they aren't just rat-crazy, but we were the people who laughed, told stories, had silly parties and generally loved life. We had the attitude of CrapCan racers—"winning" was never the point, the experience was. If you were a flagger, you were an equal. Nobody competed. Choppy had an exobrace all up his back and legs, kind of a crappy version of these Flexy bionic walkers I've got, and it didn't matter to any of us. We had skinplates, bionics, prosthetics—it was all good, to us. I think he really missed his early days, when people in his life were fun, not a buncha sketchy jerks puppetting him for ratings.

International Rescue Orange and white were the traditional colors for flaggers—except for the Euro leagues, where they always had to do something inexplicably weird, like, Euroduel had peach colored jumpsuits for volunteers, and lavender for Chiefs. Really! Well, Choppy never seemed to feel better than when he got out of his shill clothes and into his orange-and-whites. And let me tell you, when it was time to work corners, Choppy had it tight. He said he had a fan who was connected, but whatever the real story was, fact was that Choppy had a suit of milgrade power armor in glow-orange and reflective white stripes, just like the replica over there, and he carried the gold axe on its back where the ammo hopper would have been. I mean, we had armor, but nothing as cool as that. That was big-leagues stuff.

That suit gave him six times the strength of a regular guy, was shockproof, blast sealed, just wild capabilities. You see new versions in emergency services now, and their origin was miltech, of course. Crazy-expensive, and nowhere approaching cost-effective for infantry, but for fire and rescue, pilot retrieval, or high-risk diving, those suits were the best things ever.

Being around him was good. I was a noob compared to him, but he was never angry about a call. So. We were in a mid-stage flag stand on the PEP—that's Posthumous Estate Processors—Rally. Truth is, they treated us great, Choppy especially. They had this thing, that if their name was on it, it had to be reliable, because being someone you could count on was a big part of their image. The flag stands were early-model SaffBox cubes on a stick, basically, B40 boxes with popouts and two lifts. A Heavy would carry it out, drop it in its cradle on a concrete pylon, then we'd step out on top of it, and cycle the lifts. Heavies then were composite flatbed gondolas under triple honeycombed helium envelopes then—they weren't fast, but they looked great, and could carry fifty tons or more. Just like now, megacorps loved Heavies because they were giant flying billboards. That honeycomb meant they could be shot to hell without going down—bullet goes through, cells seal up behind it.

I came from far north circuits—ice tracks and wilderness mainly, what you call Rally-duelling down here. You know, in case bullets weren't danger enough, add in cliffs and ice. And moose. We used a lot of SaffBox cubes up there. Don't see B20s or B40s around much these days. Probably all got turned into ice fishing cabins. That setup for the PEP Rally was smart—bring in your people and the SaffCube from the air, plunk it out of reach, pick it back up the same day when you were done. Theft wasn't a danger.

We'd racked and secured the flagger tech back at staging. Everything was standardized in the Rally's SaffBoxes, like thirty matching ones, which was weird to get used to after so much time with decades-old surplus radios and scrounged-up junk. Hell, we used flags on wooden sticks, like that set on the wall over there. We wouldn't retire a flag until it had a dozen bullet holes or more. I'd brought coolers and hooked us up, then tested the flag semaphores. Every flag was huge now, and lighted by a G-cell, so instead of waving them by muscle power alone, we had levers with springs on a shared rack. They were weirdly-analog tech.

We had an hour to kill, at least. Our screens showed referee drones making flybys, and a commentator Heavy loped along following the course, probably shooting B-roll. We stepped out onto the platform and waved at 'em, and we made it onto the feeds! Choppy waving with the gold axe probably helped with that. He was used to being on feeds, but for me, that was a big deal. So, since there was spare time, I ran the feed back and threw it on the cube's big screen. Landscape rolled along below the network Heavy, dotted with abandoned ramps and overpasses, blown-out trailer hulks, and burned-out civvie wrecks. Then the camera looked up ahead on the roadway and zoomed in, and there we were on the flag stand. Nice as sixty-nine. Thing was, the Heavy had shots from a different angle than us, and I noticed a discrepancy between what they showed and what we could see. I ran it back again, paused, and showed Choppy what I'd seen.

From the feed, an overpass and ramp about a quarter mile away looked completely filled in, but from the flag stand, there was sunlight coming through evenly just below the bridge and a shadow that didn't match. It wasn't unusual for concrete and other debris to be dumped under an overpass, or for that matter, dwellings built under them. A roof's a roof. But what was unusual was for a dump bridge to not be filled all the way to the top. My TX drone and I were inseparable, and Choppy nodded when I suggested I'd fly it out to get a closer look at this little mystery. I powered it up and linked its feed to Control. He was getting in his power armor early for a system check, because experience had taught us all that finding a problem with your gear doesn't help much if there isn't time left to fix it. Jumping into power armor that doesn't turn on could cost someone their life.

And, I mean, it was Choppy, so yeah, I wanted to impress him with my drone skills, so I took the TX right to the edge of the overpass and lowered down. Funny how that rock-n-rubble looked pretty flat up close. Then my cam caught someone moving. Several someones, unaware of the drone, removed the camo drapes from a BiGMiG semi—BiGMiG was a store chain with a talking MiG-19 mascot—and some civvie vans. It was only then that the drone got a thermal image of' em. They'd been ambient-temperature thanks to the camo drapes. When I swung the TX around, some weenie grunts were bringing the big rig out. I checked my shadows and dropped the TX down so it wouldn't imprint against open sky, and Choppy allowed as how he didn't care for what he was seein'. He called it in to Control and requested an Enforcer head their way at high cruise. Everyone loved "having" to drive at high cruise or intercept speeds.

Enforcers were the same as now in road autoduelling. They were fire platforms, pretty much, with a squad of first responders in heavy armor, and a couple of powerlifter exos. Each Enforcer took on their own personality, turning into marketable characters themselves. "Trixy" was our assigned Enforcer for this leg of the race, stationed forty miles away at a former Highway Patrol base. Twenty wheels, articulated in the middle, big fire suppression tanks, boom arms, huge twin plows at either end, and, oh lord, the guns and missiles. Like her driver, Trixy was a mean pink drag queen of a supertank, and once she got to speed nothing would stop her. By the time Choppy had his helmet on and pressure equalized, Control said that she was on the way. An Enforcer smoking all twenty tires with its lights on caught the attention of a network camdrone, and a couple more joined it, matching its speed from the air.

Choppy rode halfway down on the lift, then jumped the rest of the way. The armor's legs had shock-struts, which made that a kind of jump a breeze, and lengthened a stride by ten feet a step. He humped off in the direction the drone showed us, hi-viz orange and blazing white against the landscape. All he lacked was a disco ball. No, wait. He had the gold axe on his back. Yeah, he was about as far from stealth as he could get without setting off fireworks, and Trixy had that angle covered.

The TX drone showed these weenies were too busy setting up something ugly to pay thought to rocks crunching a quarter mile away. The BiGMiG-logo trailer was opening up. The sides tilted outwards, and the roof retracted towards the cab, rattling like hell. No wonder they didn't hear Choppy.

It was a missile launcher, a good twenty feet long, and it was powering up.

Choppy walked up the overpass and peeked closer, racking his optics. I saw two ruggedized screens on a folding pedestal and a mess of cables through his cameras before he retracted his struts and hunkered down. The weenies had sidearms and SMGs, and the launch control screens showed an arming interface on one side, targeting on the other. It was miltech—around fifteen years old by the look of it, and hardwired—not jammable, not vulnerable against EMPs—not that we had any—it was the kinda kit that couldn't be hacked without a bucket of nanites poured into a cooling vent.

I zoomed in on the screens from a snapshot, and Control, Trixy, and Choppy all got the bad news from me at the same time. From what was on the screen, the target appeared to be the Rally's Special Stage in the Atlanta Autoduel Stadium. That's where a rally is routed into a stadium or an autoduel arena for a close-combat show. Fans loved them. Sponsors loved them more. They'd pull in thousands of people, and these weenies had a twenty-foot missile launcher hidden in a fake commercial trailer, aiming at one.

No bueno, my friends, no bueno. Trixy was hauling ass our way, but wasn't in range for the Big Kid, her high-yield missile with the glossy red lips painted on it. Hell, even the missile had fans. We've got the toys for sale, too.

I landed the TX with a view of the vehicles. Weenies were piling into the vans they'd likely driven there and camped in for days. They left the BiGMiG tractor doors wide open under a camo drape, because it was all disposable at that point. They weren't going to be around when the missile launched—their job was done. What I could see of the screens showed the missile was on onboard targeting and control. It couldn't be stopped now.

Unless you were Choppy.

Choppy had no guns on him—we were flaggers, not combatants. The armor was strong and fast, but also stripped down. No grenades, no arc guns, nothin'. When the last van pulled away in a cloud of dust, Choppy started a dead run, struts extended, to reach the big rig. He told us that the launch clamps were still on, but they'd pop open maybe ten seconds before firing—whenever that was. In the dust cloud from the weenies leaving, neither of us got a clear view of the countdown. Could go off in a minute or a second, we didn't know. Well. Looking back on it, it woulda probably waited a couple of hours to launch, for when the cars would in at the Special Stage and all the cameras were on it.

You've all seen the footage from before my TX was vaporized.

Choppy leapt from the overpass onto the missile, gold axe in both hands, over his head. As the dust cleared, that axe gleamed, chop after chop, as he went to town on the missile's guidance fins. Gashes were left in two of them, and a couple more strokes took off their air rudders too. The next two chops were into the thrust bell gimbal, before he flipped the axe in his hands to use the spike end of the fire ax on the rocket motor itself. Aerozine gushed out onto the ground, giving off boiling clouds of vapor, and I guess that was enough for Choppy to quit that end. He jumped to the front of the launcher and took off the three grid fins he could see near the nose, then put the axe blade hard into the sensor nose. If it was gonna launch, it wouldn't hit its target. It might hit—something. It might spin in circles on the ground. It might explode in the next instant. Choppy was having it his way. He nearly fell off the launcher and grabbed the cab's camo drape to steady himself.

That's when Trixy yelled, "Big Kid is on his way! Get outta there, Chop!" over our com. Choppy's helmet feed showed him glance at the sky, where a bright dot was getting bigger.

Well, I don't know what went through his mind at that moment. His audio was switched off. Maybe he didn't say anything. Maybe he was pretty happy with his life and didn't have any last words. He didn't have any jokes. Silently, he ran back towards the flag stand, and the video feed was a shaky, artifacted mess then cut out completely. The Big Kid was at apogee, maybe twenty seconds to go.

The TX feed—and the TX, obviously—vanished when the Big Kid struck.

We had nothing to say for a second, then Trixy said really softly, "We're showing a direct hit on target." Control replied, "Copy that hit, Trixy. Continue to incident vicinity and clear the course." None of us knew if Choppy was vaporized, or dying in a dead suit, or what. The event had to go on. And me, I got knocked on my ass by the blast wave even inside the flag stand, probably a couple of PSI strong. I swiveled the cams for any sight of the suit while debris rained down on the road, the cube, and probably a mile beyond, from the epicenter a quarter mile away. Rocks thunked off of the SaffBox for minutes afterward and peppered the roadway, and the impact site was just a wall of dust clouds, but there was one thing I could see right away.

The gold axe was embedded in the roadway, blade down. Trixy rolled up, side skirts out plowing rocks-n-rubble, and stopped right in front of it. That's the picture right there, the one you probably already know. Trixy's crew retrieved it, and it made its way to me. The Rally went on, and I made the calls from the 'stand. That's how he would want it. Handle what's now, feel bad later.

Choppy, well, he was never officially found. Neither was the suit. People have a lotta theories about what happened, like, maybe he was buried by debris and is still out there somewhere, maybe he hid in a culvert, maybe a cave, maybe he went dark and lives under another name, maybe, maybe, maybe. The way we tell it here is the way it is: he was one of the good ones. Choppy knew what mattered. Whoever those weenies were, they were nabbed that week. Buncha nobody terrorists, but whoever hired 'em had deep pockets. There isn't much more that isn't redacted.

And me? Well, Choppy and I were close. We still are, because his story lives on in my heart. He left his estate to me, sorted out by PEP, and so a couple of flagger friends and I bought this place. A comfortable little roadhouse, with good food, drinks, live music and that case there, with the gold axe just as it was pulled from the roadway.

And these curtains here, well, it became a tradition that flaggers, drivers, everyone in the sport came by sooner or later, and left a patch in the helmet held by that replica of his orange-and-white power armor. A team patch, a rally patch, crew or flagger or Ref or pilot, they show respect. They bring a patch with a story that's important to them and share them with the memory of old Choppy. I collect'em every night at closing, and I secure the patches onto the curtains behind the stage. Thousands of 'em.

There must be one for every seat in the Atlanta Autoduel Stadium, by now.

16 | P a g e

Crossed for Gold
by Monica Valentinelli

I lie awake staring at the ceiling, mentally tracing the cracks my crappy landlord still hasn't fixed. Shifting onto my side, I pluck my phone off the nightstand and check the time. 4:30 a.m. Frack. Stifling a sneeze, I roll out of bed and throw on a ratty T-shirt and some yoga pants. It's too early to call the hospital and find out if Tessa's blood transfusion got approved, too early to beg Gold Cross to postpone her evaluation, too early to hop on my bike and meet my prospective buyer.

Lifting the bed up, I secure it to the wall, then pull out a mat to work on my stress. Pulling my hands behind me, I stretch my neck and roll my shoulders. My neck crinkles in three or four places, and I feel a pinch just below my shoulder blade. My brain weasels won't let me relax, but I shift to a cross-legged position and do a couple of breathing exercises anyway.

"What if I can't close the deal before Gold Cross evaluates her?" I say aloud. The words stick in my throat like stale crackers. "What if I get the money and they still pull the plug? Or cloning her doesn't work?"

"Sorry, I didn't catch that," my virtual assistant, Zephyr, intones. I keep forgetting that I'm never alone. "Did you need something, Edgerton?"

I am feeling peckish, but I don't want breakfast just yet. Instead, I tell Zephyr what I really want: "I want five grand deposited into my account. Yesterday."

"I'm having trouble understanding your request," Zephyr replies calmly. "Could you rephrase your query?"

Ignoring Zephyr, I inhale deeply and slowly let the air out of my lungs. Zephyr is an amazing piece of tech—but an AI can't conjure cash just because I asked them to. I'm not thinking clearly, and that won't help me right now. Of course, I'm upset. What's happening to Tessa is something I can't fix with the right bolt or screw. Not only did she get into a car accident that claimed her mother's life, she fell into a coma, and her internal bruises wouldn't heal. I don't remember her diagnosis. I just can't accept the fact that my six-year-old niece is dying.

"Not today, dammit." Frustrated, I punch the foam mat and grit my teeth. My brother was skeptical about cloning until Tessa inexplicably dropped another twenty pounds. Then, he begged me to help his frail little girl. The solution? A Gold Cross policy—a body backup drive that was a favorite among autoduelers—to guarantee Tessa's survival through the miracle of cloning. When I visited them in the hospital a few days ago, I remember asking Rex if he understood that five grand wasn't easy for a mechanic like me to scrounge up. I didn't tell him the situation was more hopeless than he realized; there was a chance Gold Cross might refuse to insure a kid that young, too.

"Do whatever it takes," Rex told me, fat tears welling up in his bloodshot eyes. "Rob a bank, fix a race, join a gang for frack's sake. Gold Cross won't evaluate her unless they can confirm I can afford the procedure." His desperation rattled me. I'd never seen Rex cry before. Then, he forced a thin smile. It was the expression of a newly-widowed father convincing himself to be brave for the only family he had left. "I'm sorry to put this on you, Edge. I've got three days to figure something out. And I can't…."

"You don't need to explain," I remember telling him as I got up from my chair. "If you don't hear from me in a day or two…"

"I understand." Rex nodded glumly and collapsed by the side of Tessa's bed. "I know you'll do your best. I just hope it's enough."

Mentally, I conjure the last time I saw my niece in her hospital bed. Beneath the maze of wires and tubes keeping her alive, Tessa's legs were elevated in casts, her tanned skin ashen, her brown hair tangled. I remember wanting to yank every piece of machinery off her body and squish her into a hug—but that was impossible. Gold Cross is the only chance she's got. Shaking my head, I remember gripping the edge of her bed, swearing under my breath.

"Why is Edge so mad, Papa?" I imagined Tessa asking. Of course, hearing her voice again was just a fantasy. She hadn't told a joke or cracked a toothless smile in weeks. Storming out of the room, I left the hospital, hopped on my cycle, and rode to my storage unit-slash-garage. I knew exactly what I had to do. It was time to sacrifice one of my dreams for something far more important: Tessa's life.

To cough up five grand in a day or two, I'd sell my one true love: a vintage Shelby kit car that, when assembled, was worth about 50 grand. Original or not, an ultra-rare 1965 Shelby S/C Cobra CSX Series 6000 was the kind of mid-20th century car many nouveau riche collectors would be proud to own—with or without weapons modifications. Except, kit cars were as common as algae. I needed an immediate buyer for *mine*.

The con I plotted was simple and harmless enough. First, I'd try to pass my replicar off as an original to a naïve buyer. If the oh-so-smart customer realized the Shelby wasn't genuine, we'd haggle for a fair price. Ideally, I'd be able to scrounge up a lot more than five grand and recoup some of my costs, too.

Whipping through traffic, I rode straight from the hospital that day and arrived at the storage park a few blocks from my apartment complex. Punching in the security code, I parked inside my unit, slammed the door shut, and grabbed a lukewarm beer from a cooler. The Shelby was almost finished, but still needed tinkering—even after fifteen years of love, sweat, and fine tuning. After I 3D-printed the remaining aluminum parts, I finished assembly then polished and waxed the striped body. Snapping a few pics of the cherry red-and-white roadster, I posted them to a local collector's group, the kind of yacht-owning clients who didn't autoduel but loved fast cars, claiming the roadster was an original.

Sure, I could've posted that *this* Shelby was just a carefully constructed replica—but that wouldn't lure an interested buyer within hours. I did not like to lie, but I convinced myself my ruse was harmless enough. After all, I skipped the bells and whistles commonly found in chintzy counterfeit versions: mirror-chrome pipes and garish roll bars. Of course, I didn't expect anyone to believe a mechanic could afford an authentic Shelby. I just needed to show *my* car to impress the right car enthusiast and start negotiating. When I wanted to, I could sweet talk just about anyone, even those know-it-all gear heads who'd pull out the AADA Vehicle Guide to try and one up me. Still, I hoped the Shelby'd be an instant sale; over the years, I'd paid far more than five grand for the schematics and parts, after all. Plus, my "sob story"—that my niece was dying—was true.

As soon as I finished in the garage, I rode home, parked out front, and tasked Zephyr with monitoring responses to my listings. Thankfully, I got a bit just hours after I uploaded pics and set up a meet. 9:00 a.m. sharp. 2981 Redtree Avenue. The Hills. Now, all I had to do is transport the Shelby to one of the wealthiest areas in Los Disney just after breakfast today. No pressure. Sure, I'd never driven her before, but that wasn't a problem. Was it?

"Incoming call from Chad Ritter," Zephyr drones. "Do you want to accept? Yes or no."

"Yes?" I don't know Chad very well. He's a friend of an acquaintance I met when I was still autoduelling. The last time I saw Chad was at a bonfire. I remember he's a tall, gangly dude who has a reputation for liking money he doesn't have—as evidenced by his preference for "nothing but good algae." Wait. Does he know about the Shelby and think I'm loaded? Is that why he's calling me at oh-shit-o-clock in the morning?

"Connecting in 3… 2… 1…."

"I want in." Chad's voice sounded gruff. Impatient. "You're gonna need backup."

"Good morning, Chad," I taunt him in a sing-song voice. "Been a while. It's so lovely to hear your–"

"–That Shelby's gonna get boosted, Edge. Heard the chatter," Chad said, interrupting. "Not sure about firepower, though. Word is nobody wants to risk scratching the paint."

I snort. "By who?"

"Deadeyes, Cobras, the Bu Chun De, Maledictus, and Temhota for starters."

"Frack." A knot forms in my stomach, and my heart races. My body taut, I picture my worst fear: a gang steals my Shelby—my one chance to save Tessa—and that's it. Game over. Tessa will be gone. Rex will drown himself in cheap beer. And I'll have nothing left. Still, I wonder if

Chad isn't trying to pull a con of his own. "That's a lot of gangs, Chad. Never heard of the Cobras or the Maledictus before. How'd you hear about–"

"Don't you trust me?" Chad whines like a kicked puppy. "I'm trying to do a friend a favor. For a small fee, of course. I'll even help you plan the route, avoid trouble, and drive you back if you sell it."

"Just… just give me a second to think."

"Tick-tock, Edge. 5:30 now. If you want my help, I'll need to know by six."

"Oh look, somebody's at the door," I lie to him.

"But–" Chad protests.

"I'll call you *right* back," I hiss at him. "Zephyr, end call."

"Ending call," Zephyr confirms.

"DAMMITALL," I yell, pounding my fists on the mat. Wresting back control, I rub my temples and take a deep breath. Okay, Chad is either a) telling me the truth and just wants a cut or b) is trying to con me out of my "original" Shelby. It's one or the other—especially since he doesn't know the Shelby *isn't* real. Unless he's guessed it isn't? Ugh!

Weighing the risks, I check the time. 5:45 a.m. I have three hours to get ready and drive over to the Hills with or without Chad. I wish there's a way to check up on him. Nobody I know will be awake, but that doesn't mean I'm powerless.

"Zephyr, scan criminal records for keyword 'Chad Ritter'. When you've finished with that, dig up public records for the last week. Search keywords 'gang activity'."

"Scanning…."

"Great." Hopping up, I press a button, and my closet doors slide open. I flip through hanger after hanger, passing over the business casual suits that scream "desperate," and linger over a silver-sequined pant suit.

Shaking my head, I pluck out a pair of worn jeans and a fitted black T-shirt. I'd rather look like the mechanic I am than pretend to be the slick saleswoman I'm not, even in bourgeoisie Hills.

"No records for Chad Ritter." After a few minutes, the AI reports back: "Gang activity found. In the past seven days, there were two hundred sixty seven reported crimes. Shall I list them?

"No, that's okay," I mumble. I change quickly and grab an artificially-flavored chocolate-banana algae shake from the fridge. I unscrew the cap, take a sip, and make a face. Oh, the food corps can add all kinds of artificial flavoring to make ocean-sourced algae more palatable, but it's still too salty for me. "What about an increase in gang activity? En route to the Hills?"

"Please clarify search parameters. What would you like me to calculate?"

I frown. How can Zephyr predict a car theft that may or may not happen? Even if I ask the AI to scan for specific keywords, a lot of thieves swap coded messages only their gang members will understand. I don't have the bandwidth to run query after query. Guess I'm left with two options: either hire Chad because there *is* a real threat or don't and risk an attack. I sigh. "Cancel that. Record all incoming and outgoing calls until midnight tonight. Then, return last call."

I hear two rings. Then: "Hello, Edge?"

"Ten percent. Payable within thirty days. That's my offer."

"You've got to be kidding. Why would I waste–?"

"Look, Chad," I say, swallowing my frustration. I want to call him "asshole," but getting his help is more important than a moment's satisfaction. And I am recording this call in lieu of a written contract. That way, if Chad plays dirty, I can play back our conversation and his buy-in. "My niece is dying. I just need to move the Shelby ASAP to raise some cash. Otherwise, I wouldn't be selling her."

"Shit."

"Yes, Chad. Shit. As in: 'this *is* a shitty situation I'm trying like hell to fix.' Nothing's going to get in the way of me helping my niece. Nothing."

"Fine," he says. "Sure there's no wiggle room?"

"Your cut's a firm 10 percent," I tell him. I expect to raise far more than five grand, and having some extra muscle can't hurt. "I won't budge on that cut. My niece is really–"

"–sick. Yeah, yeah. I get it," he drones. Then, a sigh. For a second, it sounds like Chad is hesitating.

"So, Chad," I prompt him. "What do you think?"

"I'm not sure."

Hitting hard, I push for a quick decision: "Time's up, Chad. Do you want to save a dying girl or not?"

"Fine, Edge. Fine. Guess I'm on my way," he replies. Damn, I hope Chad isn't fracking with me. Can't afford another complication. "Where am I meeting you?"

"Confirming we have an agreement. I'm sending you the address now. Be outside the gates at 6:15 a.m. sharp." I cross my fingers and mutter a prayer. I promised Rex I'd get back to him today. "Bring a decent ride."

"Don't worry about my ride. See ya in a few."

"Bye, Chad," I sign off. My hands are trembling, and my eye twitches. Chad "guesses" he's on his way? In what vehicle?

I slam the rest of my shake, shove my phone in my back pocket, and rush to the bathroom to brush my teeth. That gnawing pit in my stomach tells me I should have met Chad somewhere *else*—but where? The clock is ticking, and there's no telling what morning traffic will be like in an hour or two.

Swishing mouthwash, I spit into the sink and glance at my reflection. I don't care what I look like, but I know some buyers will hesitate to fork over cash if I seem "too" desperate. And right now? I'm a hot mess. My eyes are bloodshot, my black hair isn't curled, and my lips are cracked. I spend a minute or two trying to make myself presentable with a little powder, tinted lip balm, and grey eyeshadow. Then, I quickly throw my hair up in a messy bun, grab my boots, and take four flights of stairs to the front entrance.

Breathless, I rush through the glass doors anxious to hop on my bike. I cough. The pungent smell of spilled gasoline fills the air. I pull my T-shirt up over my nose to filter the air and sprint to my parking spot. I barely register what I see: my bike lying on the ground like a dead horse, both tires shredded, gas tank punctured, brake lines cut.

"Who the FRACK punched a hole in my bike?" I hear my demand, but I can't believe *I'm* the one asking the question. I scan for a nearby security camera. The two I spot are fixed on me. The cameras probably captured who damaged my ride, but I do not have time to chat with a cop or move the bike to my garage. Either way, fixing my bike is going to cost me. "Tires I can fix but… FRACK!"

I pull out my phone. "Zephyr, I need a ride. What's the average wait time?"

"Calculating… Nearest service can pick you up in twenty-seven minutes."

"Argh! Chad, you better not be responsible for this." I hunt the parking lot outside my apartment for something

I can ride or drive. It's too risky to hotwire a car—especially before my meet in the Hills. Time to run. "Zephyr, message Chadrick Ritter. Tell him I'm going to be a few minutes late."

For the first time since I've moved to Los Disney, I'm grateful for the clouds strewn across the June sky and the cool fog rolling in from the ocean. Picking up my feet, I sprint toward my garage. A block or two later, I pause to catch my breath at an intersection and spot a garish vehicle: a chrome-trimmed, mossy tow truck with an oversized grill and neon green flames painted on either side. My mouth falls open. The truck is obnoxious and its polished weaponry—a torpedo launcher, flamethrower, and machine gun—are on full display. Even in this part of Los Disneys, that kind of vehicle draws far too much attention. Parking in front of me, I read a sign painted on the back window: "Gator Aid. As seen on TV."

"Edge, hop in!" Chad shouts back over the loud, purring motor. My inner mechanic kicks in trying to guess how big the engine is. Probably a 12-valve, gas-guzzling hog that only gets eight miles to the gallon. If that. "We need to settle up."

I clench my teeth and fan away billowing plumes of exhaust. Of course Chad would be driving an arena truck to show off. "Real" motorheads know the cars, trucks, and bikes that autoduelled in the arena wouldn't last on the streets no matter how well they were waxed. Not when compared to actual drivers in cars with better armor and munitions. "What are you talking about?"

"Your Shelby is gone," he says. Then, he pouts. "You didn't tell me it was a fake."

My temper flares. If my rage had a color, it'd be as bright green and as venomous as Chad's stupid arena truck. I spit out a question: "How do you… Know That?"

Chad shifts his grip but keeps both hands on the steering wheel. At least he's not pulling out a gun. "For starters, the VIN number doesn't start with CSX. I mean, you're smart enough to use aluminum when you printed your replicar's parts, but the fitment's perfectly aligned. That was a tip-off."

I grip my phone so tight my hand hurts. I want to throw it at Chad's thick head, but there are cameras everywhere. Somebody's watching, *always* watching. "Aren't you a genius."

Chad misreads my signal to shut-the-hell-up and continues: "Most collectors won't care about aftermarket head rests—not unless you're asking for several mil. But the silicone cup holders? Dead giveaway."

I swallow my rage, desperation, and pride. Tastes like chlorinated tap water. I glance up at a traffic cam and make sure I'm visible when I hop into the truck. If Chad did destroy my bike, the cops will eventually track him down if I wind up missing or worse.

"Let's settle up then, Chad." I try to force a smile, but all I can manage is a cocky smirk. "What do you want?"

"Money."

"For…" I am genuinely confused. I'll bet a million dollars Chad can't tell the difference between a lug and a spark plug wrench.

"Keeping quiet."

Zephyr interrupts: "Call from Rex."

"Not now, Zephyr."

"Emergency message. Relay override. Message reads: 'Blood transfusion canceled. Gold Cross visit moved up to

Noon. Last chance for Tessa's eval. Any news?' End message. Shall I reply?"

"No!" I spit. Without a bike, my mobility's limited. Without a car, I am a goddamn pedestrian in Los Disneys. It'd take time to call in favors for a ride or figure out public transport. "God, no."

Chad speeds past the next intersection and makes a U-turn. He reeks of gasoline, leather polish, and pine. "So you're telling the truth about your niece. She really is dying."

"You fracked over an innocent six-year-old child, Chad." Then, the truth fell out of my lips. "I should have listened to my gut."

"We can still fix this, Edge."

"How?" I sit up. I'm too pissed to realize that maybe Chad is trying to help after all. "I don't even know what condition she's in. And the meet…"

"There is *no* interested buyer, okay?" Chad says, thumping his hands on the steering wheel. "You've been catfished."

I shake my head. "You played me for a sucker, because *you* thought the Shelby was real."

Chad nods, then corrects her. "*We* played you."

"Who's 'we'?"

It is Chad's turn to frown. "I should never have taken this job. If I'd known a kid was *actually* sick…"

"You must think I'm a shitty person." For some stupid reason I must find out why Chad targeted me. I'm a mechanic, for frack's sake. I don't even autoduel—at least, not anymore.

"What? No!" Chad protests. "It's-it's-it's this new fixer I met. Some older dude calling himself Black Vinyl. He-he-he set this whole thing up. I just…"

"I. Don't. Care!" Lava-hot rage bubbles inside of my chest. I can't keep my anger in any longer. I yell: "Do you really believe I'd lie about my dying niece just to sell a fracking *car*? Maybe you should check your priorities, Chad*rick*. You think a job is worth more than her *life*? Who the frack are you, anyway?"

Chad shakes his head and grips the steering wheel so hard his knuckles turn white.

"Are you going to say anything, Chad? Or are you going to keep driving?"

"When... When do you need the money?"

"Today, Chad. You heard Rex. I need the money before noon."

"I heard. I... No, you shouldn't meet him. I need to make this right."

"Who?" I can tell Chad is wrestling with his conscience. Good.

"Black Vinyl," he says, turning a corner. "He has money. Connections. Five grand is nothing to him, but he won't loan or talk to strangers."

I rub my jaw. Fixers don't typically "hand over" cash because their hearts are generous. Most of 'em want to exchange something of value. "What are you suggesting?"

Chad sighs. "I'm suggesting that I ask Black Vinyl to cut you a fair deal for the Shelby. That way you get your five grand no matter what."

I tilt my head. "My bike's ruined–"

"–Let's get through this mess first. I've got a lead on a couple of arena cars. One of my buddies works on set during the arena battles. You can drive one around until you get a new bike or fix your old ride. Nobody's gonna care. Networks love free advertising so much they pay the cops to ignore drivers."

I let his offer sink in. Maybe Chad's just a greedy idiot who leapt to the wrong conclusion. Finally, I ask: "And my Shelby? Did you break into my garage, too?"

Chad checks his side mirror and passes an early morning commuter. "Didn't have to. Black Vinyl's got greasy fingers in all kinds of places. Storage yard owner gave him easy access. The car's gone. Dunno about the rest of your shit. But the car? Definitely boosted."

My head falls against the headrest with a loud *thunk*. Cops won't care about a stolen kit car—especially one that isn't properly registered and hard to trace. The only other things worth taking from my garage are my 3D printer, which isn't even top-of-the-line, and my stainless-steel set of mechanic's tools.

Squirming in my seat, I check the time. It's almost eight. Does Tessa know her future will be decided today? I'm too angry to break down in tears. I feel like a blue crab fighting the morning tide. No matter how hard I try, the salty water pushes me back, back, back up on the shore. After a minute or two, I say: "Fine, I guess it can't hurt to talk to Black Vinyl. Do you have a plan?"

"No plan. Just the truth," Chad says, rounding another corner.

"I approve," I tell him. "Playing it straight sounds like the way to go."

"Good," he says. Pulling into a parking lot, Chad turns off the car and looks at me. This is the first time I notice his brown eyes remind me of fresh motor oil. "Wait here."

"Yeah, okay," I reply. I'm still furious, but part of me refuses to hate him.

While I'm waiting for Chad, I call the hospital back. Before I can leave a message, Rex picks up the phone. "H-h-hi, Edge," my brother says, his voice cracking. "Bad news."

"What now?"

"Gold Cross… The hospital… It's just too much."

I sense Rex's strength is faltering, so I pretend to be the older, more responsible sibling. "Just tell me what's going on."

"The hospital administrator refuses to keep Tessa on life support."

"What does her doctor say?"

"They're arguing right in front of me. He says Tessa wouldn't be this sick if she hadn't gotten into that car accident."

I frown. "That sounds ominous. Is he implying she got sick in the ER?"

My brother sighs. "I don't know. Everyone's tight-lipped around here, like they're expecting us to sue them for malpractice."

"Rex, it doesn't matter if Tessa got sick in the hospital or not," I gently remind him. "What would change the admin's mind? More blood tests?"

"Nobody will authorize them. Even if Tessa had more tests, we wouldn't get the results before noon," Rex says.

I want to channel my frustration and drive Chad's truck right into the hospital, but I've got fumes in my tank and miles to go yet. "I'll figure something out."

"Sooner or later, Edge, we've got to face reality. We've got to. I can't let her suffer like this, but I can't let her go. They said they'll pull the plug today with or without Gold Cross. I…."

"I know, Rex. Just give me another hour. Okay? If I don't have a solution by then…"

The silence between us hurts my ears. Then: a knock on the window. It's Chad.

"Rex, just give me until noon. Promise?"

"I promise. Just hurry. Please!"

I hang up the phone and peer out of the window. Chad motions for me to get out of his truck.

"What's up, Chad?" I pretend it's just another beautiful day in Los Disneys. "What did he say?"

"He didn't believe me."

"Why am I not surprised?" I snort. "Is that it?"

"No, Edge. He's driving up to meet you."

"Fine," I sigh, gesturing wildly. "It's not like my day can get any worse."

"Can't guarantee that, love," a tall man whispers in my ear. His hot breath on my bare neck sends chills down my spine. I ball my hands into fists. "Turn around. Slowly."

I pivot and come face-to-face with a black clad man wearing sunglasses, a mask, and combat gear. I immediately take a step back. "Chad, please tell me Black Vinyl isn't a cop."

Black Vinyl wags a finger at me. "That's gunner first, security guard second, and former cop third. 'Course I offer the occasional lucrative job for my buddy, Chadrick, here. You know, help him afford the good algae to impress fine dates like yourself."

"You're not a fixer, then?"

"Hardly. Just an opportunist. Like yourself."

"Ooh!" I lunge for Black Vinyl, but Chad steps in front of him. I pause, then sock Chad in the stomach. He groans and steps out of my way.

"Now, now, l'il one. Set aside that righteous rage of yours and let's have a chat."

"Chad?" I feel my cheeks flush. "I don't have time for this."

"Just hear him out."

I spit. "Fine. Thirty seconds."

"So, Edge," Black Vinyl says, clapping his gloved hands. "I hear you're a mechanic."

"That's right."

"And your niece is supposedly sick."

"*Actually* dying," I reply, keeping my answers short. "Twenty seconds."

"Ever duel with a car?"

"Ever steal from a desperate woman before?"

Black Vinyl laughs. "I've done both. Have you?"

I roll my eyes. "I'm a concerned auntie first, unemployed mechanic second, and pissed off cyclist third. I haven't autoduelled in months because my family comes first. I spend more time at Sacred Heart Hospital than I do at home. You got me?"

"So, you *have* driven…aggressively."

"What's your point?" I ask, tapping my foot impatiently.

"Right. Face off against Chadrick, here. You win and I give you five grand with no strings attached. He wins and you still get five grand. Only, I become your puppet master."

"Hey," Chad steps up. "That's not what we agreed."

"Look, Chadrick. I like you. I really, really do. But you fracked up, bro. I've got anxious investors who want to pay me lots of money. You confirmed the Shelby was authentic. It wasn't. You told me her niece wasn't sick. She's dying."

"I thought Edge was telling a sob story! C'mon, Black. You can't be serious."

"Doesn't matter. I am holding you responsible. This is the only way to settle our account. You feel me?"

"Are you canceling my policy, too?"

"What policy," Black Vinyl says. "You have no insurance. You hear me?"

"Asshole!" Chad shouts.

"Three questions," I say, ignoring Chad. I don't know who Black Vinyl is, but I agree with him. Ultimately, this is Chad's fault. I did not have to hurt him, I remind myself, I just have to disable his truck. "What vehicle am I driving, will *I* have an insurance policy, and can we race in an hour?"

Black Vinyl turns his attention back to me. His expression is unreadable beneath his mirrored sunglasses and mask. If circumstances were different, I'd hop in Chad's truck and leave the city. "You'll be driving *my* modified Shelby, you'll have a complimentary Gold Cross policy courtesy of Chadrick here, and you can race in half an hour."

"Contract?"

"Later," he says.

I grit my teeth and stick out my hand. What choice do I have? Chad did say Black Vinyl has money. I'm afraid to ask where he gets his cash from and who his "investors" are. "Deal. Where?"

"In the arena. We'll tape the race to air tonight. You can wear a helmet if you like."

"No, no, no, no, no," Chad whines. "Gator Aid has no speed. She's built to run an obstacle course, not race."

"That's your problem, Chadrick."

"No!" Chad shouts. "I'm not taking your deal. Frack this!"

Chad dashes past Black Vinyl, but his "friend" tries to grab his shoulder. Chad spins out of the way and sprints to his truck. Fumbling with his key fob, he punches a button, hops inside and slams the door. Frozen, I'm not sure what to do. If Chad drives off, will Black Vinyl hold up his end of the bargain? If he doesn't, where does that leave Tessa?

Before I have a chance to think, Black Vinyl pulls out a gun and aims at Chad's tires. I scream and slam my body into the gunner-slash-guard just as he takes a shot. *Crack!* Thankfully, the bullet misses the truck. Chad guns his engine and peels out of the parking lot, leaving ugly tracks behind. The truck inches into morning traffic, but for now he's safe, surrounded by commuters half a block away.

Black Vinyl shakes his head and spins his hands, making the "let's roll" signal. A goon pulls into the parking lot driving my stolen car. "There's the car I want you to drive, love. Sorry she's not finished yet. Short on time and all that."

I channel all my venomous rage and shoot Black Vinyl a dirty look. The goon pulls out a gun and aims it at my chest. "What the frack are you talking about?"

"Drive my Shelby, catch up to Chadrick, and disable his vehicle. That's all."

"That's all?" I check the time. It's ten o'clock, and I haven't even gotten in my car yet. I can still spot Chad, but traffic was unpredictable… I can't autoduel on a crowded street and risk hitting an innocent bystander. Then: a deep sadness threatens to drown me. "It doesn't matter who wins or loses this fight. Tessa will die. Won't she?"

"Listen closely, Miss Edge," Black Vinyl quips. "I am a man of my word. Take out Gator Aid, and I'll make sure the money gets to your family on time."

"And if I refuse?"

"Then you'll find out why I'm 'gunner' first, 'guard' second, and 'former cop' third."

I bite my lip, then nod. Whoever Black Vinyl is, he's not a man who understands the meaning of the word "No". Holding out my trembling hand, I ask: "Keys?"

"In the ignition."

Breathlessly, I sprint to my Shelby and don't waste precious seconds staring at her. I slide into the driver's seat, inspect the control panel, and fail to recognize a couple of switches. Looks like Black Vinyl—or his goons, no doubt—managed to rush install a pair of flaming oil dischargers and God-knows-what-else. Hot oil? Is that my *only* weapon? I search for anything else I can use and pop the glove box. It's full of grenades.

Closing my eyes, I try to convince myself catching up to Chad is the right thing to do. Then, I picture Tessa's sweet, freckled face. I hear her tiny laugh. I feel her thin arms hug me.

"Frack it," I say, cranking the engine. Black Vinyl nods, gives me the thumbs up signal as I roll past him, and waves me off. I pass under a camera and mouth the words "help me"—just in case the police are actively watching that feed.

Back on the road, I inch through morning traffic. A few commuters whistle at my cherry-and-white striped roadster—the Shelby is a beauty, after all—but I don't bother to wave. All I care about is finding an obnoxious tow truck. Unfortunately, Chad is nowhere to be seen. I shift my hip, pull out my phone, and place it on the seat next to me.

"Hey, Zephyr, scan for local chatter. Keywords 'Gator Aid', tow truck, green flames."

My phone blares to life. "Scanning…."

A cyclist whizzes past me, and I try not to think about my damaged bike. Instead, I focus on hunting Chad. He's desperate, panicking, and knows Black Vinyl is dangerous. Where would he go? Would he stick in morning traffic and risk someone catching up to him? Or would he find a new route and stash his garish car? If so, where? "You know what? Scratch that. I have a better idea. Scan for routes with the least amount of traffic."

"Cancelling previous query. Scanning… Route to Newport Beach, Laguna Beach, Shreve Heights and–"

"Zephyr, plot a course for Newport Beach. Fastest route."

"Course plotted."

"Let's catch up to Chad," I whisper. Then, just in case my gut is wrong I say: "Zephyr, resume keyword search."

Instinct tells me Chad isn't sticking around to wait for Black Vinyl. Chad is not the kind of guy who'll carefully plot his next move, stash his car, or ask for help, either. Guess he's panicking and desperate to get as far away from Los Disneys as possible—just like me. No, he's heading to the Pacific Coast Highway. If I'm lucky, I'll face him on a stretch of road under construction with minimal traffic. If I'm not, he'll head for the beach or an island, killing any chance of an autoduel.

Driving during rush hour is challenging with a stick shift and a car designed for high speeds, but not impossible. Half an hour later—almost eleven a.m.—traffic finally thins to a trickle and the fog begins to clear. I take the next exit, shift into a higher gear, and speed up. Five minutes (and a *lot* of prayers) later, I'm almost blinded by sunlight reflecting off the high-polished sheen of chrome trim and glittering, neon green flames.

"Whoo-hoo!" I shout. Shifting again, I drift into an empty lane and pull up alongside Chad's truck. Then, I roll down my window and yell at him.

"Pull over! Chad, it's the only way."

Chad ignores me, slows down, and waits for me to pass. When he's behind me, he fires his flamethrowers. I swerve to dodge jets of fire, and narrowly miss a tour bus. Shifting gears, I speed up to put some distance between us. Once I'm far enough ahead, I cross my fingers and press the button marked "oil," to shoot behind me. Nothing happens. I press it again. Still nothing. What else do I have in my arsenal? Grenades?

Swearing under my breath, I press an unmarked button and hope for the best. I don't see what weapon is deployed, but it has an immediate effect. Chad hits his brakes and his truck skids. No doubt he's trying to avoid whatever I just—

BOOM!

I pull over as fast as I can, fling my door open, and run out into the middle of the road. I watch in horror as an angry pillar of fire erupts in front of me. The flames swirl, engulfing everything in their path, licking the land mines—*Oh frack, no! That's what I dropped?*—strewn across the road.

BOOM!

"Chad! CHAD!" I shout his name over and over again until my throat is raw. Did I kill him? Oh god! I leap off the road, sprint down the shoulder, and fight through billowing clouds of smoke. I hunt for a silhouette, hoping Chad's still alive. I spot the outline of his truck first, swallowed in flames, then a body lying on the ground.

Hopping around the mines, I rush toward Chad. I crawl to his prone body and check for a pulse. It's weak and Chad's unconscious—but he's very much alive. I crane my neck, hoping to find a traffic cam. Sirens scream, brakes screech, and I sigh with relief. Nobody needs to die today. Nobody, I remind myself, except Tess? I fall onto Chad's body and collapse in a puddle of tears.

"Call from unknown number," Zephyr tells me. "Will you accept?"

"Y-y-y-y-yes?" I assume Black Vinyl is confirming his end of the deal.

"Hello, love. Nice job," Black Vinyl says. "You can check with your brother. Tessa will be fine."

"H-h-h-how do you know their names? How'd you know how to find them?"

"You told me which hospital, remember? Sacred Heart? From there I had a lovely little chat with the hospital administrator. She always did like a man in uniform."

I pause, then state the obvious. "So, you *are* a cop."

"I won't tell if you won't. Doesn't matter now, Miss Edgerton. I own you. I own your Shelby, your wreck of a bike, and now *you*."

I close my eyes and sit back on my heels. I can't be *that* screwed. Can I? Remembering I asked Zephyr to record my incoming and outgoing calls earlier today, I allow myself a smirk. Then, I put Black Vinyl on speakerphone, stand up, and head over to the nearest cop. Throwing my hands out, I declare: "Take me in, officer. I am responsible for this terrible accident, but I was roped into autodueling Chadrick Ritter by a man who promised me money to save my niece's life. His name is—"

"Doesn't matter what you confess, Miss Edge. You're still mine. You hear me? You. Are. Mine."

A confused look crosses the officer's features. Then, she asks the one question that holds the power to not only guarantee my freedom and my family's safety, but the return of my car, money for my bike, and damages, too.

"Sarge, is that you?"

Black Vinyl hangs up on me. Stunned, the cop runs off to confer with another officer. Even if I do get arrested, I'm not worried. Not anymore. "Zephyr, call Rex."

"Calling…"

Surrounded by police, fire trucks, and ambulances, I collapse to the ground and stretch my neck and it doesn't crack. For the first time in months, wave after wave of relief washes over me.

"Hello? Edge! You did it! I don't know how, but I got the deposit and Gold Cross approved Tessa's policy. No matter what happens, I don't have to say goodbye to my little girl."

"Glad to hear it, big brother," I say, playing with a piece of gravel.

"Miss?" The cop says, standing over me. "You'll need to come with us."

I nod sagely.

"What did you–"

"Rex, I gotta go."

The officer helps me stand up, zip-ties my wrists, and leads me to a waiting car. I mentally review today's events to prepare for my conversation with the cops. I snort, then start giggling.

"What's so funny?" the cop asks.

"My brother… He…" I say between chuckles. "He told me to do whatever it takes to save Tessa."

"And?"

"That's exactly what I did."

Desert Merengue
By Benjamin Tyler Smith

"These Desperados just won't let up!" Beryl shouted over the roar of the tractor-trailer's engine. Bullets bounced off the hood, gouging the sand-scratched paint.

More rounds struck the bullet-resistant windshield, leaving dents and cracks along the glass. A few penetrated the cab, and her older cousin Red yelped and jerked the wheel. The rig slid to the left along the desert road before he compensated and pulled it straight again. Blood ran down his arm from a hole in the bicep.

Beryl set the roof-mounted turret to sentry mode and grabbed the medical kit. It wouldn't fire unless it detected incoming rounds, a necessity when riding in a convoy. She dug through the kit until she found an auto-tourniquet. "Hold still."

"As if I had a—*choice!*" Red screamed the last as the tourniquet cinched itself tight.

A siren wailed throughout the cab. The gunner's monitor switched to a silhouette of the rig, with the bulk liquid tank they were hauling colored red. The word "LEAK" flashed across the screen.

First, one patch job, Beryl thought as she reached for her toolbox, *and now another.* "You all right here?"

"Never been better," Red said between clenched teeth. "Why? Where're you headed?"

"Outside."

"Are you crazy?"

"We can't lose any more water." They were already down a truck before this trip even started, an electric rig as old as Beryl. While fifteen was young for a human, it was ancient for batteries. Until they could get replacements, it wasn't going anywhere except the boneyard.

As it was, if they lost even a single tank out of their five-truck convoy, they'd be forced to ration their supply to dangerous levels or worse: pay their employer/owner AlgaLife for an emergency delivery. They'd have clean water by the end of the week, sure, but how much more debt would that put Posthole in? The town was already deep in the red over the new algae tank AlgaLife had made them install to increase output.

Beryl stuffed a patch kit into her overalls, then pulled on her goggles and headset. The earpiece was awash in chatter from the rest of the convoy, and she considered muting it, but then Uncle Caleb's calm voice cut through it all: "Mayday, mayday! This is Wagon Train, en route to Posthole from Phoenix. We're under attack by the Desert Desperados! Requesting any and all assistance! We're getting chewed up out here! I repeat—"

Beryl shook her head. She'd rather have been nose-deep in her phone, watching Glitzy Gear or another VDueller stream on Clutch, but here she was instead. *No time like the present.* She took a deep breath, then unlocked the armored door and shoved it open. "Close it once I'm out!"

"Are you crazy?"

Beryl's hands shook as she grabbed the handles on either side of the open door. "You said that already."

"And you never answered!"

"Isn't this answer enough?" With that, she climbed out into the madness, heedless of her cousin's shouts and her hammering heart.

The wind buffeted her as soon as she was outside, tugging at her short hair and her loose-fitting overalls. With the wind came the bitter tang of diesel exhaust and smoke. Someone up ahead had taken engine damage, by the smell of it. She hoped it was one of the Desperados.

Beryl used the handholds mounted to the side of the door to pull herself into the space between the cab and the tanker they were hauling. As she did, she heard the high-pitched whine of dirt bikes. A trio of Desperados zipped past, whooping and firing handguns with wild abandon. One of the bullets shattered the passenger-side mirror. She flinched and ducked. Overhead, the roof turret returned fire with a short burst. She risked a glance out and caught sight of a dirt bike tumbling end over end, its driver nowhere to be seen in all the kicked-up road dust.

A survey of the tank's right side revealed no damage, so Beryl stepped over to the left side. At first, she couldn't make out anything through the haze, but after a moment she saw it: water flowing out of a bullet hole halfway up the sidewall, close to the middle of the tank. *Of course.* Had it been near the top, it wouldn't be so bad, but add gravity to the equation...

Beryl stared at the handholds and footholds that had been welded alongside the tank for just such an occasion, her stomach churning with fear. *No time like the present. No time like the present.* She repeated that thought as she reached for the first handhold.

The rig slid to the right, the sudden movement knocking Beryl off-balance. She flailed her arms and did the only thing she could think of to avoid getting pitched over the side: she jumped for the handhold. Her fingers closed around it as she started to fall, and she slammed against the tank's metal side wall. With a grunt, she held on with only one hand until her boots found the closest foothold.

Beryl pulled herself from one foothold to the next, the movement quelling the rising terror in her heart. Her "No time like the present" mantra was replaced with another: *Move the hand, move the foot. Move the hand, move the foot.* The chaos around her faded away, replaced only with the sensation of hot steel against her fingertips and the road vibrations reverberating through her boots.

She was so focused that she might've clambered past the bullet hole had the leaking water not struck her smack in the torso. She muttered a curse and reached into her overalls for the patch kit. It was a metallic tape that would adhere to just about anything wet or dry and create a seal capable of preventing gas leaks, let alone liquid. She hooked her arms through the handhold to keep from falling and removed the tape's backing. Once the adhesive side was exposed, she slapped it across the hole.

Laughter rose up behind Beryl, startling her to the point she almost fell. With a shriek, she latched onto the handhold with both hands and risked a look over her shoulder.

A dusty red sedan drove alongside her, matching speeds with Red's tractor. Its axial machine gun looked straight ahead, its twin barrels silent for the moment. The gunner's window had been rolled down, and a young punk in dusty overalls and tinted goggles leered at her. "Nice work, baby! Don't you be wastin' none of my water, now!"

A mix of anger and fear warred inside Beryl, and the anger won. "If you dumb lugs hadn't shot in the first place, it wouldn't be getting wasted!"

"Hey, it was an accident, but some good came from it." The Desperado grinned. "We got a nice view out of the deal, didn't we?"

The driver whooped his approval.

"Take your stick shift and shove it up your—Gah!"

The insult died in Beryl's throat as Red once again jerked the rig's steering wheel. She lost her footing and had to hold on for dear life until she could get her boots back onto the rail. The two Desperados cackled at the sight. Pure rage coursed through her, and her vision narrowed until all she saw was the laughing driver. She drew her revolver and started blasting. Both Desperados ducked, but the rounds went wide except for one that bounced off the armored door.

The gunner leaned out to survey the damage. When he looked back up at her, all sense of levity was gone. He drew his own pistol. "This is for scratching Big Mama's paint!"

Machine gun fire raked the top of the sedan. Some of the rounds ricocheted, but others punched through the thin roof armor. Both Desperados screamed as the bullets tore into them. Their vehicle veered off course and slid to a stop in the desert scrub.

Over the cacophony of gunfire and roaring engines came a different kind of rumble: the *whump-whump-whump* of rotors. A singsong voice that somehow sounded familiar piped up from the headset: "Wagon Train below, Wagon Train below! It's death from above calling. Keep your guns earthward, and we'll take care of the rest!"

A shadow fell across Beryl, and she looked up. A brightly painted Falcon helicopter flew directly overhead, its pilot holding the bird steady as stray rounds bounced off its armored fuselage. Two machine gun turrets hung off either side, each manned by a gunner wearing goggles and flak vests over what looked like business suits.

The helicopter continued to pour fire onto the Desperados. A total of six vehicles ended up disabled or burning wrecks before the gang broke contact, stopping long enough to pick up anyone still alive.

Uncle Caleb called for a halt so they could treat the wounded and assess damages. The woman who'd called from the helicopter announced she'd be landing and could also help with the wounded. "We're bound for a mining facility nearby, and they have a hospital. Bring your most critical cases to us, and we'll get them there in a hurry!"

Why did she sound so familiar? Beryl pondered the question as she waited for Red to stop the rig. Once he did, she climbed back into the cab to see how he was doing and found him fussing at his tourniquet. "You know you shouldn't touch it, Red."

"I know, but... Damn, it hurts!"

"You heard the lady on the radio. You're getting a free helicopter ride today, and an all-expense paid trip to the hospital."

"I'm sure it'll get put on the town's tab," Red grumbled.

Beryl's phone chimed, the sound a distinct engine rumble from Clutch, the top autoduel and racing streaming service. Glitzy Gear, one of the most famous VDuellers on the platform, had started an unannounced stream while Beryl was outside. "Bonus IRL Travel Stream!" the video was titled, with an image of Glitzy's avatar riding in a hot air balloon. She was depicted as a beautiful anime girl with long black hair, big blue eyes, and a tight-fitting race suit that looked like it fell out of a steampunk novel with all the golden gears hanging off it in various places.

Curious, Beryl brought up the stream. Glitzy sat on a plush seat in what appeared to be a hotel room, one with a very noisy air conditioning system. She was using her 3D avatar today, something she typically only did when putting on virtual concerts or when she visited tournaments or conventions.

"—we really let 'em have it, didn't we, chat?" Glitzy's avatar gave a wicked grin, her eyes narrowing to slits. "Those road bandits didn't know who they were messing with!"

The video feed changed from her to an aerial view taken by a drone or a helicopter? The road below was in an open desert, and the vehicles on the road were eerily similar to the Posthole convoy.

"Wait, that's us!"

The Falcon landed several minutes later, and three people got out. The two gunners Beryl had seen flanked a woman in a business jacket and knee-length skirt. Her diminutive height put her in stark contrast to the men on either side of her, but what really made her stand out was the tinted racing helmet she wore.

Beryl stood in the back of a small crowd of convoy members, next to a pale-faced Red and an even paler Joshua, his chest and neck covered in blood-soaked bandages. Red kept to his feet, but Joshua was lying on top of a blanket, his eyes shielded from the sun by another blanket Beryl held above him.

Uncle Caleb stood in the lead, his back straight as an arrow, a grim expression on his heavily lined face. He wasn't a day older than forty-five, but they'd all been hard years, and the desert sun was unforgiving.

"Hello, Wagon Train!" the woman said, her voice coming through crystal clear despite the helmet's presence. That same voice was picked up by Beryl's phone, where Glitzy's stream was ongoing. A glance at the screen confirmed it: despite the video feed from a drone camera showing the real-life surroundings they stood in, the figure on the screen emulating the woman's movements were all done by the 3D avatar. "We're here to assist however we can."

"We're ready to accept that assistance, Miss." Uncle Caleb held out his hand, and she shook it. "Not that we have much choice."

Uncle Caleb and one of the gunners escorted Red and Joshua back to the helicopter, while Glitzy and the second gunner waited with Beryl and the others. Beryl fidgeted, unsure of what to do. Her virtual hero was here, in the flesh! And she'd saved their lives! It didn't get much cooler than that.

Glitzy turned her way. "I didn't expect to see someone so young working a convoy!" She looked over her shoulder at Red's retreating back. "And there are two of you! Is it normal for kids to do this sort of thing?"

That took Beryl aback. "I'm fifteen. By the region's standards, I'm only a few months from adulthood." Life expectancy in the more rural towns and villages was quite low.

"Are you a driver, or a gunner?"

"Mechanic, mostly, but gunner by necessity." Beryl pointed at Red. "That's my driver."

"So, you're down a gunner and a driver, then? Matthew, a private word?"

The bodyguard pressed his hand to his earpiece and nodded along. "It's risky, ma'am."

Glitzy looked back at Beryl. "These bandits… What are they called?"

"The Desert Desperados."

"Will they be back?"

Beryl hoped not, but hope didn't always go that far in the wastes. "Most likely."

She conferred quietly with Matthew again, her words going straight into his earpiece. Matthew nodded one last time, then jogged away to join his partner and Uncle Caleb. Glitzy watched him go for a moment, then she turned back to Beryl. "Now that *that* is settled, let's go."

Beryl blinked. "Go where?"

"Car shopping."

Twenty minutes later, Beryl sat in the gunner's seat of a yellow compact. A single round had punched through the door armor, killed the driver, and wounded the gunner. Glitzy was strapped into the thoroughly-cleaned driver's seat, humming to herself as she ran her fingers along the instrument panel and the steering wheel. She'd mounted a wide tablet to the dashboard, and it showed the chat feed of her stream alongside her 3D avatar. "I haven't seen a Mako in this kind of condition before, chat. Did you see that machine gun turret up top? And those rocket pods?

Those are recent offerings from the factory, and they're *expensive!*"

The anime girl avatar mimicked every action that Glitzy took, even the facial expressions hidden behind the helmet. "You look like you're enjoying yourself," Beryl said.

"I love anything with wheels. That diesel Long Hauler your uncle drives? Is that a '35? There's a distinct curve to the front fenders that—Oh, shut up, chat!"

On-screen, the chat had blown up with multiple users bemoaning yet another 'car gusher moment' from Glitzy. Beryl tried to hide a smile behind her hand. If she'd been part of the audience today, she might've made the same complaint.

Glitzy glanced her way. "You, too?"

Had it been that obvious? "Maybe I need a helmet, too," she muttered.

"Oh, that reminds me. Hold on, chat. Girls need to do a little bit of talking." Glitzy punched a couple of commands into the tablet, and her avatar went into an idle animation. The red light in the top right corner switched off. Glitzy then removed her helmet, revealing pale skin and almond-shaped eyes almost as dark as her long black hair. "Ah, so much better."

Beryl's jaw dropped. *This* was the real Glitzy Gears? She'd expected a homely girl, or possibly a man with a voice changer, but this young lady was gorgeous. And not much older than Beryl. What a difference upbringing and circumstances made. By contrast, Beryl felt every bit as awkward as her ill-fitting overalls.

Glitzy looked at her. "You said your name was Beryl, right? My real name's Garnet." She smiled. "I'd appreciate it if you kept that to yourself. One gemstone to another."

"Contact, contact, contact!" Uncle Caleb's deadpan voice cut through the frantic radio chatter. "Watch your sectors! Don't shoot across each other."

Beryl used the gunner's controls to pan the Mako's turret around until it was aimed behind them, her heart beating like a hummingbird's wings. The Desperados had laid an ambush with their vehicles camouflaged beneath desert-patterned tarps. They'd also positioned themselves with the late afternoon sun at their backs; no one had seen anything until the shooting started. Now they were all around, zipping up and down the road, firing machine guns and lasers at the convoy in an attempt to disable the rigs without damaging the water tanks.

"Jet here! Could use some help in the rear! We're running low on ammo!"

Garnet took the Mako off-road and circled around toward the rear of the convoy. No matter how much the rocky soil caused the compact to shake and bounce, the turret's camera feed remained steady. Beryl lined the crosshair up on an enemy buggy, engaged the target lock, and squeezed the trigger. A stream of bullets shot after the vehicle. Most of the rounds impacted, sending sparks and smoke into the air.

The buggy bobbed and weaved in an attempt to shake her, but her targeting computer followed it without fail. She fired another long burst, and the vehicle's engine caught fire.

Garnet's hands gripped the wheel so tightly that her knuckles were white. She brought the vehicle around in another wide circle until they were behind the convoy, but still off-road. Beryl used this opportunity to shoot at several Desperado vehicles they'd managed to get behind.

Jet's truck opened up on the vehicles, and the Desperados scattered. Several horns blared, and the bandits broke off their pursuit, their whoops and shouts caught by the microphones mounted to the Mako's cameras.

Uncle Caleb called for a sound-off. Beryl went first. "Wagon Leader, this is Scout. We're good to go."

"Wagon Leader, this is Bodyguard," Matthew said. "Good to go."

"Bodyguard?" Garnet rolled her eyes, the motion caught and repeated in exaggerated fashion by her Glitzy avatar. "So unoriginal."

"How often do you do this?" Beryl asked.

"Complain about my escorts' lack of creativity?"

"No. This." Beryl waved a hand around her. "All this."

"On my profile you can see how many hours I've sunk into a particular vehicle or mission type. I've done a fair number of convoy escorts, and I think I've got around three hundred hours logged into this vehicle. Chat, correct me if I'm wrong."

Beryl had to let that sink in a moment. "Wait, are you saying all your experience is from a *simulator*?"

"Well, yeah. VDueller, remember?"

"How are you not scared?" It was all Beryl could do to keep her breath steady.

"Oh, I'm scared." Garnet held up her right hand, slender fingers trembling. "See?"

On the tablet screen, the chat became flooded with calls for the heart monitor to be brought on. Garnet noticed and laughed. "No, no, no, chat. We've got enough going on right now, don't you think?

"Think of this as a stage performance, Beryl," she continued. "A play, or even a dance. I've done many of those, from simple merengues to intricate waltzes. And while the stakes on stage are a bit less life-and-death than they are now, the fear is no less real in the moment."

Everyone else gave the all-clear, although Jet's truck in the rear was running low on ammo. Matthew offered to change positions with him, and after a few moments Jet was in the middle of the rolling pack. "I'm surprised he's willing to lose sight of you like that," Beryl said.

"It's a calculated risk. We're guarding the front of the convoy under the watchful gaze of your uncle, but the rear needs protecting, too. Matthew and Jeremy are the most experienced here by far, with your uncle a very close second. Did you know he used to run a road repair crew out of Vegas?"

"Where'd you learn that?"

Garnet tapped her earpiece. "Matthew's been talking with him and feeding me any pertinent information. With him watching our backs, we can focus on the fight in front."

Beryl shook her head. "We've barely met, and already you know more about my family than I do."

"Information gathering's one of my specialties! It's one of the things I do for my father's company." Garnet tapped her phone screen. "That said, I've got nothin' on some of my chat. They're real internet sleuths."

'Sloot!' one person wrote in chat, and then a steady stream of 'lol sloots' and 'Internet sloots, unite!' rolled in.

"You know what I said, chat!" Garnet's avatar reddened. "I said sleuth! Slllllooooooo-tha! These people, man."

Beryl smiled, but it faded. Garnet hadn't mentioned her company's name, or even her own last name. What did they do?

"And speaking of people," Garnet went on, "these Desperados are really starting to grind my gears." She puffed her cheeks out, and her avatar did the same in an exaggerated pout. "They're like an ex-boyfriend who just won't take the hint that it's over."

"Then we need to stop hinting and start hitting." Beryl tapped her phone screen, her finger resting on a landmark on the map. "If we can reach Demon Arch Rock, we should be able to shake them."

"Ooh, spooky! Right, chat?"

Beryl's cheeks flushed. *Does she always need to remind me we're live in front of thousands of people?* "It's not as spooky as it sounds. It's the name of a desalinization plant AlgaLife owns. The rock that the name comes from isn't even there anymore. Knocked over during construction like it didn't even matter."

"Isn't that where they distill salt water into something drinkable? How close is it to your town?"

"It's a few hours away. We sometimes pass by it, depending on the route we take to Phoenix."

Garnet quirked an eyebrow, and her avatar made a show of looking thoughtful, eyes distant and fingers stroking her chin. "Why not go there to purchase your water? It has to be safer than driving all the way to Phoenix."

"It's too expensive. We can purchase twice the amount of water in Phoenix as we can there."

"And is this the same company you sell your algae to?"

"One and the same." Beryl sighed. It used to make her mad, too, but over time she'd become as jaded and resigned as the rest of the town.

Chat lit up with a slew of comments, most expressing shock and moral outrage. A few defended the company's actions, while even fewer questioned whether or not Beryl was telling the truth. *That* annoyed Beryl, but that's how any kind of online discussion went, even with a friendly audience. Some people just knew it all, and they loved to show that to the world.

"I see." Garnet frowned. On-screen, Glitzy's face darkened, and her eyes flashed with menace. "Shouldn't they offer you a discount of some sort?"

"If they weren't greedy pigs, sure."

Garnet looked surprised, then she giggled. "You've had that prepared for a while!"

Beryl's cheeks grew hot. "Don't laugh!"

"I'm sorry! It's just... there wasn't any hesitation at all!"

"Why would I hesitate? It's the truth! The people running the company are worse than pigs fighting over trough scraps."

Chat lit up again, this time with people cheering Beryl's savage tongue. A message tone pinged. "CountDuckington, thank you for the DollaHolla!" Garnet said. He says, 'Woah, Beryl be rollin' in it if she has pigs! How rich is she?'"

Other messages streamed in, from '$$$' to pig face emojis to a slew of marriage proposals from men looking for 'the bacon life with a sugar momma.' Now it was Beryl's turn to giggle. "Lord, I wish. I'm sorry to disappoint the chat, but there hasn't been a pig in Posthole since I've been born. Grandpa raised them when he was my age, and he wouldn't *shut up* about the taste of real bacon." She leaned back in her seat and closed her eyes. "He could describe it so well that it was like I was eating it alongside him. I'd always hoped I could earn enough to get him some of the real thing, but..."

A wave of sadness struck her, and she left the thought unfinished.

"I'm sorry, Beryl," Garnet said. "I didn't mean to bring up bad memories."

Beryl wiped at her eyes. "They weren't bad at all. I... haven't thought of Grandpa in a long time. I miss him, but you have to keep moving forward, you know?"

"I miss my grandfather, too." Garnet smiled, and her avatar blushed. "A self-made man who built his own company, but he still had time for his family. A rare thing."

Beryl thought about how much time her father spent slaving away at the algae farm. "It's rare for the blue-collar man, too."

"I have no doubt of that. So, tell me, what was your grandpa like? What did he do once he stopped raising pigs?"

"Are you sure this isn't gonna bore chat?"

"No! And even if it does, it won't bore me." When she smiled, her avatar looked positively evil. "Sorry, chat. Sometimes you just have to indulge me, right?"

The chat messages were a mix of 'Grandpa story time!' to 'Uh oh, Glitzy's history obsession!' to a rolling argument about the best brand of algae bacon on the market. "Are you sure?"

"It'll help pass the time," Garnet assured her. "It's not like anything else is going on right now. With luck, we'll be swapping grandpa stories all the way to your home."

A bunch of 'Don't say that!' and 'Jinx!' messages flooded the chat.

"What's wrong, chat? Don't worry so much. It'll be fine."

Tracer fire and laser beams lit up the moonless night, nearly all of the rounds inbound. Enemy vehicles swarmed the roadway up ahead, the rumble of their engines combining into an all-encompassing roar. The only thing louder were the sounds of bullets chewing up the pavement and glancing off the Mako's rounded armor.

Garnet maintained a light touch on the steering wheel, gliding to the left and right to dodge bursts of enemy gunfire. "Looks like the Desperados had the same idea as you, Beryl!"

The convoy had reached the outskirts of the Demon Arch Rock desalinization plant when all hell broke loose. One minute they were passing through a field full of water tanks waiting to be processed, and the next they were under heavy fire from up ahead. The Desperados had somehow gotten ahead of them and were now between the convoy and the well-lit fortress that comprised the facility's main compound.

It should've been too dark for Beryl to see, but the cameras on the Mako had built-in night vision and infrared. And last gen, by the looks of it, stuff that only just hit the general marketplace. Raiding convoys for their water and ore must've been a very lucrative business if the Desperados could afford this kind of hardware. "You said it yourself, Glitzy. They're like an abusive ex who just can't take a hint."

She took aim at an approaching truck and squeezed off a long burst from the twin machine guns. Tracer rounds flashed bright across the camera before the night vision compensated and dimmed the image. By then, the rounds had struck their target. "Fortunately for us, we've got more than just teeth and claws to fight back!"

Garnet laughed. "So it would seem!"

A heavily armored pickup truck rumbled into view next, its machine guns and laser cannons blasting away. Garnet pushed the pedal to the floor and pulled off the road. The wide tires struck the hard dirt and kept rolling without any hint of slowing down. "They're gonna get us sooner or later!" she warned. "Light 'em up!"

Beryl fired a long burst at the vehicle, but the rounds couldn't penetrate the armor. Its turret started to turn their way. A flash of fear shot through Beryl as she switched to the targeting laser and painted the side of the truck. "We could use a bit of help, Uncle!"

Within seconds, a barrage of armor-piercing .50 rounds tore into the truck. Fire flared out of the engine compartment. Another burst of rounds punched through the driver's door, and the truck veered off the road and crashed into a power pole.

"Thanks for the save, Uncle!" Beryl said as she shot past the disabled truck.

"No, thank *you!* Any chance we get to end a water thief's miserable existence, we're gonna take it."

"Remind me never to get on your uncle's bad side," Garnet said. Her avatar shivered, blue eyes as wide as they could go. "He sounds like he's serious."

Chat heaped praise on Uncle Caleb, calling him things like 'road warrior' and 'convoy commander' to 'Based Uncle.' Beryl shook her head at the antics. "Just don't tell him any of this. It'll go to his head."

"Honey, you know I can hear you, right?"

Beryl froze, and it was only then she realized her mic was hot.

The convoy's radio erupted in laughter, despite the battle going on around them. "Caleb, you know it's true!" one of the other drivers said.

"Was I arguing against that? Stay focused, people. Oh, and Beryl?"

"Yes, Uncle?" Beryl asked in a small voice.

"Next time, make sure your mic isn't hot. And I want to know what chat's saying about me when this is all over."

That brought another round of laughter that Caleb quickly silenced. He couldn't silence the chat, though. They were busy heaping still more praise on him, along with mockery for Beryl's hot mic moment. "Skill issue!" and "Get good, noob!" were the most common responses.

Beryl thumbed her mic off, her cheeks hot enough to melt her headset. She cursed her own foolishness. Why was she worried about *this* when there was a real battle going on around her?

A strange chime came from Garnet's tablet, and a window opened up to reveal a private chat stream for those with upper-tier subscription packages. Garnet skimmed the words, her expression darkening. "Is that a fact, Broker? Should I fill the rest of the chat in on this?"

Beryl fired a burst from her machine guns, and whooped when the rounds shredded the right rear tire of the buggy up ahead. "Fill them in on what?"

Before Garnet could reply, Beryl looked over at the mirror. The message read: "I've got proof that the Desperados are working with AlgaLife." Beryl's mouth fell agape, and hot anger flooded through her. "If you don't, then I will."

Garnet laughed, but there was no mirth in it. Even her avatar looked unamused, the top half of her face darkened so much her eyes were invisible. "Be my guest!"

Beryl tapped her headset. *Might as well kill two birds with one stone.* "Wagon Leader, this is Scout. We've got some information that'll be equal parts liberating and infuriating."

"I'm a little busy trying not to get shot, Scout. What is it?"

Garnet jerked the wheel to the left, and a burst of tracer rounds zipped past the space they'd just occupied. Beryl aimed and fired. The rounds glanced off the enemy sedan's armor, but it spooked the driver. He swerved to the right, and then a long burst of gunfire from one of the rigs' heavy machine guns lit him up. A few of the .50 rounds went wide and struck a water tank off to the side of the road. Water sprayed, and an alarm sounded.

"Watch your fire!" Uncle Caleb yelled, his calm demeanor finally breaking. "The company suits will bury us in debt!"

"Maybe not, Uncle."

"Like I said, I'm busy. Get to the point!"

"It would seem our company overlords are paying the Desperados to harass us."

There was a long pause. "How do you know this?"

Beryl pointed at Broker's message. "How does he know this?"

"Never underestimate the obsessive nature of Otaku and dark web denizens, my friend!" Garnet looked at the camera and winked, her avatar making an exaggerated version of the same motion. "Right, chat?"

Another message arrived from Broker, and Beryl read it aloud. "'That's not all. I've got proof that one of AlgaLife's shell corporations is directly responsible for polluting the region's water table with seawater.' Or so he says."

"Trust me, he's reliable." Garnet grinned. "He's not called 'Broker' for nothing." She then muted her character long enough to add, "He's a real-life friend of mine. Works for my father's company."

"Well. Well, well, well." Uncle Caleb's voice was cool as ice. "That changes things, doesn't it?"

"It does, and I've got a plan." Garnet tapped her tablet and brought up a satellite view of the area. "Instead of skirting around the facility, let's take the road straight through like we'd originally planned."

"Didn't the original plan include getting the security team to protect us?"

"Yes."

"Isn't the company working with the Desperados?"

"Also yes."

There was another long pause. "Then why would they help us?"

Garnet's wicked smile returned. "Because of what my chat's about to do to their stock price."

The chat stream was alive with links to social media accounts and snippets of messages attacking AlgaLife for its crimes against towns like Beryl's and against the consumer in general. Their "best practices" were non-existent, all serving the singular purpose of maximizing profit while minimizing quality, ethics, and safety. Broker joined in with links of his own, videos and documents detailing illegal slant-drilling operations. It seemed AlgaLife was as rotten as they could be, which came as no surprise to Beryl. She made a low whistle. "Chat doesn't mess around."

"No, they do not."

Beryl checked her ammo supply. The rocket pods were down to three missiles each, and the twin-mounted machine gun turret was down to two hundred twenty-six rounds in each gun. That left roughly nine seconds of trigger-squeeze. She'd have to be sure of her target before she even thought of firing.

Fortunately for her, the area ahead was a target-rich environment. "Let's get 'em, Glitzy!"

Garnet grinned. "That's what I'm talking about!"

"You heard Little Miss Hot Mic!" Uncle Caleb shouted. "Weapons free! Let's punch through these Desperados and make for home!"

The radio erupted into cheers, and the convoy opened up with all its guns. A thick blanket of machine gun tracers, bright laser beams, and whistling missiles flew downrange. Several big explosions overloaded the night vision, leaving patches of white on Beryl's monitor that took a few seconds to fade. When it did, two Desperado vehicles were burning wrecks, and a third slid off the road on two wheels.

This sudden aggressiveness by the convoy caught the Desperados off-guard, but only for a moment. The remaining vehicles opened fire with everything they had, and it was all Garnet could do to avoid them. Even with her expert handling, bullets still struck the vehicle, scratching the armor's paint and cracking the windshield. A bullet pancaked against the windshield directly in front of Beryl. It didn't penetrate, but a tiny glass shard broke free and grazed Beryl's cheek. She grunted and put a hand to her face, then pulled back bloody fingers.

Garnet swerved to the left, jumping the sandy median and entering the opposing traffic lanes. When they straightened, Beryl lined the crosshairs onto an armored pickup truck, and let fly with the missiles. One went wide, but the remaining three slammed home against its grill and windshield. The hood blew off, glass shattered, and the truck careened to the side and crashed into a trike that had been attempting to pass. The smaller vehicle was crushed *beneath* the jacked-up truck, and then the road forward was clear.

"Chat, did you see that?" Glitzy asked as they blew past. "That was a Sandcrab! And it looked like it was in good shape."

"*Was* being the operative word."

Glitzy laughed. "You said it!"

There were still many more Desperados ahead. Beryl wiped her bloody hand against her overalls, then got back to working the guns. She fired at another trike, a tricked-out sedan that looked like it should've been at a car show somewhere, and then a truck obviously pieced together from at least three other vehicles. Whatever the Desperados threw at her, she kept shooting.

And then her guns ran dry. Fear flashed through Beryl, and she checked and rechecked their supply before saying, "I'm out!"

Garnet kept the pedal to the floor. "Nothing left for it but to ram our way through, then!"

No sooner had she said that then missiles struck the Desperados *from behind*. Vehicles poured out of the desalinization plant, their weapons chewing into the bandits. "Wagon Train, this is Rock Security Force. We're here to assist!"

Here to assist the company in saving face. Beryl didn't dare voice that aloud, not with her reputation as "Little Miss Hot Mic".

"Rock Security Force, this is Wagon Train," Uncle Caleb said. "We appreciate the help! We're just trying to get home."

"We'll make sure you get there. And that the Desperados never trouble you again."

Was that satisfaction in the man's tone? Maybe not everyone in AlgaLife's corporate employ had been happy with the local arrangements.

Between the two forces, the Desperados stood no chance. What was left of them drove off into the desert, with the Rock Security Force chasing after them in vehicles better suited for off-road action than any of their vehicles were. The members of the convoy cheered until Uncle Caleb told them to pipe down.

As they drove beneath the streetlights lining the roadway through the desalinization plant's main property, Beryl let out a slow sigh of relief. She sagged against her seat, all the tension draining from her body. "Some beginner's merengue that was," she muttered.

Garnet laughed, then heaved a sigh. Her Glitzy Gear avatar did the same in an exaggerated motion, much to the delight of the chat. "Well, that was a close thing, wasn't it?" She looked sidelong at Beryl and smiled. "Do you think chat deserves to see heart monitors on us both?"

Beryl laughed. "I'd rather not, but they did us a solid back there. I have to admit that."

Garnet's Falcon met them a few miles out from Posthole. Once he was in radio range, the pilot radioed a successful drop-off at a hospital. Red and Steven would be fine, but they'd both need treatment and monitoring.

"We'll put the medical bills on my expense account," Garnet said. She shrugged. "It's not like I use it for much, anyway."

Garnet pulled off the side of the road close to her helicopter. Uncle Caleb's rig stopped behind them, followed by the one driven by Garnet's bodyguards. "Everyone else, keep going!" Caleb barked. "We'll be along once Beryl sees Miss Glitzy to her ride."

A chorus of affirmatives crackled through the radio, and the convoy continued on without so much as a hiccup.

Beryl and Garnet climbed out of the Mako and were soon joined by her bodyguards. Uncle Caleb switched to the now-empty rig. They'd drive with their roof turrets in sentry mode, with Beryl driving their newest—and littlest—acquisition the last few miles to home.

"Excellent work, Matthew, Jeremy," Garnet said to her bodyguards as they walked toward the helicopter."

"Right back at you, Miss Higurashi."

Miss *Higurashi?* Beryl knew the name Garnet had sounded familiar! She was the daughter of the current owner of Higurashi Motors. Despite the name, it was an American-based car company out of Los Angeles, known for its cutting-edge electric motor and internal combustion technology. They threaded the needle between both styles, and as such were quite popular even in the Free Oil States.

"You did well, too, Miss Beryl," Jeremy added.

"Yes, you did." A cold desert wind tugged at strands of Garnet's long hair as she looked over her shoulder at Beryl. "What do you say? Father's company could use you."

Beryl stopped. "You want to hire me?"

"Why not?" Garnet turned and counted off her fingers. "You're a crack-shot with a gun. You're no slouch when turning wrenches. You're able to think quickly on your feet. You've got great comedic timing. Should I go on?"

"What does that last thing have to do with it?"

"I'm a streamer, remember? Entertainment's a critical part of the gig, and you'd be utilized there, too. In a few years, you'd have enough money socked away and enough of a Clutch following that you could do your own thing. And with my backing, you'd be very successful at it." She shrugged. "Who knows? After today, maybe we'd cut back on the VDuelling and give the real thing a shot, you know?"

Beryl couldn't believe her ears. The day had started off horribly, but now it was looking up so much she wondered if she'd been killed, and this was the afterlife. She'd be a fool to not accept the offer. This was *the* Glitzy Gear, after all!

Still...

Beryl shook her head. "As much as I appreciate the offer, I can't accept. I'm a Posthole girl. She ain't much of a town, but I can't leave her. Not unless all of us can."

Garnet frowned, but that was quickly replaced with a smile. "Then I'll make you a different offer. If this mine survey and purchase works out, my company will have a foothold in the region, and hundreds of miners to clothe and feed. An algae production line could go a long way to making our operation self-sufficient."

"You'd buy us out?" Sure, Higurashi Motors could afford it, but....

"It'll take time," Garnet continued, "and I'll need to convince Father. That last part shouldn't be too difficult." Garnet's smile broadened into a grin. "I *am* his only beloved daughter, after all."

"And *the* Glitzy Gear. You can't forget that part."

Garnet laughed and held out her hand. "Is it a deal, then?"

Beryl returned the grin, and the handshake. "Deal!"

END

Fourth Time Lucky
By: David W. Hensley

There are a lot of ways to wake up from being dead. At the top of the list is waking up in a Gold Cross premium suite attended by the best nurses your money can buy. Soft lighting, soothing sounds of the ocean or a spring thunderstorm playing in the background. You wake up seated in a thickly cushioned chair, fully dressed, warm, safe, and comfortable. As waking from the dead goes, it's first class. On the other end of the spectrum are the back-alley meat markets. No soothing sounds in the background. No well-trained, attractive nurses to see to your reemergence into the land of the living. If you're lucky, you wake up dry and in one of those shitty gowns the hospitals love so much. I wasn't that lucky.

I woke up shivering and coughing the last bit of nutrient solution from my lungs. I rolled to my side and opened my eyes. Bright light stung my new eyes, made them tear up, everything a smeared blur. They say they use light stimulation to ensure the eyes grow and develop properly, but that's the boys up in the Gold Cross facility. Down here in the grit and muck near the bottom of the socioeconomic ladder, the odds are better that the body farmer cuts a corner or two. Then again, any time I woke up in a Gold Cross suite, they had the lights turned down real low and took the better part of an hour to let me acclimatize.

Across the room, a TV blared. Don Northcraft's smarmy voice kept yammering about the showdown of the century at The Pyramid. I tuned out Northcraft and focused on wiping the goop out of my eyes and clearing it from my nostrils. This was not a Gold Cross location. Hell, this wasn't even one of those New-U kiosks. Even the bottom-tier services gave you a flush and wash down.

I got to my hands and knees in the puddle of nutrient gel. Soft padding squidged between my fingers. I was still in the grow tube. I coughed until I gagged, which set off a fit of heaving and vomiting, bringing up a thin watery substance mixed with more gel. Using the edge of the tube for support, I climbed to my feet. My legs shook and wobbled like a newborn foal standing for the first time.

I stood shivering ankle-deep in piss-warm nutrient gel, trying to take stock of my surroundings. I couldn't see more than a few feet through the blur. What I could see were hand railings surrounding the edge of the tube, a series of backlit arrows on the floor pointing the way to a narrow exit, and an aluminum walker. I clambered from the tube on unsteady legs and with the aid of the walker, followed the lighted path.

The arrows led to a shower where I managed to scrub the last vestiges of the nutrient gel from my skin and hair just before the hot water ran out. I stood in front of the TV, not a holovid but an honest to God flat-screen television, hanging on a bare brick wall. I did my level best to get dry using the threadbare scrap of fabric I'd found hung near the shower entrance. I guess you could call it a towel back when it was new, probably when there were still fifty states.

On the screen, Don Northcraft did his oily best to convince everyone to stay tuned in to Dead Man's Run, whatever the hell that was. The chyron crawl across the bottom of the screen said it was the first of November. Based on that information, I had been out of circulation for roughly two and a half months. The last thing I remembered was sitting down in an upload chair shortly after turning in my expense and after-action report to my boss at Allied Atlantic Insurance and Indemnity for a skip trace on a killer that had jumped bail in Atlanta and was hiding out with the Bloodmouths in the Hampton Roads Dead Zone. The paper had offered the bounty dead or alive, and the skip had chosen dead when he started lobbing grenades at me from the hangar bay of a half-sunken aircraft carrier in the Elizabeth River. That was mid-August.

Given the missing time and the quality of my decanting, I was in deep shit. The question was, how deep? I took a better look at my surroundings. The lights were turned down real low, leaving the corners half shrouded in shadow. It was a large space. No windows. One end, where I stood, had a small shower stall, a table with a couple folding metal chairs, and that giant television. Opposite the TV stood several tall lockers. Six clone storage tubes took up the bulk of the space in the middle of the room. The holovids and movies show clone tanks as tubes made of glass large enough for a person to float around in with streaming hair and tastefully covered genitalia. Like so many other things in the movies, it was complete bullshit. These tubes were all metal, likely Durasteel, with a full-length pressure hatch that hinged on one side. An LCD touchscreen mounted in the hatch displayed all of the information that a body farmer might need. Shrouded in shadow beyond the tubes sat an upload chair. Behind it was a bank of MMSD servers—floor-to-ceiling, wall-to-wall consciousness storage.

While the amenities were sparse, the equipment was top-of-the-line. Those meat jars were the same as the ones Gold Cross used. The spartan utility of the space, combined with the luxury-grade equipment, told me where I was. Uncle Lou's. Someone had managed to punch my ticket three other times if I was waking up here. Or I'd done something to get fired from Allied Atlantic, and all I had left was my off-the-books backup. Either way, I was in deep shit.

I shuffled to the lockers on increasingly steady feet. They were big steel affairs like you'd find in a gym, six or seven feet tall and a couple feet wide. Each door had a scrap of paper in the little metal placard holder with a number scrawled on it. Mine was the one on the end. I glanced at the other doors; all five had their own scraps of paper with numbers on them. Seems Lou was doing a brisk trade down here at the bottom.

There was an old-school dial combo lock on the door of my locker. I got it open on the third try. I can never remember if the sequence starts right or left on those things. Inside was my minimum necessary kit for bugging out or laying low. A change of clothes, some cash, a monocrys and Kevlar trench coat, a model 1911 modified for caseless, a burner phone, and a beat-up old fedora.

It took me about twice as long as usual to slip into the faded jeans and Sam's the Hero t-shirt. I didn't bother tying my boots. My hands were too shaky for that. The last time I'd felt this rough was the month I'd spent sobering up to start working for Allied Atlantic. The burner was on and fully charged, and the pistol was fully loaded. Handling the weapon helped settle the shakes. The clinical term for my weakness, shakes, nausea, stiffness, splitting headache, sensitivity to light and sound, and general sense of unease, is Clone Transition Syndrome, or CTS for short. Everyone I know calls it meat sick. Gold Cross and the other mainstream outfits pump you full of medications I can't pronounce that dampen the meat sickness, and they send you out the door with a bottle of pills designed to continue damping it until you've fully integrated your consciousness with the new meat. Lou wasn't in the comfort business. He was in the off-the-books resurrection business.

I sat in one of the folding chairs and unlocked the burner with a thumbprint. There was one missed call and a message waiting in my voicemail. Odds were good that I'd left myself some sort of heads up on why I was waking up in Uncle Lou's instead of one of the backups Gold Cross had waiting for me on the company dime.

I pushed the burner away and rested my head in my hands. The voicemail was a confusing mishmash of static, sporadic talking, and background noise. What I'd left myself wasn't a usable brief on the situation. It was a recording of my death. I slid the phone back in front of me and hit play on the message again.

The first thing I noticed every time was the sheer volume of static rising and falling like surf hitting the beach. In between the waves was heavy breathing. It's measured and deliberate, so I'm not sprinting, but running. For an insurance investigator, I'm in unusually good shape, a relic from my days in the Ranger Battalion. For me to be breathing like that, I had been running for a while. Between breaths I was trying to leave myself some sort of message. It's not the running that makes the message mostly unintelligible, it's the static. The only words I could make out in this section were "Don't trust" and part of an address that could be in any one of a dozen cities in the U.S. or the Free Oil States.

I'm pretty sure the next sounds on the recording were gunshots. After five or ten more seconds, the static-surf cuts off; you can hear footsteps and two people talking. One of them had a soft drawl that sounded like it came straight out of the Louisiana bayou. The other's voice was a high-pitched nasal twang with a bad habit of mushing up his words. Not squeaky, but high, in the upper end of the range for most men, though I suppose it could be a woman. After the third listen, I'd taken to calling one Bayou Billy and the other Jethro.

"He dead?" Billy asked. He sounded out of breath.

"Probably." Two more gunshots rang out. "Definitely."

"Not nearly as tough as they said."

"Mos' folk ain't," said Jethro. "Not if'n you catch'em out."

"Now what?"

"Burn 'em," Jethro said. "Papa G said burn 'em an dump whas lef in the river."

The rest of the message was roughly two and a half minutes of those two bitching about how heavy I was and how far they had to carry me to get back to the car. It cut off about thirty seconds after they stopped bellyaching and got to work. I took some satisfaction in imagining two soggy assholes dragging my 270 pounds of dead weight all the way back to their car.

This was bad. Person or persons, unknown, had set an ambush and killed me. Most likely, me number three. That should have been a lot harder than those two yokels made it sound. Especially if me one and two had already come to a similar end. Me three should have been a hell of a lot harder to catch. Come to think of it, where the hell was my backup? Allied Atlantic was a big outfit with deep pockets. Whatever this case was, it should have rated more than just one investigator. Especially after having that investigator killed or vanished two other times. The price of my previous three downloads alone would have justified at least a two-man security team.

Somewhere around the third or fourth time I listened to the message, my hands stopped shaking. I tied my boots, shoved the cash and burner in my pocket, and strapped on my pistol. I shrugged my way into the knee-length coat and crammed the battered hat onto my head. I checked the long mirror hanging in the locker door. Looked like Randall Wade was back in action.

"Time to get some answers," I said to the man in the mirror.

Waking up from the dead a fourth time did have a couple of advantages. For one, no one knew I was back. Well, no one but Lou, and he wasn't talking. Lou isn't really the name of the off-the-books meat doc. He used to be a promising young geneticist specializing in human cloning. Turns out he had a thing for betting on the wrong driver in the arena. That left him owing substantial sums of money to the sort of people you don't want to owe the least amount. I helped him out of the jam when I got assigned to investigate his alleged death and subsequent payout of his sizable policy through Allied Atlantic. It turns out that when you're a world-class doctor in the biotech field, faking your own death is pretty easy. Covering it up? Not so much. I helped him out. Say goodbye to life as a biotech researcher heavily indebted to very bad people and say hello to Louis P. Moretti, owner of Uncle Lou's Delicatessen and off-the-books resurrectionist.

I'm no boy scout, and it didn't take a lot of work to see the percentage in helping Lou. So, I help him disappear, go into business for himself as it were, and in return he keeps a fresh meat suit and backup on hand. Off the books. What he does with the other five meat jars is totally up to him.

I made my way from the basement into Uncle Lou's on the book business. The smell of fresh baked bread, high-grade algae, and cured meats bypassed my brain and went straight to my guts. I was hungrier than an Anarchist Relief Front hostage. Lou was behind the glass case displaying an array of cured meat options. In this neighborhood, few could afford the smallest sliver of actual meat. Except Lou sold his at prices that would have been cheap back when people still drove gas guzzlers. Everyone in the neighborhood knew he was connected, just not how. The how was the very large cash payments he received for his other meat services.

"How's the Reuben?" I pulled out a chair and sat heavily.

"Randall!" Lou looked through the glass case at me. He was short and round in a fleshy kind of way. Bright blue eyes peered at me over his chubby cheeks. He closed the door on the meat case. "Did you take pills I leave you?" No matter how often I talked to Lou, his thick Russian accent always threw me.

"There weren't any pills, Lou." I shook my head.

"Sure there are." He walked around the end of the counter to the front door, locked it, and flipped the hanging sign around to closed. "I take them out of pocket and…" He trailed off, patting his apron. It rattled.

"Those the pills?"

"Sorry, Randall." He shrugged, walked over to my table, pulled out the other chair, and flopped into it before placing a small bottle of pills in front of me. "Take two now, two more every four hours 'til gone. Do not miss dose. Otherwise, you meat sick."

"Got it." I popped the top, shook out two pills, and dry swallowed them. "Now, how about that Reuben?"

"You want with dressing?"

"No." I shook my head. "Horseradish if you've got it. And the algaekraut."

"You should eat with sauerkraut." He heaved his bulk up out of the chair and went back behind the counter. "Is best with sauerkraut. I make it fresh."

Lou turned out to be pretty good as a proprietor of a neighborhood delicatessen. He was even better as a (XXX clone doc). I suppose not getting tortured to death is a good incentive for learning a new trade. Or maybe he always had a passion for fresh baked bread and cured meats. Who knows? In any case, he made the best Reuben sandwich in Memphis, and I'd stack his food up against any deli east of the Mississippi.

He slid a plate onto the table in front of me, along with a bottle of water.

"What's this?" I held up the bottled water.

"You drink."

"A bottle of Ol' Muddy would go better." I cracked the top and took a swig anyway. It was good water, cold and crisp.

"Not with pills," Lou shook his head. "New formula not mix so well with alcohol."

I picked up my sandwich and took a bite. My new taste buds sent little signals of bliss through my brain. One of the things they probably should market when selling you on clone services. Old memories and new synapses interact, making everything a strange Deja vu first-time experience.

"This is wonderful, Lou," I said.

"You are mad man, Randall." Lou shook his head. "Eating solid food on new stomach."

"I don't have time for a week of eating bland mush," I said. "Someone's done me in at least once and likely three times. I got to fuel up and get on the move before they figure out where I am and do me in in a more permanent way."

"Figured you in trouble," Lou said. "Man and woman in here couple days back. Show me picture of you. Ask if you been in. I tell them no. They ask again, tell me I have nice place be shame if something happen. I tell them you eat here sometimes."

"What did they look like?" I took another bite of bliss and groaned as the horseradish sprinted up my sinus passages and set the top of my head to tingling.

"Both medium size. One long blond hair, light skin, nice ass. The other dark skin, bald. Good shape. Voodoo Mafia ink on arms and necks." Lou said.

I chewed on that and another bite of my sandwich. Whatever I was doing when I got hit, I'd run afoul the Voodoo Mafia. Not a big outfit as outfits go. Word around the campfire was they specialized in entertainment of the adult variety. Ran their operation from an old plantation down in Louisiana. No taste was out of bounds with the Voodoo Mafia, or so the story goes.

"What did they sound like," I asked.

"Sound like?" Lou pulled a rag from his apron pocket and wiped the sweat from his face. The dining area felt cool to me, but Lou was able to break a sweat in a meat locker.

"When they talked," I said.

"The blond one, she talk through nose, hard to understand," he said.

"And the bald one?"

"No talk, just stare." He went back to cleaning behind the counter.

So, Jethro was a woman. A woman that handled hits for the Voodoo Mafia. I chewed on that for a bit while I finished my sandwich and my water. And for some reason, she'd come sniffing around here. I must have hidden something they wanted. So, Jethro and Bayou Billy were still on the hunt, trying to retrace my steps. I needed to figure out what the hell was going on, and I needed to do it before Jethro and Billy found me again.

I'd left myself an address, but the message quality was shit, so I would have to get that sorted. I'd been killed three other times, which meant there was a solid chance I'd been set up at least once. No way around it; I was going to have to report to Colonel Allison direct. See if the big cheese himself could shed a little light on the subject for me. First things first. I needed to get the hell out of Memphis.

I'd picked up an old Tate Bombardier IV. I paid five hundred dollars more than it was worth, but it was starting to rain, and I didn't have time to haggle. It was a rust bucket, but the powerplant was new, one of those sixth-generation jobs that got four hundred miles to the charge. The quad .50 caliber machine guns mounted in the hood were well-oiled and fully loaded. Patches scabbed over a series of holes in the gunner's door didn't fill me with much confidence in the side armor, and I wasn't too sure that the chaff and flare buckets were fully operational. On the plus side, she did have smoke and oil dispensers and dual gunnery controls. I named her Molly.

I picked up the pace. I knew someone in Little Rock who could sort out my garbled message, so that was where I was heading. Not that there weren't plenty of shops in Memphis that could help me out, but I didn't want one of them looking to make a quick buck by selling me down the river. Keeping half an eye on the road, I punched in the number to Colonel Allison's office. It picked up on the second ring.

"Allied Atlantic, Mr. Allison's office." The voice on the other end rumbled like a freight train. It belonged to Reid Montgomery; he was the Colonel's secretary, personal assistant, bodyguard, dog robber, and all-around flunky. In earlier days, he'd been Corporal Montgomery, later

Sergeant, later still Sergeant Major, and the unofficial personal aid to the Captain who'd gone on to full bird Colonel before retiring and moving into Allied Atlantic as head of a satellite investigation office up north. Detroit, I think. Reid had stuck by the Colonel and followed him into the private sector.

"Monty," I said. "It's Randall. Put me through to the Colonel."

"Wade?" Monty asked.

"Yes. Randall Wade." I steered around a big-rig hooked up and hauling tandem. "You know any other Randalls with this number?"

"No." Monty sounded mildly confused. "I was unaware that Gold Cross was finished growing your new meat."

"How long?" I asked. I was missing ten weeks of time thanks to the lag between my last visit to Uncle Lou's and waking up there, but I doubted I had been out of proper circulation that long.

"You'll have to ask the Colonel," he said.

"Bullshit, Monty." I set the burner to speaker and clipped it into a holder mounted to Molly's dash. "You know down to the minute how long I've been out, what I was working on, my last report, and probably what I ate for breakfast that day."

"Of course," he said. "And you know it is policy for all revived agents to debrief with Mr. Allison in person. In fact, you, Wade, are the reason for that very policy's existence."

Monty was right. Say what you want about Reid Montgomery, he's always been a by-the-book guy, while I have what some might call a cavalier attitude towards The Book.

"Sticking to the book, are we?" I shook my head and laughed. Made sure Monty could hear me.

"Policy exists for a reason, Mr. Wade." I could hear the disproving look he was giving the air in front of his desk.

"Fine; is the Colonel in?"

"Afraid not," he said.

"What the hell," I asked. "I need to talk to the Colonel direct."

"When he returns, in the morning, I will inform him of your premature reemergence from the land of the dead. I assume you are headed back to the main office for brief and reassignment."

"I'm headed to Little Rock," I said. "Following a lead that's probably ice cold at this point, but it's what I got."

"A lead?" I could hear fingers tapping on the other end. "On what?"

"A murder," I said.

"Whose?"

"Mine." I stabbed the disconnect button on the phone in frustration and mashed the accelerator to the floor. I hate bureaucratic rule followers. But that was why Reid was up on the sixtieth floor with the Old Man while I was down here in the mud and the blood.

Little Rock was as busy as a yellow-jacket nest and twice as deadly. Part old west boom town, part sin city. Like Deadwood and precrash Vegas got together and made a megacity.

I eased into the parking lot of a strip mall off John F. Kennedy Boulevard. The place I was looking for was nestled into the second story above a Chinese take-out called the Lucky Panda and a twenty-four-hour nail salon. I parked Molly where I had a clear route back to the street and headed for the armorglass door with 'Rusty Velvet Audio' frosted onto the surface around a stylized microphone. The lights were on upstairs, so the odds were good that Val was still working. I made my way up the narrow stair, the smell of Chinese food mixed with the acrid-sweet odor of acetone leaving me with a craving for General Tso's chicken and a manicure.

The door at the top of the stairs was locked. I hit the buzzer anyway. When no one moved, I leaned on the button. After about ten or fifteen seconds, mag-locks buzz-clacked, and the door swung inward. Val filled the door frame. To call her a big girl would be an understatement. Valerie Wienszcyslaski was six foot two if she was an inch and the better part of two hundred eighty pounds. She was what my grandpa would have called a handsome woman. Attractive in a sturdy sort of way.

"Randy," She eased the hammer on a .50 caliber hand cannon down, stowed the big gun, and stepped aside, waving me into the postage-stamp-sized waiting area.

"Easy, Val," I said. "What's with the artillery?"

"Had a customer that thought he was buying more than a session in the sound studio. I broke his arm and rolled him down those stairs last week. He was back yesterday with some friends."

"How'd that go?" I stepped aside while she shut the door. The maglocks buzzed and clacked back into place.

"It took a restoration crew the rest of yesterday and half of today to get the blood out of my carpet." She shook her head. "I lost a full day of scheduled recording."

"Feel like making back a little of that lost cash?" I asked.

I'd met Val several years back. She'd been on the wrong end of a wrongful death suit, and I owed her old man a favor. It was a happy accident that she turned out to be a fantastic sound engineer. So, when I have a tricky bit of forensic sound analysis I need done, Valerie Wienszcyslaski is my gal.

"Is a duck's ass watertight?" She stepped around the end of the reception counter and through a beaded curtain into the bowels of Rusty Velvet Audio.

"That's pretty rough." Val pulled the large headset from her head and let it rest around her neck.

"Tell me about it," I said. "I can't make out much until near the end."

"I was talking about you getting executed." She looked up at me. "Sounds like you had a real shit day there."

"Sounds that way," I said. "Not that I remember, I'm working from a ten-week-old backup. Can you clean that up at all?"

"It's pretty bad," she said. "The static is sinusoidal."

"What?"

"Like a wave, a Sine wave. Rises and falls at predictable intervals. Look here." She reached into the holodisplay and expanded a window to display a waveform model of the message. I'm sure it made perfect sense to Val. To me, it looked like a batch of worms all trying to crawl along a tube with one big worm running along the middle.

"What am I looking at here?" I squinted at the display.

"See this thick line here in the middle, how it hits the top and bottom of the scale?" She pointed at the squirming mess.

"Uh-huh." I nodded.

"That is the static you hear."

"What does it mean?" I leaned in for a closer look.

"It means someone was jamming you, your signal." Val leaned back in the chair and stretched. It did interesting things with the thin T-shirt she wore.

"Can you get rid of it?" I forced my gaze back to the issue at hand. I wasn't her type anyway. Or maybe she wasn't mine.

"Who're you talking to?" She leaned forward and expanded another window. This one seemed more organized to me, less jumbled. "Here it is without the jamming interference. I'm surprised you got anything through that mess. You must have been close to a cell tower."

Val played it without the static. There were large chunks of nothing where the static had been, but it was easier to concentrate on the things that were there. Running water, a train whistle, distant shouts and cheers, and glory of glories, the address all sharp and clear: 9901 Sherrill Boulevard. I had left something at that address.

My bankroll was lighter to the tune of five hundred bucks. Valerie was damned good at what she did, and good service cost good money. I climbed into the driver's seat of the old Bombardier. 9901 Sherrill Boulevard. No city. No zip code. I opened a navigation app on the burner and punched it in. Of the options that appeared after I hit the search button, I only recognized one—The Big Bill's Dine and Dash in Knoxville. Odds were I'd stashed something there. Something that the Voodoo Mafia wanted badly enough to kill me at least once.

I was so lost in thought I didn't see them coming. My first hint of trouble was the staccato thump of high-velocity lead on the hood of the Bombardier. I dumped the burner into the center console, stomped on the accelerator, and laid on the trigger paddles. The puncture-resistant tires spun and smoked before catching and launching me across the now-empty lot straight at my assailant. I expected there to be a rolling roar from the quad .50. All I got was silence. Rounds continued to thump off my hood and crack against the Armorglass of the windshield. From the sound of the impacts, the other guy was using a smaller caliber, probably 5.56. Light, high velocity but no real penetration power against an old arena queen like Molly.

The headlights and flashing muzzle of my assailant's vehicle were closing fast. I'd expected to give them a head-to-head pass with steel-cored .50 rounds knocking holes through their powerplant and cockpit. With the gun controls not responding, I was trapped in a lopsided game of armed chicken. Why weren't my guns firing? Considering action being superior to inaction, I activated the smoke and oil dispensers. At the last possible second, I flicked the steering wheel left then right, juking around the oncoming car. I checked the rearview in time to see them hit the oil slick and break into a spinning slide. Good enough for me. I powered into a sliding turn onto John F. Kennedy Boulevard and accelerated away.

I'd managed to sort out the inoperative weapons problem not long after I broke contact with my assailants. Turns out there was a switch that allows the driver to select where the weapons controls are assigned. Molly's were still assigned to the unmanned gunner's station. It's the little details that kill you. I checked my rearview for the hundredth time. Still clear. Not that I had gotten a good look at the shooter's car. It was low-slung and black, but that describes two-thirds of the armed cars on the road.

The better question was, how the hell did they know where to find me? Was it some shitbirds looking for an easy score? Val's place was in a rougher part of town, but that didn't matter much. Little Rock was a city where self-defense was encouraged, so hit-and-rip attacks didn't happen much, even in the worst neighborhoods. Besides, what dumbass goes for a rusty old Bombardier? No. That attack was a half-assed attempt to rub me out. It was sloppy and felt rushed.

I drove around Little Rock for another hour, making turns at random and backtracking more than once just to be sure my tail was clear. Definitely amateurs, definitely a rush job. I kept turning the problem over in my head. No one knew where I was. Bayou Billy and Jethro had come sniffing around Uncle Lou's, but anyone with two brain cells to rub together could have figured out that I stop in there every time I'm in Memphis for a meal. I rave about the food there to anyone who'll listen. Makes my visits slightly less conspicuous.

Only one other person knew I was headed to Little Rock: Monty. Well, Monty and Colonel Allison. I'd bet a shiny new nickel Monty had called the Colonel as soon as he'd recovered from my abrupt end to our call. If the Colonel really was unavailable. Odds were good that he'd been in his office doing whatever it is he did in there. Maybe the Voodoo Mafia had bugged Allied Atlantic's home offices, or I'd been sloppy getting out of Memphis. Or, maybe, there was a leak at the office.

There was another possibility. I shook my head. I couldn't imagine it was Monty or the Colonel. We'd spent way too much time in the shit together. If either one of them wanted me dead, I'd be dead. No half-assed hit. No. It would be a .50 caliber round through the head from so far off you'd need a week of hard digging to find the shooter's perch.

It was likely that I'd not been as careful as I should have been getting out of Memphis. I'd made a beeline for Rusty Velvet and hadn't really bothered to check my six for tails. Whatever I'd been working on, I'd pissed off some serious people. Too bad for them; I worked for serious people.

A restless night in a place where you pay by the hour and two-hundred twenty miles later I picked up the burner and dialed the Colonel. I was stopped at a Jumpin' Joe's on the far side of Jackson, recharging Molly and jamming some waffles and fried algae down the hatch while I waited. Predictably Monty picked up.

"Allied Atlantic Insurance and Indemnity, Mr. Allison's office."

"Monty," I said around a mouth full of waffle.

"Mr. Wade," he said. "How did your lead pan out?"

"You do care." I finished off my lukewarm coffee and signaled the waitress for a refill.

"Only in the sense that one of our investigators is on his own fragging program."

"I'm not OFP, Monty. I'm simply working my last assignment on very limited intel." The waitress refilled my cup. I smiled my thanks at her. "Which I wouldn't be if you'd unclench your sphincter for thirty seconds and give me a proper brief."

"As I stated yesterday, Mr. Wade." I could hear fingers punching keys. "Policy requires you to return to the main office for debriefing and reassignment."

"Look, I was on to something that got me dead, what, three times?" I sipped steaming coffee.

"You have been rebooted two times, not counting this one. I cannot tell you more than that over an unsecured line, Mr. Wade."

"Then switch me over to a secured one."

"If you were calling on the device issued to you by the company, you would be, but since you are not, the only real insurance, if you'll forgive the pun, is to debrief you in person at the home office in Rich— "

"I don't have time for your bullshit." I cut him off. "Get the Colonel."

"He is unavailable."

"You didn't even check!"

"I don't need to," Monty said. "I keep his schedule. Mister Allison is in meetings all morning. Try back around 15:30. Better yet, get here and see him in person. He's been rather concerned since hearing about your early resurrection."

"Look," I lowered my tone, dialed for conciliatory or at least less hostile. "I'm at loose ends here. Something squirrely is going on. I had someone take a shot at me last night. I don't know how they knew where I was, but they did. What was I working on?"

"I can't tell you," he said.

"Can't or won't?"

"Can not, Wade." He lowered his voice. "I don't know what you were working on, something for the Old Man. It came down from on high, boardroom level."

"Well, hell," I finished my coffee in one large gulp and signaled for the waitress. "Tell the Colonel I'm headed east. Got to pick up something."

"Where at?" he asked.

"I'd rather not say." The waitress approached with the coffee pot. I put a hand over the cup. "Check, please?"

"What," Monty asked.

"Unsecured line, Monty," I said. "Maybe, whoever's trying to drop me tapped your line and that's how they found me last night."

"Sure," he said. "What do you want me to tell the Old Man?"

"Tell him I need to talk to him direct. Tell him I need a supply drop that includes expense money, encrypted coms, and a damned brief." The waitress slid my check onto the table. I counted out what I owed plus a ten for the tip. I thought for a couple seconds. "Tell him I'm picking up a package at Sarge's favorite greasy spoon. He'll know the place."

"Which one?"

"The original." I said and ended the call.

The trip from Jackson to Knoxville was listed as four and a half hours by my outdated Ada. That was two hundred ninety miles on good roads passing through Nashville. It took me six hours on roads that probably hadn't seen a repair crew in a decade, and that was passing straight through the burned-out remnant of Nashville. Modern-day Ada's won't even give you a route to Knoxville. All they do is flash a warning about the danger level and needing a well-armed convoy. Lucky me, I was working with an Ada at least fifteen years out of date.

I had no way of knowing how many hitters the Voodoo Mafia had looking for me. Or why they were looking for me. And I didn't really know how they'd found me at Val's in the first place. What I did know was that I'd left something valuable to the case at Big Bill's, and dead me was cagey enough to leave an address rather than the name of the place. Had to mean something.

With the sun setting and a cold wind blowing in out of the northwest, I sat in the driver's window, rested my elbows on Molly's roof, and glassed the Big Bill's compound from a nearby overpass. A recon drone or two would have been nice. Instead, I had a pair of fourth-generation Maxwell binoculars. Got 'em on special from the Uncle Al's kiosk at the Jumpin' Joe's. At least they had thermal imaging, range finding, and light amplification.

I was just about ready to pack it in and head on down to the diner when they made their first big mistake. I'd given the front of Big Bill's another look when Tyrone came lumbering out of the front doors carrying two large bags of take-out boxes.

Tyrone is the owner and head cook of the Knoxville Big Bill's Dine and Dash. He's six-foot-eight if he's an inch, and probably tips the scales around four-twenty-five. He's not just big. He's mammoth. Not only is he mammoth, he's as close to fearless as I've ever seen in a human being. So, when he came stomping out of the front doors of the diner and made for a big rig with Conroy Algae emblazoned on the trailer toting two bags full of take-out boxes and taking nervous-looking glances over his shoulder at the diner, I knew something was up. That, and the fact that he never runs food out to the lot. He's had a long-time policy that if you want to eat, you can come in and order. He even has several large signs posted in the diner windows to that effect.

That was their second mistake. I hadn't noticed it at first, but with Tyrone looking back at the building every few steps, I naturally turned the binoculars to see what he was looking at. A blond woman sat looking out of the window, watching Ty all the way to the truck. Across the table from her sat a muscular man, dark-skinned, bald. I increased the magnification on the binoculars. They both had stylized zombie heads wearing a top hat ink of the Voodoo Mafia on their forearms. Bayou Billy and Jethro were here, waiting for me.

One of my previous incarnations really kicked over a hornet's nest with these Voodoo Mafia pricks. I watched Tyrone bang on the rear door of the Conroy Algae trailer. After a few seconds, it opened. Food went in, and a stack of cash came out. I gave the trailer a closer look. Odds were good that it was loaded up with a hit squad. There had been eight or nine takeout boxes in the bags Tyrone had passed into the trailer. On my second inspection of the trailer, I spotted several pancake antennas mounted on the roof. Either they had recon drones, or a mobile bollix. I pulled out my burner. No signal. That was a piece of good news. They were running a bollix. No signal for me. No signal for them to control drones either.

What I should do is drive away. Point Molly east and run like a scalded dog. There's no shame in strategic withdrawal when faced with a superior force. They taught us that at nearly every level of training, from basic all the way through Ranger School. I slid back through the window into the driver's seat. I'd have resources and backup in Richmond. The only problem was that I was pretty sure it was someone at corporate that put these pricks on to me.

I'd been pretty nonspecific about where I was headed. "Sarge's favorite greasy spoon" could have been any one of a thousand truck stops and diners east of the Mississippi. Someone listening in on a wiretap would have to spend a lot of time running down my past known associates to figure out which Sarge I was referring to. It was possible but highly unlikely. Occam's Razor suggested the source of my leak was much closer to home. Either Monty or the Colonel had put these pricks on my trail. Withdrawal to Richmond was out.

I could run, disappear into the vastness of the U.S. or the Oil States. Whatever it is they thought I knew might keep them looking, but I could stay ahead of the Voodoo Mafia goons indefinitely. Could I evade the Colonel and Allied Atlantic's investigators? Not unless they decided the juice wasn't worth the squeeze. If they thought I had something that could hurt them or, worse yet, damage an insured client they would keep looking until they found me. They would assign another special to the job, someone with similar skills and background. Another hammer to drive down this nail.

The kicker to the whole damned box of snakes is I didn't really know what it was they thought I knew or had. The key to the whole thing was down there, hidden away under the watchful gaze of a giant brown squirrel and a truckload of killers.

When you can't run, and you can't call for help, you only have one option: fix bayonets and attack. I put Molly in gear and drove down off the overpass. Time to teach these assholes a thing or two about picking a fight with Randall Wade.

I was staging a one-man assault on a strong position. Assets? A twenty-year-old Bombardier, a bullet-resistant trench coat, a .45, three magazines of caseless ammo, a combat knife, and a burner phone. Liabilities? Too many to count. My only chance was to hit them hard and fast. Surprise is something that happens in the mind of your enemy. It engenders both chaos and confusion. And where there's chaos, there is opportunity. If your enemy is well-trained and experienced, the window of opportunity is small and shrinks with every passing moment. I was counting on the Voodoo Mafia not being very well trained. And I was counting on Tyrone and his people to take advantage of the chaos I was about to cause.

I waited until the sun was nearly set and shining straight into the faces of anyone looking west. I barreled through the gate and made straight for the Conroy Algae truck. I squeezed both trigger paddles tight on the steering wheel. This time the quad .50s roared to life. Thumb-sized and steel-cored, the .50 caliber armor-piercing rounds tore through the side of the trailer. I hit the smoke dispenser and powered Molly into a large doughnut, pouring hot lead into the truck from every angle.

Satisfied that the occupants of the truck were either dead or wounded, I slid to a stop, nose facing the front doors to Big Bill's. I punched open my door and slipped out, keeping below the protection of Molly's armored door and hood. Relying on smoke and confusion to hide me, I ran to the trailer door. It was partially open, kept that way by the dead man hanging head down. Poor bastard had tried to make a run for it. I pulled him the rest of the way out of the door. He was armed with an M-4 carbine. I picked up the weapon and checked the load before peeking inside, weapon ready.

There was no need. The inside of the trailer was a charnel house. There had been nine or ten inside. Hard to tell without time to sort through the pieces. I turned back to the front of Big Bill's. I'd left the smoke dispenser running, reducing visibility to feet. That worked in my favor. Under the cover of the smoke, I pulled a couple of road flares from the center storage compartment between Molly's driver and gunner seats, lit them, and tossed them inside the trailer. More fire, more smoke, more confusion. I grinned and jogged through the smoke toward Big Bill's Dine and Dash.

By the time I'd worked my way into the warehouse portion of the truck stop and on into Big Bill's proper, Tyrone and his crew had the Voodoo Mafia thugs all sewn up. Turns out there had been four more keeping everyone penned up behind the lunch counter. Big mistake. Tyrone hadn't built a profitable truck stop on the outskirts of Knoxville by being a pushover. When I came tearing into the compound guns blazing, Ty took the opportunity to hit the panic button. This transformed the diner into a fortress with Durasteel shutters sealing off the windows and a similarly armored barrier that turned the lunch counter and the area behind it into a small bunker complete with weapons ports. Safe behind the barrier, Tyrone and his crew tooled up and handled business. I arrived in time to find Ty and his crew stripping corpses and stacking the bodies for disposal.

"Damn, that was quick work." I looked at the bodies.

All four were sporting the characteristic zombie head in a top hat ink, signifying full membership in the Voodoo Mafia. Bayou Billy and Jethro were sporting a lot more ink than that. The collection of skulls, coffins, crossroads, and X-eyed effigies identified these two as serious players in Papa G's organization.

"Not our first rodeo." Tyrone pulled a thick stogie from his apron pocket, bit off one end, and wet the other before sticking it in the corner of his mouth. "I tried to tell them you weren't to be fooled with, to take some food and go on back down to the bayou."

"They stayed put?" I started going through pockets for intel. Both Billy and Jethro had phones in their pockets. I took Jethro's and used her thumb to unlock it.

"They were pretty confident you were headed this way." He pulled a match from another pocket, struck it with one well-chewed thumbnail, and lit the cigar before perching on a stool at the counter. "Said you'd be here to pick up something you left behind."

"Like maybe someone was passing them intel on my whereabouts?" I opened the recent calls tab. The last seven calls were to a number with an 804 area code. Richmond's area code was 804. The number didn't match any of the numbers I kept memorized for Allied Atlantic. But that didn't mean much.

"Sounded that way from this end." He shrugged. "They tore the hell out of the lockers and my short-term storage."

"Find anything?" I opened the settings on Jethro's phone and added my thumbprint to the login options.

"Nudie mags, spare clothes, spare parts, and ammo. The usual crap truckers leave behind." He exhaled a thick cloud of heavy blue-gray smoke.

"So, you don't know what I left behind?" I opened Jethro's clutch app. Turned out her name was Carol Landry; she was born in '42 and had a cat named Baron Samedi. I liked Jethro better.

"Didn't say that," Tyrone said. I looked up at him.

"Let me guess, you got it locked up in the office safe, and they hadn't gotten around to beating the combination out of you?"

"Bitch, please." He exhaled another cloud of smoke and laughed. "These half-assed swamp thugs? Besides, I opened the safe for 'em. Weren't nuthin in there but cash, ledgers, and documents."

"What did I stash here?"

"Me." Her voice was small and soft as a fleece blanket. I looked up from Carol Landry's phone. The voice belonged to one of Ty's staff. She was older and must have been a real beauty in her younger days; even now with the iron-gray hair pulled back in a severe ponytail and wrinkles pulling at the corners of her mouth, she was striking. The name tag on her apron said Doreen.

"I'm missing something here," I said.

"Look closer." Ty dragged an ashtray carved from an old piston over and flicked ash into it.

I jammed the gangster's phone into my pocket and took a closer look at Doreen. Someone, someone with serious skill, had transformed a young woman in her twenties into an old lady. There was something about her face that nagged at me. Poked me in the back of my brain like a splinter. I looked at Tyrone grinning around that fat stogie, then back at her. Slowly it dawned on me. I'd seen that face all over the news feeds. Hell, you couldn't turn on a screen without seeing it or the sorrowful visage of her father. But that was ten years ago. Since then, the story would resurface around the anniversary each year. I was looking at the face of Alissa Conroy. Kidnapped and presumed dead daughter of billionaire Devon Conroy. I had somehow found and stashed the missing person of the century before being murdered by the Voodoo Mafia.

"You're Alissa Conroy." She nodded. I glanced at Tyrone. "You've been hiding her in plain sight as a sixty-year-old waitress named Doreen?"

"You didn't leave me a lot of options," he said. "You blew through about a month back, late I might add, dropped her on my doorstep, and begged me to keep her out of sight until you came back for her."

"Begged?"

"You gave me this," he pulled a thick, grease-stained envelope from his pocket and tossed it onto the table. I picked it up and looked inside. It was fat with hundreds.

"I gave you the better part of fifteen grand to look after her?"

"More like twenty-five," he said. "I kept ten for my trouble."

I looked at Doreen/Alissa. She'd stood there the entire time, quiet. Her hands twisting and working at her brown apron. "You're not dead," I said.

"You said that when you found me."

Alissa spilled as much of the story as she knew, which wasn't much. She'd been deep in the throes of gooferdust withdrawal when Randall Three found her. A month later and the marks of it were still present, now that I knew where to look. He'd hauled ass to Knoxville and dropped her and an envelope full of cash on Tyrone. She vaguely recalled Randall Three shooting at someone several times though her recollection was very disjointed. Not much help, all things considered.

She did have one thing, though, that was helpful: a datacube for a holocomputer. What I didn't have was time to dig through it. Somewhere in the next hour or so, someone would be checking in on these assholes. When they didn't answer that someone was going to know something was up. It was time to figure out who was on the other end of that 804 number.

I pulled Jethro's phone out and called the number. It picked up on the first ring.

"Did you get him?" I recognized the voice on the other end. Not counting my last couple years in the service, I'd heard that voice more than my own mother's. Hearing it now, asking if my enemies had gotten me, the same way it'd asked me if I'd completed one task, or another hit me like a punch to the gut.

Surprise is a thing that happens in the mind of your enemy. I should have been surprised. I wasn't. Betrayed, angry, a little confused? Sure. Surprised? No. I'd reported in to Monty more than once since waking up at Uncle Lou's. Shortly after, people turned up taking shots at me. When I'd glassed Big Bill's and spotted that Conroy Algae truck and the goons in the window, I knew there was something rotten in Denmark, or someone. Now I knew who.

"Sorry, Colonel," I said. "I got them."

"Randall?"

"Anyone else still call you Colonel?" I walked around behind Tyrone's lunch counter and poured myself a cup of coffee.

"I tried to warn them off." The Colonel sounded tired. "I tried to warn you off."

"That why you weren't taking my calls?"

"Yes."

"Now what?" I added a little creamer and a lot of sugar.

"You weren't supposed to have another backup," he said. "You'd done what I needed— "

"So, you had me killed?" I took a sip of coffee. It was sweet enough to qualify as a desert. Perfect.

"Not the first two times." His voice grew sharp with frustration. "Those were legitimately at the hands of Papa G and his thugs."

"The third one?"

"You know," his tone shifted, sounding almost amused. "You're a hammer. Hammers get used to hit things. When the Chairman of the Board calls you up in the middle of the night and tells you to sort shit out in Memphis and spare no expense, well, that's when I call you."

"I don't follow." I eased onto a stool at the counter. Tyrone was busy on the grill while the rest of his crew went about getting Big Bill's back in business.

"Devon Conroy stumbled onto his long missing and presumed dead daughter in a Beale Street brothel," he said. "One that indulges those with wealth and deviant sexual tastes. If you catch my meaning?" I did. Places like that were illegal, but for the right price, you can scratch any itch these days."

"I'm listening," I said.

"Mr. Conroy is very good friends with Allied Atlantic's Board Chairman. He called up the Chairman in a drunken stupor raving about Alissa. The Chairman called me with orders to sort it out. I put you on it. Told you to figure out what the hell was going on in Memphis. Told you to take off the gloves if you had to."

"Let me guess," Tyrone held up a plate and cocked one eyebrow. I nodded. I hadn't eaten since Jumpin Joe's. "I stirred up a hornet's nest when I did."

"You don't know the half of it," he said. "When you turned up face down in the Mississippi without your hands, feet, or brain, I knew Papa G was involved." That was no surprise. Papa G ran the Voodoo Mafia, and the Voodoo Mafia was in the itch scratching business. "The Chairman said spare no expense, so I activated your backup and put you back to work. You wound up in a Jumpin' Joe's bathroom. No hands, no feet, brain scooped out."

"I'm sensing a theme here," I said.

"Now the Chairman is pissed so I activate your other backup and put you back on the— "

"Wait a minute," I said. Something wasn't adding up. "I can understand Papa G's crew getting me the first time. I didn't know what I was getting into, I probably asked the wrong person one too many questions and they got the drop on me. But the second and third time I know they're coming. Unless you don't fill me in on all the details. Why? What kind of game are you running here?"

"Well, that's the thing," he said. "I couldn't just turn you loose on Papa G."

"Why the hell not?" Tyrone dropped a plate loaded down with Memphis Red and fried potatoes in front of me. There was something the Colonel wasn't saying. Papa G had to have his hooks into the Old Man. It's the only thing that made sense. "Does Monty know?"

"Monty?"

"Yeah," I forked a pile of algae and potatoes in my mouth and chewed. "Does Monty know you work for Papa G?"

"Who said I— "

"Don't piss down my back and tell me it's raining hot water." I cut him off. "Only way you'd keep rolling me under the bus like that is if you owed Papa G. How deep are you in his pocket?"

"As deep as it gets."

"Monty?"

"No. Reid's clean."

I ate and thought for a minute. I owed the Old Man; owed him my entire life. After the court martial's decision to discharge me with a dishonorable, no one in the security business worth working for would hire me. No one except the Colonel. He knew the discharge was bunk. He took me on as one of his specials. "I'll let the rolling me under the bus slide."

"What about the girl?" So, he knew what I'd found, just not where I'd stashed her. I looked at Alissa plating up food and toting it out to the rest of Ty's crew. Looked over at where Jethro's body had been. They were of a similar build. Dental records were probably different, and a DNA test would certainly tell the difference. I looked out the window at the burning Conroy Algae rig. An idea forming.

"Dead," I said. "She caught a flamethrower shot trying to run across the parking lot. Ran right into the damned thing."

"All right," he sounded hesitant, like he suspected I was bullshitting him but not wanting to push the issue. "And us."

"Like I said," I washed another bite of Ty's cooking down with coffee. "I'll let it slide. I owe you that much."

"Papa G won't stop coming for you," he said.

"That sounds like Papa G's problem." I leaned back and watched Tyrone work. For a big man, he floated around behind that grill like some kind of cigar-chomping, spatula-wielding kung-fu master. Every movement precise, controlled, no wasted motion. I wondered, not for the first time, if he had to have his implements special made.

"He'll make me help."

"I know," I said. "How about this, you help me take him down, and you help him find me, you know, double agent style."

"You're gonna take on the Voodoo Mafia?" He sounded incredulous.

"Do I have a choice?" I looked at Alissa again. Hers was just one of hundreds if not thousands of lives ruined by Papa G and soft bureaucrats like the Colonel. I could run. Hell, if I couldn't stay two steps ahead of Papa G and the Voodoo Mafia, I deserved to be found floating face down in 'Ol Muddy, missing my hands, feet, and brain. But running from trouble has never been my style.

"You tell Papa G I'll be seeing him."

Gun Bunny Blues
By William Joseph Roberts

"Al is going to kill me," Cass mumbled to herself. "Just my luck too. Everything on this trip has been nothing but smooth sailing, and just as soon as a sure thing falls in my lap, boom, Lady Luck kicks me in the teeth and leaves me to rot." She poured sugar into her coffee and began to stir.

Five days, she thought. *Five days to make it to Dallas/Fort Worth for the trade show or Uncle Al will kill me. It's only our biggest money-maker of the year. All hands on deck and I'm stuck here in the middle of nowhere.* "The only gun bunny to screw up the easiest gig ever. Drive around the country, enjoy the scenery, and work over the parts stores as only one of Uncle Al's official Al's Gals can."

She let out a long sigh that turned into a scoffing laugh. *But noooo. Betting a classic '32 Vulcan model Moose coupe and losing it was not the bright, shining moment of this trip. I just have to come up with five grand, and he'll let me have the Moose back.* She shrugged to herself. "Even if I wanted to bail and come back, there isn't even a rental place in this podunk town."

"Thanks, Chuck," the announcer on the vid screen caught her attention. His plastic, painted-on smile looked painful. "I've always enjoyed fieldwork," the announcer continued. "But chasing down story leads is a game for a young reporter. I'm afraid my days of footwork like that are over, but that's why we have a younger generation chasing the stories to give you the scoop on the latest from the world of Autoduelling."

The other announcer smiled and chuckled. "I take it you have something special for us then, Alex?"

"That I do, Chuck. That I do. It isn't every day I come across a reporter that reminds me of my younger self. She has a fire in her belly and an eloquence with her words that I'm sure you'll agree are beyond reproach. Let's turn it over to Bridgit Tassin with our affiliate for a special report on the state of affairs in the South Florida autoduel circuits.

"Hon, are you okay?" The waitress asked as she leaned down on her elbows over the counter.

Cass blankly stared at the mug and stirred the steamy brown liquid like a mindless robot on a factory line.

"Hey, hon!" The waitress slapped her hand down on the counter.

Cass blinked, startled, and looked up at the waitress. "If you stir that coffee much more, Sug, you're going to bore a hole through one of my good mugs."

Cass looked down at the coffee, dropped the spoon, then rubbed vigorously at her face with both hands.

"I have been there and done that honey." The waitress blew out a breath with a dismissive wave and shook her head. Pouring herself a mug of coffee, she came around the counter and sat on the stool next to Cass. "Trust me, if you're feeling like that, he isn't worth an ounce of that worry you're putting into him. You'd be better off by yourself. I've seen it a thousand times." She sat the coffee cup and saucer on the counter, then patted Cass on the back of the hand.

Cass let out a snide-sounding chuckle. "If only. My luck isn't that good. I wish it were that easy."

The waitress gasped, then gently rubbed Cass's back with that motherly sorta touch. "Oh, sweetie. Did he leave you with an extra little gift?" She glanced down at Cass's midsection and then back up at her with an inquisitively raised eyebrow. "Pants that tight won't be good for either of you for very long, sugar. Been there done that myself a time or two." The waitress daintily sipped at her coffee, pinky finger extended as if it were a formal tea party.

Cass looked down at her own midsection before the reality of what the waitress was hinting at struck her. "Oh, no. No, no, no, no." She smiled and let out a laugh before nervously raking her fingers through the chaotic chop top hairdo, pushing her bangs to the opposite side and out of her eyes. "That's about the furthest thing from the realm of possibility for me." She eyed the waitress. The other woman wasn't skinny, and she wasn't voluptuous, but she did have curves in all the right places. Cass turned in her seat to face the waitress full-on, then waggled her eyebrows. Her tongue flicked out like a hungry serpent, then slid across her lips before slipping away. "But I am…available in the right situation." She smiled, then smoothed down an eyebrow with the tip of her pinky finger. The waitress's eyes went wide with shocked embarrassment.

"Oh, no, sweetie. I'm not into all that. If that's the sort of *entertainment* you're looking for, you'll want to go down the street to see Mindy Thobbs. She's down at the Fearless Banjo, two blocks down right next to the hardware store. They've got the coldest beer in town too."

Cass turned back to her coffee and sipped, grimacing at the overly bitter brew. "I wasn't really in the market for *entertainment*, anyway." She tapped out a slow, repetitive beat on the countertop. "I just need to figure out a way to make some quick cash, so I can get my car back and get out of here." She looked back at the waitress. "I didn't see a help wanted sign in the window, but you wouldn't happen to have anything a girl could do to earn a few bucks, would you?"

"Nope. Sorry. Wish I could help. To be honest," the waitress started to say, then covered her shameless smile, "there's barely enough work around here for me most days, but the owner doesn't need to know none of that. Have you checked the boards?"

Cass shook her head. "The boards?"

"Yeah," the waitress smiled and nodded. "It's a community bulletin board sorta thingy. Has a little of everything. From wedding announcements to lost dogs, stuff for sale, and help wanted ads. Midland isn't the biggest place around, but there are enough folks around that you might find something on there."

Cass perked up and glanced around the dinner. "That sounds great. Where is it?"

"Oh, no," the waitress said, waving Cass off. "It isn't a physical board. You just have to do a search on your phone."

"Pssh," Cass laughed, retrieving her phone. "That's easy then." She punched in the search and in no time was scrolling through several entries before coming to a reward notice that caught her eye.

$10,000 Reward

Removal of public nuisance.

On charges of being a danger to the public of the tri-county area.

Serious inquiries only.

"This almost looks like a bounty…" Cass stared at her phone for a moment then showed it to the waitress.

She glanced at Cass's phone. "That's because it is. It was posted by the sheriff's office. That's for that pack of Tinkers that sorta moved into the old quarry site south of town. They've been more nuisance than anything. Heard they'd started getting more aggressive recently. Maybe that's why the Sheriff posted a bounty."

"Why doesn't he take care of it himself?"

"Oh, lord, honey. With it being only him and Deputy Marvin, they don't have the manpower to do anything about it."

"Says here the last place they'd been seen was a small farm. Hey, do you happen to know where this address is?" she asked, turning her phone toward the waitress once more.

"Yeah, that's Jerold Cortez's place. It's down the road a piece just outside of town. He use to be some kind of celebrity or something way back when, but he passed away last year. He was a nice guy and always tipped well when he came in."

"Might not be a bad idea to find out what they were doing at the farm. How far is it?"

The waitress hummed to herself as she thought. "Maybe a mile or so down the road."

"What about the old quarry?"

The waitress tapped her nails on the countertop, thinking. "It's a bit farther. Maybe ten miles or so. I'm not exactly sure."

Cass tapped on the screen and marked the listing as active. "It isn't all that far." Grabbing her jacket, she leapt off the stool and headed for the door.

On an average day, a mile wasn't anything for Cass. She'd regularly run four or more a day at the gym when not on the road traveling for work, or wherever she could when the hotel had a gym. But a mile traveled under a Texas noonday sun in an all-black outfit was something wholly different.

Walking alongside the asphalt pavement turned out to be cooler on the soles of her steel-toed boots. Dust puffed up and trailed away slowly on the light breeze with each sweltering step.

"I really didn't think this plan through so well," she mumbled to herself through chapped lips. Swallowing had become dry and difficult under the baking sun.

Turning off the main highway, she strolled onto a dirt road leading up to a weather-worn farmhouse. Its once white-painted walls and fence were now grey from age and exposure, the paint all but removed by time and dust-laden winds.

This has all the makings to be some serial killer trap to lure in an unsuspecting victim like out of a bad horror movie, she thought. Stepping up into the shade of the porch was a welcome reprieve from the scorching noonday sun. Dry wooden boards creaked under her weight. The wooden framed screen door bounced as she knocked.

She waited, but no one answered. She knocked again.

"Hello, anyone home?"

Someone please be home, she thought, *if for no other reason than I really need a drink of water.*

Stepping off the side of the porch, she walked around to the back of the farmhouse, finding an old barn just down the rise a hundred or so feet from the house. The barn had the same weather-worn features as the farmhouse but seemed somewhat older. She continued down the dusty rise toward the barn. Abandoned farm implements, tractor parts, and parted-out carcasses of cars surrounded the ancient barn. The scene almost looked like one of those quaint, picturesque paintings of country life you'd see hanging on the wall of a dealership or a doctor's office.

"Hello? Anyone?" she shouted, then mumbled, "Anyone besides a maniac serial killer, preferably."

Still, no one answered. Continuing to the rough lumber entrance door that was built into one of the large main double doors, she knocked.

"Anyone at all besides psychopath killers home?" She whispered. Still, nothing. She lifted the simple wooden latch and stepped into the barn. An assortment of body panels hanging from the walls greeted her once inside. Automotive parts and components from all sorts of makes, from Fnord to Conquistador, to Indra and Imperial Motors lay scattered about on rusted metal shelves that lined the walls.

Examining this or that as she stepped deeper into the cavernous barn, she stopped when something caught her eye. Lifting the edge of a canvas tarp, the chrome from a bit of bent fender trim caught her eye. She pulled the tarp up and folded it back, revealing the front end of an older model Iron Horse.

She smiled and muttered, "Well hello, beautiful," continuing to fold the tarp back, letting the bulk of it rest on the trunk lid.

Cass took a step back and let out a low whistle, admiring the lines of the classic Iron Horse autodueller. "Even with the dents and dings, she's still an absolute thing of beauty. Gotta be at least a '35 if not a '36."

"Actually, Sarah is a '37," came a soft voice from behind her.

Cass spun on her heel to find a petite Latina woman standing in the doorway she'd left open after entering the barn. She threw her hands up to show she didn't mean harm.

"I'm sorry. I saw the trim, and curiosity got the best of me."

The woman took another step further into the barn and crossed her arms. "Can I help you?"

"Oh, yeah, sorry about that." Cass laughed nervously. "You just totally caught me off guard."

The woman rolled her eyes and rotated her wrist, motioning Cass to get on with it.

"Yeah, right. Um… I came across the bounty on the community board and the waitress at the Detour Cafe said the bandits were last seen out this way, so I thought I'd learn what I could about them before I blindly wandered into an ass-kicking."

The woman shifted her stance and glanced away for a moment in thought before turning back. "You think you can take out an entire bandit camp by yourself?"

Cass shrugged. "That all depends on a lot of factors. That's why I wanted to do my homework first."

She looked Cass over, sizing her up before she opened her mouth and sucked in a long breath, preparing to speak. "I don't really care if you wipe them out or not, but if you think you could steal back my property, I'd make it more than worth your time."

"What sort of property?" I wouldn't be the first time she'd jacked a vehicle. She'd had to repo vehicles and gear from autoduelling teams that couldn't pay up.

"Marge, my father's old combat camper. He drove that thing through nineteen years of amateur night and minor league autoduels all across Texas. Lots of great memories of traveling in that RV with Dad, and I'd really like to have it back."

"What if they've already scrapped it out for parts?"

She shook her head. "No, I've driven by the old quarry where they've been camped out and recently saw it. It's still intact. There's just no way that I can do anything about it myself."

That's good, but that doesn't mean they haven't gutted the engine and weapons, she thought. "Alright," Cass nodded. "How many of them are there?"

She shrugged. "Seven, eight, maybe a dozen at most."

"And that's where it becomes problematic," Cass said. "Two or three, maybe even five I can handle without any trouble. It's just a matter of sneaking in and sneaking out. With that many, there's no way that I could sneak in and steal the RV back. I'd have to fight my way in and out."

"Okay," the woman nodded excitedly, "so do it. I don't care how you do it. I'll even pay you extra for getting Marge back for me."

"Well, see, that might be a problem."

"Why is that? You were ready to go a minute ago."

"The odds of getting away fast enough and evading that many of them is sketchy at best. I'd need a car to pull it off."

She looked strangely at Cass, tilting her head sideways. She shook her head, not understanding. "Then how did you get here?"

"I walked," Cass admitted, lowering her head in shame. "I lost my ride in a bet last night. I need the cash to buy it back. That's kinda why I'm here."

The woman craned her neck looking around Cass at the Old Iron Horse behind her. "If you think it can pull it off, then take Sarah," she said, chin nodding toward the car.

Cass turned glancing at the car behind her, and awkwardly smiled when she turned back. "You mean you want me to take this car?" she asked. "You want me to take this classic 37' Iron Horse autoduelling masterpiece to recover your dad's old RV? I mean, yeah, she's got some dents and dings and she's not exactly in mint condition, but still…"

"Si."

Cass narrowed her gaze toward the woman. "What's wrong with it? Let me guess – it doesn't run, does it?"

"Oh, it runs, or at least it did the last time Dad worked on her. The key is probably still in the ignition, right where he left it." Her eyes screamed hopefully, almost pleading to take the old dueller.

"But it's your dad's car."

"Sarah was just a side project my dad was fiddling with to keep himself busy during his retirement. Marge, the RV was Dad's primary vehicle in the arenas when a vehicle wasn't supplied. She got us there and brought us home safely every time." Her gaze momentarily drifted off, and she smiled as if she were reliving a happy memory.

This might be the icing on the cake if I play my cards right, Cass thought. "So, what's the RV worth to you, that is, if I can recover it?" Cass suddenly threw her hands up. "Now, you also have to keep in mind I cannot guarantee there won't be any damage. I won't be able to control what the other guys do when the shooting starts, and there's no telling what they might have already done to the RV."

The small woman turned her attention back to Cass with a look of seriousness. "Dad left behind more than just memories after all the hospital visits, so about the best I could do is a thousand."

Excited, Cass stepped forward with her hand outstretched. "You've got a deal, uh…" She stopped. "I don't remember catching your name."

The woman took Cass's offered hand into hers. "Maria. Maria Cortez."

"It's a pleasure to make your acquaintance, Maria."

Maria's father must have installed brand-new power packs before his passing because it took less than an hour to get them fully charged and ready to go. While she waited, Cass carried out a full systems check on the Iron Horse. It all checked out as good as anything brand new Al had let her try out or demonstrate. Then she checked the function of both machine guns before she made sure the recoilless rifle and rear-mounted rockets were operational and fully loaded.

There wasn't anything particularly elegant about the vehicle. It was as round and bumpy as the ugliest toad around, but sexy nonetheless, bristling with gun barrels and rocket ports.

Now if I can just convince them to give back the RV and move off without firing a shot, she thought. *Doubt that will go over well.*

It was still early in the afternoon, so if things did go south, there was no reason why she'd be fighting these guys in the dark. After plugging Maria's info into her phone, she set out heading south for the old quarry.

She'd seen quarries in movie scenes before, but she'd never seen one in person. The main road curved around a rise in the otherwise flat landscape and overlooked the stone quarry.

Old rusted machinery sat abandoned and forgotten around the complex, fighting the ravages of time and elements. It had an old-world industrial elegance about it.

A number of large tents surrounded what was left of a dilapidated block building. Parked alongside the building was an older RV and several other smaller vehicles.

Guess they're home, she thought to herself. *Now if I can talk some sense into them, I could be on the road before dinner if I'm lucky.* She continued along the highway, finding the access road that branched off to the quarry. Clouds of fine dust poured out behind the Iron Horse like a massive rooster's tail as she followed the road to what had most likely been the quarry's main office. Several individuals stepped out from the buildings and tents as she approached.

"I may have the advantage, but I'm not willing to take a chance," she mumbled to herself, then activated the weapons systems. Green lights illuminated across the simple sheet metal dashboard.

A blonde-haired man, who was tall, lanky, and dressed in ragged shorts and a shirtless vest stepped ahead of the others with his hand raised in greeting. The others stayed back several paces. By the number of high-powered rifles visible, there was no doubt that they were well-armed.

Probably should have thought this through a little better, just like gambling with my only ride, she thought. The drive motors hummed as she pulled ahead slowly, approaching the one who seemed to be their leader. Turning slightly to pull up alongside, but keeping her forward arc aimed at one of their parked vehicles, she eased off the accelerator, letting the resistance of the motors bring themselves to a stop.

She rolled down the window and the man took a step forward, leaning down to look through the window.

"We don't get many visitors out this way," he said.

"So I've heard."

"You must be either lost or not all there in the head," he said, a confused tone lacing his voice.

She flashed him a toothy smile and pulled her sunglasses down the bridge of her nose. "Neither, actually."

"Fine looking vehicle you have here." He passed a caressing hand over the roof of the Iron Horse. "Haven't you heard about the big bad Tinker camp? Best you go on home now before you find yourself in a mess of trouble that you can't get out of, Little Miss." The tone of his voice when he called her that grated on her nerves like nails on a chalkboard.

"I'm here to let you know that the sheriff's office has a bounty out on your heads, dead or alive."

He quirked his mouth like the news was a surprise, but not at the same time. "Really? And why would that be?"

"Honestly, to me, it sounds like folks are just scared of what they don't know. But what do I know? I'm just passing through."

The man straightened and laughed, turning to look at the others behind him. "Well, maybe you should just keep right on going, *Little Miss.*"

It was at least worth the effort of trying to talk them into leaving, Cass thought. She clicked her tongue against the roof of her mouth and shook her head. Smiling, she gave the guy a side-eyed glare and let out a chuckle. "Not gonna happen, *bud.* But I'll tell you what *is* going to happen. One," she said, flicking a long-nailed middle finger into view. "You need to get that RV unloaded of anyone or anything you've placed in it. Two," she said, ticking off another finger.

"You need to get everything you plan to take packed up and ready to go. I'll give you and your people one hour."

She slid the sunglasses back up the bridge of her nose and smiled at the man. "Clock's ticking. Chop chop."

He scowled at her. "I don't think you heard me."

"Oh, no. I heard you perfectly fine. But I don't think you heard me," she said, an angry growl tinging her voice. "You need to leave. Now!" She depressed the trigger for the recoilless rifle; it boomed. The blast's concussion reverberated throughout the frame of the old Iron Horse, the round impacted, slicing through the Tinkers' vehicle she'd aimed for.

She floored the accelerator and cut the wheel hard right, then hard back to the left, skidding around the gathered Tinkers, racing away between them and their parked cars. Clearing the space between buildings, she cut the wheel hard left once more, drifting a dusty corner around to the back of the building.

She watched the Tinkers through the rearview mirror scattering for their cars amid the cloud of dust she left in her wake.

"I guess that's gonna be a big fat no," she quipped to herself. Racing past the site's old power substation she followed the road around then cut hard right, drifting through the intersection near the main entrance of the complex.

Machine gun rounds pummeled the Iron Horse's rear and driver's side armor. Two high-velocity rounds impacted the driver's side glass. Spider web cracks raced out from the craters left in the bullet-resistant glass of the antique autodueller.

Continuing her controlled skid to the right, she brought the nose of the Iron Horse around to bear at one of the vehicles following along the dirt path behind her. Firing her left, then right-mounted machine guns as she crossed the line of sight, she continued, throwing dirt high into the air as she did a doughnut through the intersection. Once the Iron Horse's nose was aimed at the next target, she unloaded both machine guns, then fired another round from the recoilless rifle into the lone sedan charging toward her.

The nose of the vehicle exploded in a conflagration of fire and smoke. Its rear end arced high into the air, carried by the forward momentum of the vehicle, somersaulting two full rotations through the air before slamming hard into the ground, landing wheels first.

The light machine gun rounds peppering the hood and windshield left behind little damage against the thick glass. Then, a heavy impact to the rear driver's side of the Iron Horse exploded, sending the tail of the car sliding sideways.

Tapping the brakes, Cass regained control and stomped the accelerator to the floor. The Iron Horse fishtailed as it lurched forward, all four tires finding easy purchase on solid ground just beneath the thin layer of fine dust. One of the Tinkers' cars grazed the nose of the Iron Horse as it blew past her.

Directing the nose of the Iron Horse off the main road, Cass turned onto a side path, skirting past the other two cars in pursuit. She could see them following in the rear view through the cloud of dust left in her wake. Both cars slid sideways through the corner, continuing their pursuit. More rounds pounded against the rear armor plating of her car.

"Really? I don't think you really want to do that!" Lining up the rear sights in the rearview mirror, Cass pressed the right thumb button mounted to the steering wheel, launching everything from the rear-mounted rocket pack. Three of the six rockets impacted the front of the lead vehicle. Its thin front armor plating tore away like tissue paper, flapping in the wind, but it continued in pursuit.

"Didn't get the hint, huh, buddy? You gotta be either stubborn or dumb. Let's see how you handle some creative driving."

Keeping the accelerator buried, Cass raced the Iron Horse up the rise leading to the built berm surrounding the quarry pit. Cass popped the parking brake as she neared the top of the rise and cut the wheel hard to the left, spinning the Iron Horse a full one hundred and eighty degrees. She squeezed the triggers and fired everything forward facing that she had. Tracer rounds sparked, ricocheting off the lead vehicle before the recoilless rifle round impacted the front left of the vehicle's grill.

Controlling the skid, she brought the nose of the Iron Horse around to bear on the upper path that led around the top of the quarry. She cut the wheel to the left again, skidding through the turn at the top. The right rear wheel dropped over the cliff edge. Keeping the accelerator floored, the Iron Horse pulled itself clear of the edge and continued around the perimeter path.

Cass glanced at the rearview. The lead pursuing vehicle tumbled end over end across the roadbed, falling into the dark water of the quarry below. "You should have listened in the first place," she mumbled to herself.

Small caliber rounds continued to pound at the Iron Horse's rear armor, chipping away at the paint and plating. The rear glass exploded, shattering into a thousand shards that showered the inside of the cab.

"Shit!" She swerved, rocking the car back and forth to disrupt their aim. Glancing up at the rearview, she spotted a fiery flash, followed by the distinctive three-round bark of an autocannon mounted to the driver's side of the trailing vehicle.

"Oh, holy shit! That isn't good!" Quickly lining up the rear crosshairs, she pressed the thumb buttons for the rear-mounted rockets, but nothing happened.

"That's even worse. I've gotta get this guy off my tail before he frags me with that autocannon." The path ran for approximately one thousand feet before making a sharp ninety-degree turn to the right and continuing roughly the same distance to repeat the turn and run on the opposite side of the water-filled abandoned quarry. On one side was at least a hundred-foot drop to the water, on the other a steep slope of what looked like loose dirt and sand.

Unless there's a solid path at the bottom, cutting down the side of this thing will most likely get me bogged down and turn into a death sentence, she thought.

The autocannon barked again.

"Frack me!"

Her heart raced in panic.

Rounds ripped past, grazing the driver's door and ripping through the front fender as she bounced along the rough dirt road. Jerking the wheel, she zigged and zagged across the narrow roadway as much as possible. The rear quarter of the Iron Horse buckled under a direct hit from the autocannon's armor-piercing rounds.

"Seriously? If I wanted someone chewing my ass, I'd have stayed home and gotten married. One seriously big bonus to being an Al's Gal: driver training. Now, go away!"

Cass popped the brake and cut the wheel hard. Immediately shifting into reverse, she floored the accelerator. The stink of overheating electrics filled the cab. Drive motors whined and clicked at the strain of the sudden direction change. She lined up the sights of the recoilless rifle and fired. The round tore through the front of the vehicle and exploded. She popped the brake again, bringing the Iron Horse around to face the opposite direction, and stomped the accelerator. Cutting the wheel hard to the right, she drifted into the corner, close to the edge. Both front wheels skipped across the jagged edge of the cliff. Rubber caught hard against the rough stone edge, spinning the Iron Horse out of control. Cass held onto the steering wheel, white-knuckled as the Iron Horse rolled over and over, down the quarry's steep outer slope. Glass shattered under the repeated impact of the tumble, scattering razor-sharp debris throughout the cab.

Her head bounced against the driver's side door, then the Iron Horse came to an abrupt stop on its roof, leaning against a very large and very solid boulder. It struck with enough force that the front driver's side fender caved in, and the boulder dug itself deep into the hood, crushing it like thin parchment paper.

"That was not the best of ideas," Cass mumbled to herself. She shook her head and rubbed at her face, trying to get her eyes to refocus. She glanced up making sure her legs were still there, then took a deep, calming breath. "Nothing else hurts, just my head. Not like I had a lot of brains to start with, so a win for the home team I guess." She chuckled at herself, then winced in pain. "Gotta get out of here, gotta get moving. I'm as good as dead if they find me pinned in here."

She released her seat belt and fell head first, crumpling into a pile against the roof. Turning, Cass pulled herself through the shattered passenger window, the uneven edges of broken glass bit and gouged at her through her clothing. Blood trickled from several cuts she'd gained by climbing through the opening.

A great weight landed on her, pressing down on the center of her back shoving her to the ground and forcing the air from her lungs. She felt fingers wrap themselves into her hair and nails digging into her scalp. Then they pushed, shoving her face into the dirt, grinding her nose against the sandy soil of the slope.

"Why?" a man's voice frantically shouted. "Why did you do this? We didn't do anything, we never harmed anyone. We just wanted to live our lives and provide for our families!"

He had a death grip on her hair and slammed her face into the loose soil over and over. Dust filled her nostrils, and her lungs burned as she struggled for breath.

"We just wanted to be left alone," the voice furiously shouted through sobbing wails. Cass frantically scratched at the ground around her face, digging away at the soil smothering her. She fought to fill her lungs, gasping through the dust. Something hard slammed into the side of her head, the weight suddenly lifted, and hands rolled her onto her back. Someone stood over her, silhouetted in the sun. The silhouette dropped, straddling her.

Cass swung with her right, twisting to get free.

"No!" The person screamed, then struck Cass again in the side of the head with something hard. She blinked, fighting to remain conscious. The person leaned down. It was the blonde-headed man from before. Tears had cut through the dust and grime crusting his face, leaving behind clean streaks. His left hand found its way to her throat and squeezed while his right forced the barrel of a pistol past her teeth and into the back of her throat. She gagged, struggling to breathe.

"Why?" he said through sobbing gasps. "We never…." His sentence was cut short with a choked gasp for air. Cass flexed, wrapping a leg around his neck and jerked him backward.

She grabbed for the gun and his hand and twisted. As soon as it slid out of her mouth, she put pressure on the inside of his wrist, digging her thumb in deep. The gun fired, and the slug thudded into the ground nearby. The man now struggled to breathe. Cass continued to squeeze with her leg, forcing him backward and cutting off his airway.

"Because I have a job to get to," she answered, growling through gritted teeth. "You could have just driven away. They don't want you here. This is on you."

Another round fired, thudding into the ground next to her head. The man swung a left hook with all of his might, pounding his fist into her side, knuckles digging deep into her kidney. Pain shot through her torso, robbing her of breath. Cass gasped then arching her back, wrenched the man's head back even farther. He fought against the strength of her leg, fumbling, he fought to stand. Cass dangled from his neck, hanging upside down.

Digging deep with both thumbnails into the man's wrist, she fought to shake the gun free. He released his grip on her leg. He gripped the gun with both hands to regain control and fired at her again.

Cass's head involuntarily jerked back. Searing hot pain followed the burning red flash of the gun's discharge. The gut-churning stink of burnt flesh replaced the all-too-familiar scent of spent gunpowder. Dazed, she dropped to the ground, landing solid on the back of her neck. Pain shot down her spine and burned across her left eye. A spike of pain suddenly stabbed through her side. She rolled to her right and pushed herself upright, getting her feet solidly under her.

"I'm not done with you yet, bitch!" The blond-haired man rushed forward, reaching for Cass's hair. "I'm going to make you pay!"

Too late to back out now, she thought.

Staying low, Cass sprinted forward and buried her shoulder into the man's midsection. He doubled over from the impact; the breath rushed out of his lungs. Cass gripped and turned his hand as soon as he brought the pistol up, doubling it back toward him. She forced her finger between his and the trigger guard, then squeezed.

Two quick rounds popped off, the slide biting deep into the index finger on her left hand as the action worked. The blonde-haired man gasped, fighting to swallow. Blood splattered, covering his face more with each coughing gasp. His grip on the gun slowly loosened until both hands fell away to his sides. His blue eyes seemed to glow in the bright desert sun. He smiled, then relaxed, letting his body go fully limp. One bloody exhale later and he was gone. Brushing the side of her palm across his face, Cass closed his eyes and sat quietly for a long moment.

"You could have just drove away. It didn't have to come to this." She bit back a sob and swallowed down the upwelling of emotion.

Releasing the magazine, she checked the remaining rounds, then slid the mag home and tucked it into her waistband. After a search of the man's pockets came up empty, she snapped a picture of the dead Tinker for evidence with her phone and then climbed the dusty rise to the service road where the man had left his vehicle parked. After gathering the remaining evidence for the local law officers as proof, Cass pulled up alongside the old RV. No sooner had she shut off the engine and climbed out than a woman burst out of the RV's side door.

The woman's feet had barely touched the ground when she stopped dead in her tracks and pushed the camper door closed. Turning back, she crossed her arms and took a slow step forward.

"We can do this the easy way. You take this heap," Cass said, thumbing over her shoulder, "and just drive away. I'm just here for the RV. The owner would really like to have it back."

"And what exactly are you going to do if I don't want to leave?"

"It has a lot of sentimental value to her, you know. I'm sure you can understand something like that. I mean, it was her dad's and all."

"And why am I supposed to care?"

Cass pulled the front of her shirt up to reveal the pistol tucked in her waistband. "I think I can figure out at least one reason for you to care. Now, let's do this the nice and easy way. You just get in that car, drive away, and never look back."

The woman brushed several loose strands of hair out of her face. "All right," the woman said, nodding. Slowly she made her way over to the car. Even nearly an entire foot shorter than Cass, the woman stood tall and proud in front of her. Cass sidestepped and the woman climbed into the driver's seat.

"Thank you for understanding." Cass bowed slightly then turned, heading for the RV. The unmistakable sound of a revolver hammer being cocked stopped her in her tracks. She turned, slowly glancing back over her shoulder. The tip of the large caliber revolver's barrel bounced all around in the woman's trembling hands.

"You should never have come here."

Cass flashed the most charming smile that she could muster at the woman, then turned slowly to face her. "In hindsight, neither should you. You going to talk me to death or are you going to use that thing?" she asked, chin nodding at the shaky revolver. Cass turned, continuing toward the camper when the report of the revolver stopped her in her tracks.

"You'll get away from that door right now and leave," the woman ordered. An angry growl laced her otherwise pleasantly soft voice.

Cass turned back slowly to see the woman lowering the gun to aim in her direction again. She'd essentially fired into the air for effect. *Bet she couldn't hit the broad side of a barn even if she wanted to*, Cass thought, and continued toward the RV.

A dusty geyser of dirt sprung up from the ground ahead of Cass in time to the bark of the revolver and she froze in mid-step.

"I said to get away from the RV and leave," the woman warned. Her voice sounded desperate and angry.

Cass started to turn and said, "What's it going to take to get you to…?" Another round from the revolver cut her off. Dust leaped from the ground next to her foot. She jumped to the side like it was a snake about to strike. "Geez, lady. You're going to hurt someone with that thing if you aren't careful."

"That's kinda the point, isn't it?"

Cass hooked her thumbs into her pockets and rocked in place on her heels. "Listen, maybe we can make some sort of deal. What exactly is this old wreck worth to you anyways?"

"More than you'd ever know. Now go! Get out of here!" The woman squinted as she started to squeeze the trigger, anticipating the coming recoil. Drawing the pistol from her waistband, Cass dropped to her knees, aimed, and fired. Three points of red blossomed and grew from beneath the woman's shirt. The woman staggered back and fell, dropping the revolver as her body went limp.

Cass stepped over to where the woman lay on the ground, picked up the revolver, and tucked it away in her waistband.

"I'm sorry," she said, rummaging through the woman's pockets. "You had your chance to walk away, and I prefer to keep living. I've only ever had myself to count on and look out for, so nothing personal, lady." Cass pressed the woman's eyes closed, then turned her attention back to the RV.

It wasn't really much to look at. Its armor was cratered and pockmarked, with patches scattered across its surface. Machine guns protruded from the nose and looked to be manually operated from the gunner's seat, while a turret-mounted rocket pod sat idly on the roof, forward-firing flame throwers mounted high to either side, and a rear-mounted mine dropper looked to be the only armaments.

Reaching for the door latch, it felt stuck. She tugged and it didn't budge. Yanking it open, and a girl that couldn't be any older than twelve or thirteen stood there staring at her, pistol in hand. The girl fired, and Cass felt an all too familiar pain. The small caliber round grazed the side of her arm.

Cass drew the revolver from her waistband. "Jesus fracking Christ, kid! You could kill someone like that if you're not careful." Cass snatched the pistol away, removed the magazine then racked the slide, clearing the chamber. Catching the ejected round in mid-flight, she returned it to the magazine before sliding it home into the pistol and tucking it away in a cargo pocket.

The girl recoiled, stepping back away from the doorway. Cass could hear the sound of frightened sobbing coming from somewhere inside the RV. More kids? She glanced back over her shoulder at the body of the woman lying near the car, then swallowed hard. *Shit, shit, shit. If I wanted kids, I'd have had my own litter of sociopathic boat anchors. This is not what I signed up for*, she thought.

Spotting motion deeper into the RV, Cass leaned to the side, glancing around the girl. "How many more of you are in there?" she asked, a nervous waiver cracked in her voice. The girl didn't answer, her only reaction was to stare blankly at Cass and to swallow hard.

No one said anything about kids. I'd have found another way if I knew there were kids involved. Can I just leave them here? Do they even know how to take care of themselves?

Cass thought for a moment, then stepped up into the RV. The girl took another step back, tripping against the bench seat of a table. "What's your name, kid?" The child continued to stare back at Cass. "Mute? Or maybe you just prefer to be mute, huh? Don't talk to strangers and all that sorta stuff? I get it. Ever been to town?" The girl's eyes went wide at the mention of town. "Don't like that idea, huh? Or was town just the bad place your parents warned you about?" She kept the revolver at low ready, just in case any of the others had a gun and got up the courage to use it.

A sudden chill ran up Cass's spine. She glanced over her shoulder once more then pulled the door closed behind herself before sliding into the driver's seat. She glanced around at the controls and caught movement in the large rearview mirror that spanned the width of the windshield. At least a dozen pairs of eyes stared back at her in the reflection of the mirror. That's when she noticed the puffy red gouge running vertically across her left eyebrow and upper cheek. *That explains why it hurt so much*, she thought. She cocked her head to the side and touched the edges of the wound. *It probably needs stitches. Might get lucky enough for one kick-ass scar.* From what she could tell, the grubby little faces peering at her looked to be maybe four or five all the way up to maybe ten years old. Mostly girls from the looks of them, but it was hard to tell under all of the grime.

Cass glanced out the side window at the body of the woman, then looked back up at the faces in the mirror. A cold achy pit formed in her gut.

"We don't need anyone getting hurt, so find yourselves a seat and hold on. We'll be there in no time. Have you kids ever had ice cream before? I'd be willing to bet they have some stashed away for emergencies just like this one," Cass rambled as she steered the RV toward the highway. The ride smoothed out significantly once she pulled out onto the cracked and graying pavement.

Once heading for town, Cass pulled out her phone and dialed Maria.

"Hello?"

"Large Marge has been liberated."

"You're serious?"

"I am," Cass chuckled, nervously. "And then some."

"That's amazing. So I'll see you in a few minutes?"

Cass let out a reluctant sigh. "There's just a slight catch. Meet me in town at the Sheriff's office, and I'll explain."

"What catch?"

"A catch. Meet me in town."

Maria huffed, blowing a puff of exasperated breath into the phone. "Fine," she said, sounding annoyed. "I don't suppose there's any other choice, is there?"

"Nope," Cass responded.

"I'll see you shortly."

"Twenty minutes, in front of the Sheriff's office. Don't forget to bring my cash," Cass reminded her then ended the call. Before she tucked the phone away into her pocket, she dialed the sheriff's office to let them know she was on her way with proof of the Tinkers' removal.

It was almost twenty minutes to the second when she pulled up in front of the sheriff's office. The old RV was large and slow, but it could easily carry extra armor and armaments without a problem. Cass could see why some people would choose it for the arena; it just wasn't her style though.

Turning off the engine, she stood and turned, finding the wide-eyed passel of kids huddled together at the back of the cabin. They ranged from the older tween to a toddler that one of the others held and comforted. *Creepy as shit the way they just stared at you*, she thought.

"Just stay here and stay quiet," she said quietly to the older girl. "I'm going to get all of you some help, okay?" The girl only stared. No nod, flinch, or any other sign of acknowledgment. "Just stay here," Cass repeated, waggling a finger at the girl.

A knock came to the RV's door, then it swung open before Cass could even turn around.

"What in the hell…" the voice trailed off. Cass turned to find Maria standing in the doorway, looking beyond baffled at the sight of the children.

"Told you there was a complication. Do you have my cash?" Cass asked. Maria nodded, handing her a credstick. Cass checked the readout on the stick; it read one thousand dollars, just as they'd agreed. "Perfect. Is the sheriff out there?"

Maria nodded, still at a loss for words.

"Let me wrap this up with the sheriff, then Marge is all yours." Cass turned to the girl holding the toddler and held out her hands. "May I?" The girl flashed a look to the pre-teen, who nodded. Cass recoiled at first from the stink of a bad diaper, but took the toddler from the girl anyway, and placed it on her hip. *They'll be someone else's problem in a few minutes*, she thought. Maria moved out of the way, allowing Cass and the toddler to exit the vehicle.

"The hell is this all about?" The man was obviously the town sheriff, in his clean-pressed khaki uniform complete with a fancy gold-colored star on his chest. "Was it you that called in about the Tinkers?"

"That would be me, sheriff." She handed the toddler off to the sheriff then retrieved her phone from her pocket and proceeded to show him the evidence of their removal. "Where do I go to collect the bounty?"

"Just inside the office. There's some paperwork we'll have to take care of first though." He started to hand the toddler back to Cass, and she immediately took a step back, throwing her hands out to the side.

Cass laughed. "Nope, sorry. That one and the other dozen inside the RV are your problems now."

The sheriff choked, looking taken aback. "What the hell are you talking about?"

"Exactly what I just said. They are your problem now."

"I don't understand," the sheriff admitted, shaking his head.

"I removed the Tinkers just like you wanted. Now I just want to get paid, so I can get out of here."

"Young lady, you aren't making a lick of sense. What's with these kids?" He handed the toddler off to another lady who had hurried over to assist.

"Nothing in the bounty said anything about killing kids. So I didn't. What I did do was to follow the bounty to the letter, *removal of public nuisance*. The adults have been eliminated and their children relocated."

"But…"

"Can you in good conscience say that you would have wanted me to leave them out in the desert all alone?"

"Well, no…"

"Perfect! Let's go get the paperwork squared away. As soon as I can get my car out of hock I can get back on the road." Cass turned on her heel and triumphantly strolled toward the front door of the sheriff's office.

Under the Hood
A Car Warriors Tale
By Christopher Woods

L arry Turner frowned as he passed the church. He was late getting home, and he knew Garrett was going to be fired up. The man was almost unbearable, and he couldn't understand what his mom saw in the guy.

Garrett Wynott was the minister that had spoken at Larry's father's funeral. Less than a year later, he was dating Elena Turner. His father, Jacob had died in a car crash ten years ago, and Larry missed him. Garrett was hard to like with his religious fervor. It wasn't that Larry didn't believe there was a God. He just reasoned that his business with God was between him and God and no one else.

Sure enough, the lights were still on as he pulled into the drive.

"Of course they are," he muttered.

He could hear raised voices from inside the house as soon as he shut off the engine.

"…Driving around in that death machine! Just a matter of time until he kills someone!" Garrett's voice was loud enough to hear from the car.

"It was his father's car! He's not going to kill anyone!"

Larry stepped out of the Conestoga and shook his head. It was a familiar argument. Garrett tried to get rid of the car soon after he moved in, but Larry wanted to keep it. His mother let Larry have the car and used it to teach him how to drive. It was one of the few times she had stood up to Garrett.

The weapon systems had been locked down until he reached eighteen. Garrett refused to unlock them, but it was completely legal for him to have a weaponized vehicle and the car was in his name. It was the beginning of an endless argument that continued over the year since. Any infraction of Garrett's rules ended up being an argument about the car.

Larry opened the door to find Garrett with his finger already shaking under his nose.

"Not one minute of peace in this house since you started driving that death machine."

"Whose fault is that?" Larry asked.

Garrett's eyes bulged in rage.

It was always smarter to just be quiet and let the man get his rant over before saying anything. But, more and more, Larry had trouble doing so. He raised his voice.

"That's right, your fault, not mine. You're a bigoted loud-mouthed vulture that swooped in as soon as my father was out of your way. It's no secret you wanted her a long time before he was gone. Now, you've got what you wanted."

Garrett raised his hand as if he was about to swing at Larry, who smiled. The blow didn't come but it was close. "That's it! That car is going to the scrap heap tomorrow! As long as you live under my roof—"

"Whose roof? My father bought this house before your useless ass ever stepped foot inside the front door." Larry looked at his mother, whose face had paled. "What you see in this asshole, I'll never understand. But he's all yours, now. I'm through."

Larry sensed the blow coming and stepped back. Garrett had swung hard but only a fraction of the force had landed. It still split his lip.

"Garrett!" Larry's mother exclaimed in horror.

The minister had been about to step in and try to hit Larry again.

Larry glanced past the man with the copper taste of blood in his mouth. "Is this what you want, Mom? This guy?"

"Garrett is a good—"

"Horse shit." Larry looked at the man who had struck him. "He's a bottom feeder and a useless sack of shit."

He could see the rage building again. He raised a warning finger. "You hit me again and I'm gonna hurt you. Now I'm gonna get my stuff, put it in that 'death machine', and drive away so you don't have to worry about me anymore."

Larry stepped forward, staring straight into Garrett's hate-filled eyes. Garrett dropped his gaze. Larry pushed past him and his mother.

"Yeah," he muttered, and went to his room to get his things.

It was a little surprising how few things he had that he felt a need to keep, and he left the room with a single duffle bag. His mother was still in the living room. But there was no sign of Garrett.

"Son, you don't have to go," she said. Her eyes pleaded with him.

"Of course, I do," he said. "There never was anything in that man but hate for me. You choosing him after dad died is something I'll never understand."

"Your father wasn't who you think he is," she said.

He pointed toward the back of the house. "Maybe… but *he* is. He's exactly what I think he is." He shook his head.

"You'll see when he doesn't have me around to take that righteous anger out on. This was never about a car, just like it was never about curfew or the people I chose to see. But, maybe I'm wrong, and he'll be a decent guy. I won't hold my breath, though. Goodbye, Mom."

He couldn't help but feel a sense of loss as he drove away. His mother had changed after his dad died. She'd always been quiet and a bit meek, but she would still stand up sometimes. Though it seemed to be less and less. The fact that Garrett hit Larry in front of her and she didn't do anything was a sure sign that it would happen again. It was like she had given him permission.

Larry had been thinking of leaving for some time but didn't know where he would go. Maybe he would go to Knoxville. There was money to be made there.

It was even possible old Bill might have a load of whiskey he needed delivered along the way, which might give him a small stake to get started with. Bill paid decently to deliver his whiskey. The reason Larry had been late getting home was a delivery to Bean Station. The guy had been running a little behind.

It was almost midnight when he drove up Bill's driveway. The lights out in the barn were still on, so he knew Bill was still at it.

"Hey, kid." Bill stepped out of the barn as Larry got out of the car. "What are you doin' out this time of night?"

Larry shrugged. "Had a fallout with Garrett and I'm about to take off. Plannin' to head to Knoxville if you need anything dropped off."

"Matter of fact, I got a shipment to drop off in Maynardville. You got any bad blood over there?"

"None that I know of."

"You headin' in tonight?"

"I reckon. I don't rightly have anywhere to stay."

"You can sleep out here in the bullpen if you want. I'm about to call it a day anyway. We'll get you loaded up in the mornin', so you don't have to make that run at night."

"Thanks, Bill. You're all right for a no 'count moonshiner."

He chuckled. "Gonna miss you round here, kid. I'm guessin' you're plannin' to stay over there in Knoxville. If you need a little cash, you can always come make a run or two for me."

"I might take you up on that," Larry said, gratefully. "Burned some bridges at home tonight, so it may be a while before I'm back for any amount of time."

"It ain't so far away you can't come see me every now and then."

"True enough. And thanks for lettin' me use the bullpen."

"Anytime, kid. Now, I'm gonna go hit the sack."

Larry watched the old man walk toward the house and turned to push a door open inside the barn hallway. It led to a set of stalls that had been converted into a pretty nice lounge with a home-made wet bar on the far wall. There was a pool table and a seating area where Larry dropped onto a fake leather sofa. He liked Bill and knew his dad had been one of Bill's drivers. He knew a little more about Jacob Turner than his mom or Garrett thought. He'd been doing a run for Bill when he was ambushed by some fellas out of Jefferson City. His crash wasn't just a crash, but Larry wasn't supposed to know any of that.

He laid back and drifted off to sleep with ideas of his future running rampant through his dreams.

"Go ahead and dump the bucket in there," Bill said as he loaded the last case of shine. He pointed toward the ammo bin.

"How much?" Larry asked, surprised.

"No charge, kid." He smiled. "Fella going out to make a new future should be fully loaded. Fill the bins on all of em."

"That's four mini guns!"

Bill looked a little sheepish. "Yep. I owe you that much already after all I cost you."

"What happened to Dad wasn't your fault."

"He was workin' for me, kid. If he'd been farmin' corn, he'd still be here."

Larry shook his head. "Dad hated farm work."

"True enough."

"We both know he loved running the roads for you."

Bill smiled. "You're too much like him, kid. When you settle into some job in the city, make sure you get one away from the roads."

Larry grinned. "Sure thing."

"Look in that crate over there when you get the ammo bins full."

Larry poured the buckets into the bins and watched them drop into the feeder tubes before starting to fill the bins. All four bins took most of the barrel.

"You sure 'bout this? That's a lot of bullets."

"Yep, I got more barrels in the back. Your pop put those oversized bins in the car shortly after he started workin' for me. I sure wish he'd been drivin' the old girl when he took that load. Things would have been a lot different."

"Me, too," Larry said.

"Don't forget that crate."

Larry stepped over to the crate and opened it to find four rockets.

"Woah."

"No fussin' now, kid. Those are for the pursuit rockets. You get in a situation, you send those down their throats and they'll think twice about givin' chase."

"Wow." Larry didn't know what else to say.

Bill gave him a gap-toothed grin. "There's just one other thing. Your pop used to have one of these. Thought I'd give this one to you. I don't drive anywhere anymore, and I don't need it."

He held out a helmet.

"Is that a—?"

"Yep. Fully integrated targeting HUD. All you got to do is link it to the car and it'll use all of the sensor package."

"Sensor package?"

"You never found the sensor pack?"

"I just use the dash sensors."

"Boy, are you in for a treat, kid. Your pop put a full 360-degree sensor package on her ten years ago with a triple drone backup." He paused with a sad look on his face. "He never really got to test it. It was bein' installed when he took that last run."

Larry took the helmet he was handed in silence.

Bill shook his head like he was trying to shake what he was thinking out. He let out a long breath. "Put that on and we'll see about gettin' it synced up."

Larry nodded with a lump in his throat and donned the helmet.

"Everything set?" Larry asked the guy who unloaded the corn whiskey in Maynardville. Corn whiskey was a premium product since corn was a rare crop anymore after the blight.

"Sure thing," the man said. "This is so much better than the normal stuff. You tell Bill we really appreciate this."

"I'll do that."

"Is there a problem back there? Bill usually deals in cash."

"I'm on my way to Knoxville. He took an electronic payment since it'll be awhile before I get back to Tazewell."

The man nodded. "That makes sense. You watch out between here and Knoxville, though. There's been talk of some raiders settin' up shop out there." He stuck out his hand. "I'm Cody, Cody Joseph."

"Larry Turner." He gripped the man's hand. The man's eyes widened.

"You're Jacob's kid?"

I nodded.

"You favor him. I thought you might be when I saw you in the Conestoga. He bought that car from my dad at the dealership a couple of years before he died. He was a hell of a driver and a pretty good hand in a scrap."

"That's what I hear."

"I know it's ten years late, but you have my condolences."

"Thanks." I slid back into the driver seat and pulled the helmet down over my head.

Larry saw in his mirror that Cody was still watching with his hand shading the sun from his eyes as he took the left turn on Maynardville Highway toward Knoxville.

Seemed like his dad knew a lot of people around the area. Garrett and his mom never wanted Larry to know about his dad's history, but they should have known it would come out at some point.

The deep hum of the motor was comforting as he drove away from everything he had ever known. The sensors flashed red, and he triggered the HUD just as he topped Copper Ridge. The other side of the ridge was a long straight that led down to the wall around Knoxville. There were three targets on his HUD, and it only took a moment to take in the scene below.

Two vehicles the sensor package identified as Piranhas were attacking a Chameleon. The Linden Motors Chameleon, or LMC was a fairly tough vehicle, but the two Piranhas were doing a lot of damage. Like the Conestoga, the LMC was a car with a driver and gunner station. But the guns were silent.

Jacob had built-in a slave system into the Conestoga so he could run the weapons from the driver's seat, but it looked like the LMC didn't seem to have that benefit. And it was painfully obvious the gunner station was inactive. The enhanced sensor package picked up two heat signatures, but it looked like the weapons control position was damaged.

It only took Larry a moment to decide his course of action. Two on one and they'd already knocked out the gunner? It wasn't hard to decide who the bad guy was in this fight.

He thumbed the controls and the mini guns rose from their ports. His foot pressed the accelerator to the floor and the Conestoga's oversized power plant vibrated as she jumped forward.

He closed the distance with the dueling vehicles quickly. He was pretty sure the Piranhas didn't even know he was there with their focus solely on their victim.

The front left tire shredded on the LMC, and it dropped to send the car into a spin. Both Piranhas shot past the spinning car and slammed on brakes.

Larry caught a glimpse of long blonde hair as he passed the stopped vehicle. He pressed the button on the left side of the wheel with his thumb and the mini-guns began to sing. Tracer rounds showed the path as well as the sensor package did. The old girl tore up the back and sides of both cars as he shot between them. Larry spun the wheel to the right and let her skid completely around to face the Piranhas again. He shifted down and stomped on the accelerator again, tires billowing smoke as the Conestoga lurched toward them.

Bullets peppered the wagon, and Larry thumbed the trigger again letting all four mini-guns pour out a hail of bullets into both cars.

They accelerated toward Larry, but he once again shot between them. Armored glass shattered on the Piranha to his right as Larry passed between them. They hit brakes and began to turn when Larry targeted them and fired a rocket at each of them. Both impacted and engulfed the rear of the cars in flame.

They decided they'd better not finish the turns. They both fled toward Copper Ridge at a greatly reduced speed than they were moving before.

Larry skidded to a halt a little distance from the LMC. Smoke rose from the rear of the car.

"Need to get out of the car!" he yelled. "Fire!"

Both doors opened and two people exited the vehicle. The driver was obviously a woman in her tight road leathers. The gunner was a lean built man. He didn't carry a hand cannon, which was a little surprising.

"Get away from it!" Larry yelled. He motioned toward the Conestoga. "Get in before they come back!" He pointed toward the back door. "One in the gunner seat, one in the passenger."

The woman hesitated for a moment, then shrugged and pointed the man toward the back door as she headed for the passenger seat.

She slid into the seat and the man settled into the back.

Larry punched the accelerator. He needed to get further away from the now-burning car. Just then, some of the ammo went off from the fire. A couple of rounds pinged off the rear of the Conestoga.

He turned to the driver. "That was clo…" He was staring into beautiful gray eyes.

She smiled one of those smiles that lit up a room. "Thank you. I'm Liz. This is Derrick, my little brother."

"Brother?" He glanced in the mirror as the guy in the rear seat took his helmet off. He couldn't be more than thirteen or fourteen.

"My dumb-assed brother who really needs to choose his friends better."

"Come on, Liz!" the youth protested.

"Your *friends* just tried to shoot us."

"That don't seem very friendly to me," Larry said.

"Exactly," she agreed.

He removed his helmet. "Don't look like they're interested in a rematch."

She turned back to the kid. "They're rarely your friends, Der. They all want something from you."

"They didn't know who I was," Derrick protested.

"If they didn't, why did they shoot at us to keep you from leaving?"

"Maybe they thought you were kidnapping me."

"Really?"

The boy sat back with a sulky expression. "Whatever."

Larry saw vehicles coming from Knoxville. "Those look serious."

"Shit, that's Dad," Liz said.

"Those are armored trucks."

She shrugged. "He's kind of a big deal."

He nodded. "Am I about to get shot?"

She giggled. It was cuter than anything had any right to be, and he wondered what he'd gotten himself into.

As the armored trucks arrayed themselves across the road, Larry eased to a stop, keeping his hands on the wheel and his gun ports closed.

Liz grinned at him again and got out of the car motioning to her brother. "Come on, dumbass."

She walked around the car to the driver side and leaned inside the window. "The least I can do for my hero." It felt like a charge of electricity when she kissed him. She slipped a card into his hand as she withdrew. "Call me. I'd like to buy you dinner."

"Um…"

"Man of few words. I'll take that as a yes. Call me tomorrow."

She walked out toward the trucks dragging her recalcitrant brother.

"I don't even know her last name," he muttered, and looked down at the card.

It said Graven Industries, Bowling Green, Kentucky and the name was Elizabeth Graven.

"Shit."

Even out in the backwoods, the Graven name was known. They sponsored the Hoods. Autoduelling was what Graven Industries was known for, and the Hoods were at the top of the charts in the eastern half of the States.

"Charlie would never have let them catch her," Liz said as Larry drove around the curving ramp that climbed the parking garage. She looked amazing. "Unlike my stupid brother."

"Charlie?" He fidgeted with the tie around his neck.

"My sister. She's at boarding school at the moment. She loves to drive." She pointed at the tie and grinned. "You don't like wearing a tie?"

"It's uncomfortable."

"We could just call it off…" She let it drop with a pout.

"Not a chance. Probably not likely there'll be any scrappin' anyway."

She giggled. "And what's the tie have to do with that?"

"Don't get in a scrap wearin' a tie."

"I guess you probably should avoid a scrap anyway." She laughed. "No fighting at Flemings."

"True enough. But a fella needs to be prepared, just in case."

Liz scoffed. "I'm pretty certain we won't be accosted here."

"Is there a bar?"

"Yes."

"There's always the chance of a scrap if there's alcohol," he said.

"You sound like you're looking forward to it."

He tugged the tie. "Not wearin' this damn thing."

She giggled.

He grinned. He really liked the sound of her laughter. It reminded him of the sound he used to hear when his father was still alive. His mother used to laugh a lot back then. There'd been precious little laughter at home in the last ten years.

"Where did you go?" Liz asked. "You were somewhere else for a second."

Larry recovered and smiled at her. "Just a little of the past sneakin' up on me."

"Better days?" she asked.

"Better than bein' right here, right now? Not likely."

She cocked her head a little to the side. "That might just be the nicest thing anyone has ever said to me."

"Honey, you been talkin' to the wrong people."

She laughed again. "Most of the people around me say all sorts of flowery nonsense that sounds really wonderful but none of it is real. For some reason, you're different. One true word is better than a thousand of those flowery nonsense words. Most men who approach me are after something, whether it's money, connections to my family, or sex. Tell me one true word. What do you want?"

"Up until you stepped out of that car and into mine, I had no idea what I wanted," Larry said as he parked in an open spot. "I came to Knoxville with nothin' but a ten year old car my dad left me and maybe enough cash to buy one dinner at a place like this. I looked it up. When I saw you and what you did, that all changed. You drove out into the midst of a bunch of raiders and fetched your brother. Probably the bravest thing I ever seen. Turns out you're brave, beautiful, rich, and interestin' as they come. And, above all, you're completely out of my league. So what do I want? I want to spend the evenin' with a girl so far out of my league that I'll look at this day as the best day of my life for years to come. Better days? There ain't much better than that."

He turned and looked into her eyes and before he could say another word, she clicked the seat belt off and lunged across the seat to grab his tie and pulled him in close. She kissed him for a long time.

She pulled back and smiled. "That's what a tie is good for."

He swallowed. "Yep."

"Let's skip this overpriced dinner and order room service."

"I don't have a…"

She giggled.

"Oh."

"Best day ever," Larry muttered.

Liz moved beside him, "You said that yesterday… and the day before… and the day before."

"It was, at the time. Now today is."

"You're a mess."

"Could be," he said as he dropped his legs off the bed and reached for his clothes.

"You in a hurry to leave?"

"Not really. I have a job interview in a couple of hours."

"Where is it?"

"Tennessee Titan Authority. They're openin' up a division to start workin' out on the roads."

"Why don't you come back to Bowling Green with me?"

He stopped in mid-movement. "You mean that?"

"I'm not in the habit of saying things I don't mean, Larry Turner."

He swallowed. "Best day ever."

She giggled.

"…And the Hoods have taken home another victory!"

"That was a close one, Daniel!"

"You're telling me! The Yarboroughs sure gave them a run for their money this time! I'm not sure where Kelly

Hood learned that last maneuver, but, I swear, I've never seen anything like it!"

Larry tuned out the announcers as he ran the cloth along the shiny red side of the Conestoga. She was candy apple red where she didn't have damage from the scrap outside of Knoxville. He thought about making a run back to Bill's and maybe getting enough to patch the old girl's wounds.

He looked up as a black sedan turned into the carwash parking lot. He nodded in their direction and started working the cloth along the car again.

He straightened as the car stopped next to him and the back door opened. A tall man in a nice suit stepped out of the car.

He stepped toward Larry. "You're Turner, right?"

"I am." He placed where he'd seen the man before. "Mister Graven."

"Don," the tall man said. "Figured I should meet you. You did a good thing when you stepped in to save my daughter."

"She's a brave girl," Larry said.

"Stupid girl," Don Graven replied. "She should never have been there."

"I reckon she saved your boy's life."

"We were on the way to retrieve him after those degenerates sent me a ransom demand."

"You rolled up on that bunch with those trucks and I reckon they'd have put a bullet in your boy's head. They didn't expect her to drag the boy out by his ear and shove him in a car."

Don chuckled. "Perceptive."

Larry didn't say anything more.

"You're correct. She saved his life. And you saved them both." He stepped up to the car and ran his hand across several bullet holes. "That's a little more than a stock Conestoga. Where's a youngster get a car like this?"

"Inherited it from my dad. He used to run shine in it."

"Bootleg liquor? Not an overly profitable business."

"Not if you're runnin' that old algae-based shit. Bill runs some of that for the local boys. No, this was pure corn liquor."

Don's eyes widened. "Where's he getting corn around here?"

Larry laughed.

"What?" Don asked.

"You city guys always figure we don't know what the hell we're doin' out there. They grow it out in the hills still. City folk pay high for stuff like that. You never wondered where it came from?"

"How do they keep raiders from taking it?"

"Reckon they shoot the bastards."

He laughed. "I understand what my daughter sees in you now. You don't mince words. It's refreshing. What are your intentions toward my daughter?"

"Reckon that's up to her, sir. I like her a lot. She ain't like anyone I ever seen before. I reckon I'll be there as long as she wants me to be."

"I came out here to see if I could convince you to stay away from my girl, but I'll be damned if I don't like you." He motioned toward the car where they could still hear the announcers rattling about the Hoods' victory. "With that win, we're heading back to Bowling Green. Come with us and I'll see about getting you some work that fits your skill set."

"I'll take you up on that, sir."

"Good, I look forward to seeing how this goes."

He turned and got back into his car and Larry watched as they drove away.

"Sizin' up to be a pretty good day," he muttered. "Could be best day ever."

"The Hoods take Midville! What a match! Kelly barely got that one over the finish line after that knock-down drag-out with the Soul Crushers! What's next for the Hoods? Maybe—"

The announcer's voice abruptly cut off as the HUD lit up with three red markers.

"We got three bogeys," Larry said, talking into his microphone pickup.

"Where?" Jimmy, he convoy driver, sounded worried.

"Comin' from your two o'clock."

"There they are. Damn you have some good sensors."

"Best on the market."

"Enough chatter," Allen Stark said. "You're playing rear guard, rookie."

"Will do, boss." Larry said.

He watched the sensors as the three war wagons moved to intercept the incoming bogeys. He took position near the left rear of the lead tractor trailer. The trailer was a plain Jane budget box full of supplies for Wichita after the destruction from three f-5 tornados that dropped within minutes of each other. No one had ever seen anything like it. All three were on the ground in the Wichita area at the same time. The convoy of seven trucks was filled to the top with food, water, and medical supplies Don had shipped out for disaster relief.

Larry launched his three drones to keep a better track of what was going on. They reached their designated altitude and Larry's HUD lit up with more red bogeys coming up from the rear.

"Damn! More comin' up on our six. Four targets."

"What do we do?" the lead driver asked.

He thought for a moment. "Floor it and don't stop for a damn thing."

"Where are you going?" he asked, as Larry hit the brakes and dropped back along the convoy.

"Reckon I'm gonna go introduce myself, Jimmy."

"What?"

"Just move it on out, Jimmy."

Larry dropped behind the last truck and glanced back at the full loader racks for the launchers. He grimaced and started tapping the control screen right behind the gear shifter. The drones slowed and dropped back to a position closer to the four red bogeys.

The bogeys turned yellow.

"Let's light 'em up, old girl."

He punched in the directions for the seeker rockets. There were four vehicles, and the drones had a hard lock on all of them. He hesitated for a moment but knew it had to be done. He couldn't let them get to the trucks.

The two launchers fired, and the racks dropped another rocket into each. Every three seconds, two more rockets fired. In less than twenty seconds all twelve rockets were in the air and seeking their targets.

He slammed on the brakes and slid around to face the incoming trucks. As he punched the accelerator and smoked the tires, the first rockets struck their targets. Each of the trucks got three of the rockets. Although two of the twelve lost their lock and overshot the Galahad that was leading the pack, one still hit it. Two of the trucks were smoking wrecks and a third was losing speed when Larry thumbed the button on the four linked mini guns. The ammo bins were full, and Larry kept his thumb down as he closed the distance on the Galahad.

Bullets peppered the Conestoga, and the windshield cracked just before the Galahad lost its windshield. Bullets from the minis filled the cab and the Galahad erupted with flames. The truck that had lost speed slammed on brakes and was trying to run, so Larry let it go. He turned the wagon back toward the convoy and left the drones on scan to keep track of the lone survivor of the attack that was rolling east at a slow speed.

The three war wagons came into sight and Larry drove past them.

"Jesus, Rook. What the frack was that?"

"Reckon them fellers didn't like the introduction." Larry kept his voice steady even though he felt like losing his lunch.

He was pretty sure he had just killed more than one person back there and his hands were shaking on the wheel.

"Not a good day," he muttered under his breath.

"I don't think I want to kill people for you, sir."

"I understand," Don said, looking at the damage from the firefight. "It was a travesty you had to do that. But you need to understand, that wasn't for me. That was for the millions of casualties in Kansas. Son, there's war going on in the wastelands between cities. I don't even understand why, but there's always someone out there trying to take from those that have what they want. You and those drivers had something that was desperately needed in Wichita. Those men knew you carried it and knew what it was for. They still decided they were willing to kill you all and steal it. You stopped them. That's what you did. You saved untold amounts of lives by protecting that shipment. You were a soldier, and there's no dishonor in that."

Larry grimaced. "I'm just not comfortable with it, sir. Not at all."

"Nobody should feel good about it. It was necessary, and that's the only thing you can say to make it any better."

"All right, sir."

"You're a good man, Larry Turner. Now, go make sure Lizzie knows you're okay."

Larry got back into the Conestoga and let out a slow breath. He'd almost gotten past the sick feeling, but he could see that Galahad erupt in fire when he closed his eyes. It was one thing to shoot up another car in defense, but it was usually settled when someone ran like those two Piranhas. The fight in Kansas was another matter. It had been deadly.

He pulled slowly out of the lot. He would sure be glad to see Liz.

"You ready?" Larry stood next to the bathroom door. "Gotta get to work."

"I'll meet you there, baby. I'm going to be a few minutes." Liz's voice was muffled.

Larry's newest job was to work the prep crew for the Hoods. He looked forward to going to work each day, and remembered Garrett's warning that it was only a matter of time until Larry killed someone. Garrett was seldom right about things, but it had been the truth. The fight in Kansas still left a bad taste in his mouth. Just like Don said, it was a war out in the wastes. It didn't mean he had to like it.

"I'll take a cab over. You can bring Charlene," Liz called out.

"Okay."

He grinned at the name. Liz was dead set that he couldn't name his car after her. So, they settled on naming the Conestoga after her sister Charlie. Larry had met Charlie one time at a holiday dinner but didn't know her very well. Liz really looked up to her sister, so the name stuck, and he saw no reason to change it after meeting her.

He glanced back at the bathroom with a grin.

"How did I manage to get this lucky?"

He picked up his jacket and left the hotel room. It was a balmy day in Waco, and he was quite happy it wasn't the middle of summer. Texas could be hotter than Hell in the summer.

He waved at a taxi that had just let a passenger off.

"My lucky day," he muttered. Sliding into the back seat he nodded at the driver. "Double Drum."

"Going to see the *Two Fer*, buddy?"

"I work the pits for one of the teams."

"That's a pretty good gig. Which team? I thought I'd ask before rootin' for one of the others."

Larry laughed. "Dude, you root for your favorite. Don't you worry 'bout offendin' me. Who's your favorite?"

The cabbie pulled out. "It's probably a tossup between the Hoods and the Grave Diggers. If we get really lucky, they'll win their respective matches and have to go head-to-head. Now, whose pit are you working?"

"The Hoods."

"Holy shit! You really work with the Hoods?"

"Sure do." Larry grinned at the excitement of the cabbie. "Been workin' their pit crew for a few months. We went over that car with a fine-toothed comb yesterday. She's gonna be a beast in the arena."

"That's frackin' awesome!"

"You gonna be there?"

"I'm on shift too late, but I'll be listening on the radio. If I'm stopped by some chance, I'll watch on the pad." He tapped the data pad laying in the front seat beside him.

"I think you'll be happy with this one," Larry said. "The Hoods have been in prime form lately."

"I swear Kelly Hood gets better and better," he replied.

"She's Hell on wheels, that's for sure."

"So, is she as pretty as everyone says?"

"Never seen under the hood. They show up hooded and stay that way. I guess they want to live regular lives when they're not drivin' out there."

The cabbie gave a firm nod. "I guess it makes sense. There's a lot of people on the Clutch Stream that would kill to get a look."

"I'd say so. But, like I said, even the pit crew's never seen her."

"Still has to be one of the coolest jobs around," he said.

"Yeah, it's pretty awesome."

The cab stopped at the side entrance of the stadium for employees. Larry got out and looked in the front window. He handed the cabbie a fifty.

"Keep the change, buddy."

"Thirty dollar tip. Heh, you're all right for a greaser."

"I reckon you're a pretty good for a hack. Didn't even run off the road once."

The cabbie grinned and waved as he drove off.

Larry showed his ID at the entrance and took the first door to the right. It opened on a long hallway that circled the stadium to end at the pit area. He only made it halfway around before he was met by David, one of Don's assistants.

"You need to follow me, sir."

"Sure," he replied and followed David to a door on the left.

Don was inside with several other people that Larry didn't know. Don stopped what he was saying and strode over to Larry.

"We have a big problem, son, and you may just be the solution."

"What kind of problem?"

He motioned for Larry to follow him into another room where a couple of people were looking at a body on a table.

"Woah." Larry stopped. "This just got a lot more serious than I'm comfortable with."

"That's Jeremy Hood, son. Had a damn stroke right over there." Don pointed at a small lounge area where a broken glass coffee table was being cleaned up.

"Oh shit, that's not good."

"You're telling me. I need you, kid. You're the only one here with any experience as a gunner. I need you to put on the hood and run this race."

"What?" Larry blanched.

"We can't drop out of this one. There's a lot of money at stake here."

"Winner's purse is maybe a hundred thousand," Larry said.

"Son, the winner's purse is just for the driver and gunner. The real money is the gambling. The winner's purse is yours, win or lose, if you do this."

"Frack."

"So, what do you say, kid?"

"I'll run the gunner's chair, but I ain't him, and I ain't plannin' to kill anyone."

"The object is to disable the cars," Don said. He nodded and motioned for David who had followed them into the room. "David, get me the spare suit." He turned back to Larry. "You'll have to wear the hood. It's an advanced HUD linked with the car's weapons and sensor suite. Can you handle a 360-degree HUD?"

"Yes, sir. Been usin' one for a while now."

"Get dressed and get in the car. Kelly will be down in a few minutes."

Larry took the hood from Don as David brought a stack of leathers and set them down on the chair in front of him.

"Frack me," Larry muttered and picked up the pile.

"The Hoods are on fire, Jackie!" the announcer's voice boomed over the speaker system. "Literally and figuratively!"

"Looks like they have the literal fire under control with the fire suppressor, though, Willy!" Jackie replied. "I don't think anyone is going to suppress the Hoods tonight!"

Larry cursed as he used the last of the chemical extinguisher. "Sons of bitches!"

"What the hell are you doing?" Kelly yelled, as Larry unlinked the two Vulcans on the top of the car. "Those are linked for a reason!"

"I have two frackin' hands! What the hell did he do with the other one? Jerk off?"

Expecting to get screamed at, he was surprised when Kelly snorted.

Larry rolled his shoulders and grabbed both controls. "Get me between those two pricks with the flame throwers."

"Between them?"

"Hell, yeah."

"Crazy… get us killed…" she muttered. But she braked and let the two cars get closer.

The Vulcans spun to each side and spat a hail of bullets into the front tires on both vehicles.

"Full brake!"

She slammed on the brakes just as the fronts dropped on both cars. They came together as the destroyed tires pulled them. The fronts of both cars collided with a satisfying crunch and the Vulcans spun to face them.

A hail of bullets poured into the rear of both cars and Larry's sensors showed the power plants go offline.

"Two for one!" Kelly yelled, turned the wheel, and throttled back up.

"That's why they call it a *Two Fer.*"

She throttled up and shot toward the outer wall as the last of the cars rounded the track behind them. It was the Praetorians.

"This guy's moving fast," she said.

"Gotta get closer for the Vulcans to do anything."

Kelly barked out a laugh through her mask. "You want closer? Let's get a little closer."

She threw the car into a skid that ended facing the other car and stomped the throttle. All four tires smoked as the car lunged forward. The Praetorians were distracted for a moment by the wreckage of the other two, before realizing Kelly was turned around and the distance was shortening rapidly.

"Tires are the weakest point," Larry said and focused his fire on the Praetorians' steer tires.

Bullets peppered the front armored glass.

"Driver's the weakest point!" Kelly yelled and skidded the car again to get the front out of the firing line.

Without having to worry about steering the car, Larry kept the Vulcans trained on the front of the other car. The front dropped and sparks flew as the bottom of the car slammed into the pavement. Kelly straightened and passed the Praetorians. Larry grinned as he switched to target the power plant. The Vulcans spat out a stream of bullets.

His sensors showed the power plant go down, but the gunner kept firing.

"They're done. Why is he still shootin'?"

"He's an asshole."

The glass cracked on the back.

"Fine," he said and triggered the rear rocket launcher, targeting the spot just under the rear bumper.

The back glass shattered just before the rocket impacted and sent the Praetorians' car over on its top. The firing stopped.

"Well, now, that shut them up," Kelly said. "Middle gate!"

She threw the car to the side as the middle gate of the Drum opened and a bullet-riddled car entered the track.

"Let's get this done before this bucket of bolts falls apart." Kelly said. "That's not the Grave Diggers. I was expectin' the Grave Diggers."

"If they took out the Grave Diggers, they have to be some bad asses."

The other car came to a stop just inside the arena and smoke bellowed out of broken windows. They could see struggling inside of the car and Kelly skidded to a stop.

Larry was out the door before she could say a word and sprinting toward the car. As he got closer, he could see the driver trying to get his seatbelt off. The gunner staggered out of the other side and Larry yanked open the driver door. He popped his knife open and sliced the belts. Then, he helped the driver struggle out of his seat.

They were about twenty feet from the car when the explosion sent them tumbling.

Larry rolled over on his back, breathing heavily.

"Frack me," the driver said, panting. "I was a goner. Frackin' Jeremy Hood just saved my life!"

Larry shook his head realizing the guy was live streaming from the feed in his helmet.

Without a word, he stood up and returned to the car.

"Working with a fracking white knight..." Kelly's muttering could be heard over his com.

"So, now you've roped him into it too?"

Liz was talking to Don as Larry stepped into the room.

As the door closed, he strode to Liz and removed the hood.

"Oh, damn," she said.

"What?" he asked as he swept her into his arms.

"You've got that look in your eyes. Just like hers when she put the damned hood on."

"Hers?"

She looked past Larry at Kelly. The driver removed her hood. Larry gawked.

"Charlie?"

"I hear you named that old Conestoga after me."

He shrugged.

"A Conestoga? Really? I'm a fracking station wagon?"

Charlie dropped the hood and shook her head in dismay. "A Katana maybe, or a Shuriken. Yeah, that would be okay." She raised both hands in the air in disgust and walked toward the locker room. "I wouldn't even mind a bike. A Spyder, maybe. Nooo, I'm a fracking Conestoga..."

The door closed behind her, and Liz burst out in laughter.

"It's a bad-assed station wagon," he said with a shrug.

"Kid, you were pure gold out there!" Don exclaimed as he strode forward and slapped Larry's shoulder. "We're going to be working on getting Jeremy reloaded into a clone. Then we have to go through retraining therapy. What do you think about wearing that hood for a bit longer?"

Larry looked at Liz. "What do you think, Lizzie?"

"I don't like you being shot at," she said. "But, you're really good at it. Dad said you're a better gunner than Jeremy. And, I can see by the look in your eyes, you loved it."

"I won't do it if you don't want me to."

"I would say you do it until Jeremy is back. Then we can discuss it."

Larry nodded.

Don smiled. "I guess we need to head to the office, then. You have some contracts to sign, and I have a fairly large check to write."

"Let's do it," Larry said.

Liz shook her head. "First, you get in there and change out of those leathers. Take a shower and get the smell of burnt wiring off you. No one can know you were out there."

Larry opened the door to Don's office.

"Are you sure about this?" Don asked the man sitting across from him.

"I am. Kid's better than I ever was anyway."

Larry recognized the man as he turned toward the door. It was eerie seeing Jeremy Hood in the flesh. The last time Larry had seen him, he was dead on a table.

"Speak of the devil…" Hood said, "that's my cue to exit stage left."

Both men stood and shook hands.

"Good luck, kid," Hood said as he walked past and out the door.

"Have a seat." Don motioned toward the vacated chair. "We have a few things to discuss."

Larry sat. "Sir?"

"You've been under the hood for close to a year, now. I know you like it. What would you think about wearing it a while longer?"

"I'd like that, sir. But I'll have to talk it over with Lizzie."

Don nodded. "You do that. Seems Jeremy doesn't want to come back. He's been shaky ever since Kelly left, but it never was enough to make him follow suit until this."

"I reckon dyin' gives a person somethin' to think about."

"I'm sure it does," Don said.

Larry stood. "I'll talk to Lizzie and have an answer for you."

"And the Hoods take the Double Drum, Ellen!"

"Frankly, I'm a little surprised, Daniel. They haven't had a great year."

"They announced this as their retirement year, and I have to say they deserve it. Jeremy and Kelly Hood have been top competitors for close to twenty years…"

Larry started awake.

"Where were you?" Liz asked.

They sat in a matching pair of rocking chairs on the front porch.

"Just rememberin' when the Hoods retired."

"Which ones?"

"The last ones. Not me and Charlie."

They heard yelling kids as they came around the corner.

"That Tolliver kid's a bully," he said.

Bill Tolliver pursued Donnie Flynn through the front yard. He got close enough to push Donnie down on the ground.

Larry stood up but Jake rounded the corner and tackled Bill. He and Bill rolled across the lawn, but Jake came out on top, where he held Bill down until he quit squirming.

"You leave Donnie alone, now!"

Bill nodded quickly and Jake let the boy go.

"Our grandson seems to be a lot like his grandfather," Liz said.

"He's gonna be a fighter. Sure wish his dad was still around to see him." He sat back down.

"Me too, love." She reached over and took his hand. "Do you ever regret leaving the circuit?"

"Nah. I made you a promise the day you agreed to marry me, and it wasn't a hard one. When you say the word, I retire."

"And I told you I wouldn't do that just for me."

"Yep. When the time came it wasn't." He pointed at Jake. "It was for our family."

"He's a good boy, love. He's a white knight like his grandpa. A lot like his dad, too, though. He needs to tread lightly as he grows up."

"Yeah, he's got a temper, but nothing like his dad's."

The kids ran back around the corner.

"You going with me this afternoon?" Liz asked. Larry shook his head with a smile.

"I have to deliver this latest batch of shine to Bean Station. I'll run in and do my upload on Friday."

"It's getting more and more expensive."

"That it is. To get a long-term policy is ridiculous. If not for Don, I couldn't buy one at all."

"The payments just to keep the immediate family updated is insane," she said. "God forbid we ever need to use the cloning policy too."

"True enough."

The kids ran across the front of the house again.

"Sure wish his dad was here to see that boy," he repeated.

She squeezed his hand. "Me, too, love."

He squeezed her hand in return and turned to look at her. "Still the best day, ever."

Extra, Extra,
Read All About It
By Jenny E. Wren

"**H**ey, Bridgit! What do you think about that new rookie gunner Baker picked up? I thought for sure he was going to get smeared near the end." Frank, my co-announcer, called over from where he was leaning cavalierly on the wall, chatting up two of the newer – younger and cuter – members of the broadcast station staff. He had the charm and the shine turned way up. They were both giggling, soaking up the attention. Frank and I had good on-screen visuals, his black hair slicked into style and rich brown eyes compared to my shoulder-length auburn curls and blue eyes. He carefully maintained a tan to contrast with my pale. The fact that his tan made his veneers stand out what purely coincidental. Right.

Well, they'll learn. Or they won't. I thought, then sighed at my own cynicism. I had been trying to leave the studio with a minimum of fuss.

"Well, you know how it is, Frank. There's always a rising star out there, and I enjoy showing them off to the world." I said with a slight warning in my tone. Frank's shining smile flattened ever so slightly, and his eyes flicked around quickly like he was looking for someone before he waved to me and turned back to the fawning newbies.

A racer's career could be made or broken by the media, -- by the announcers, really. We could pick who the favorites were and who people hated. Frank needed to remember that we were paid to tell people who to like and who to hate. If he kept throwing his opinions around like that and the wrong ears caught wind of it, well, I'd get a new co-announcer.

"Bye, Frank, see you tomorrow," I called over my shoulder as I headed out the station door. I threw the strap of my crossbody bag over my head, settling it comfortably over my synthetic leather jacket. I glanced at the gray sky as I trotted over to my car. If I hurried, I could beat the rain and have enough time to get dinner started before Luca got to my apartment.

Luca, my younger brother, was a rookie gunner who had had his first race that morning, and I was making a celebratory dinner. Sitting in my fridge were some lovely steaks that I'd had formed out of top-shelf algae, with some of the higher-priced mock potatoes that probably came from the same algae tank.

Though, really, with what he could expect to start making winning he should be the one springing for the food.

There went my cynicism again. I shook my head as I snicked my five-point harness. I wasn't a racer and had no intentions of being a racer, but in my line of work, I'd seen enough gnarly accidents and had to get out of enough 'interesting' situations tracking down a story that I could justify investing in a couple of enhancements. One benefit of the connections I made in this job was that I had access to 'specialists' who could add modifications that sometimes weren't exactly what you would consider legal; the kind that got raised eyebrows and non-committal shrugs from the mechanic. For some of the bigger-ticket things I had even gone in for some small-scale street races and won the mods. That's the good thing about being underestimated – winning is much, much more satisfying.

Turns out I didn't beat the rain. As I pulled into the covered parking spot at my apartment building, the tropical depression-level rain had just started, and the colossal raindrops were pounding the ground between me and the front door with loud splats. In the few seconds it took me to get out of my car, it was pouring so hard that I could barely hear the beep of my car locking.

Welcome to hurricane season in Florida. All year long.

I sighed and zipped my jacket, pulling my bag around in front of me. I wouldn't really be able to do much to keep it dry, but, hey, a girl's got to try. Mother Nature proved me right though. In the fifteen feet from my car to the doors I got soaked. I dripped my way across the lobby to the elevator, boots squeaking on the tile.

By the time the elevator dinged on the twentieth floor and swooshed open, I had already started to shiver in the AC. I managed to unlock my door with minimal shaking and beelined for my bathroom. I peeled my wet clothes off and changed. Thankfully, my spiffy new synth leather jacket shed the rain like the iridescent duck feathers its color mimicked.

Someone knocked at my door as I hauled my sopping pile of clothes to the laundry room.

Well, shoot, he's early.

It had to be Luca; including him, there were only two people who were on my list to make it past the front desk. I detoured to the front door, dripping all the way.

"Come on in, you're early and I've got to get this drying." I barely looked up as I balanced my clothes one-handed to unlock the door and turned around to hurry to the laundry room.

"Bring me whatever you need dried. There should still be some of your old clothes in the guest room." I yelled out into the kitchen.

"Well, that's flattering, that you still have some of my things around here." Someone who wasn't Luca chuckled from behind me. I whirled around, surprised. Johnny stood in the doorway to the laundry room, his long neon green raincoat open and dripping on the floor, showing his violently purple three-piece suit and matching fedora. He leaned casually on the doorframe with his jacket unbuttoned and his hands in his pockets he was the picture of quiet confidence.

I tossed my clothes in the dryer harder than necessary and slammed my boots up on top of it to dry. Without saying anything I walked stiffly up to him, crossed my arms, and stared up at him. He didn't move. He just stood there, smiling down at me like he knew I wanted him to move, and he was going to make me ask him.

"Ugh, fine. Will you move please? You're in my way." I squeezed by him as soon as he started moving. "Why are you here, Johnny? We agreed that we'd stay out of each other's lives, that it was better that way." I distracted myself by getting dinner ready, the familiar pain blossoming in my chest.

Johnny and I went way back. We'd met while I was still in school and were virtually inseparable from the beginning. We made it for a few years, but eventually we realized the impact his work would have on us, and on our relationship.

Having someone in his life he cared for was a liability, a way for people to get leverage on him. He was the head of the legal department for Ironworks Corp, headed by Oscar Visoth. The cutthroat nature and the competition in the upper echelons of the larger corporations meant he couldn't afford to have anyone or anything that could be treated as a weak spot. After a long, painful few months we decided that it was safer if we weren't together. No one could get any leverage on him, and I wouldn't be worrying if I was getting in the way of him being able to do his job. Logic aside, it still hurt like hell and was just plain not fair. Plus, I still worried about him, even if he wasn't coming home to me, so twice the bad and no good.

Johnny took off his raincoat and propped it over a chair, then walked into the laundry room to hang his suit jacket up. He strolled back into the kitchen, rolled up his startlingly bright blue sleeves, and started helping me get dinner ready, unasked.

Dammit, how long does it take to forget how each other moves? I grumped to myself. We had been good together, and we still moved in sync. I didn't have the biggest kitchen so that was really the only way two people could be in the kitchen at the same time. But I didn't have to like it.

Midway through chopping the mock potatoes, Johnny sighed and put down the knife. "B, look, I need to talk to you."

I ignored him and kept salting the mock steaks. They didn't need it, but it was something I could pretend to be doing that gave me an excuse to not look at him.

"Bridgit. We need to talk. It's about Luca," he said quietly. I hated it when he used that tone.

"Ok, fine. What is it?" I asked neutrally, still not looking up.

Johnny sighed softly. I hated that too.

I slammed the salt bowl down making everything on the cutting boards jump. "Johnny, so help me...."

Johnny hesitated. "Ok, yeah, sure. So, you know the driver Luca is the gunner for, Jimmy? He's a nephew of the president of Redustries Corp, Silas Carson. They're the ones who produce the hardware for Gold Cross's cloning operation. They make the tubes, and the tanks and all of that."

My stomach dropped.

"I knew Luca had a friend, Jimmy, who was a driver who took him on as a rookie gunner."

Now I was getting angry.

"That little shit! Why didn't he tell me? Why didn't I ever think to ask him?" I snarled, grabbing a dish towel off the counter, "I should have asked more questions. It's only my damn job!" I hurled the towel across the kitchen, leaving a scattering of algae bits behind it.

Johnny put his hand on my shoulder and carefully turned me toward him. "Hey, B. Look, it's not on you. He's an adult. You can't always step in to correct his mistakes. You each have your own lives to live. Besides, he went into this with both eyes open, and from what I heard he didn't hesitate."

I rested my head on Johnny's chest, staring at the retina-melting blue of his shirt, with his purple and blue-dyed goatee tickling the back of my neck. I wondered what my brother had gotten into and how the hell I was going to get him out of it. We stood there like that in the middle of my kitchen for just long enough to get comfortable, but nowhere near as long as I wanted to.

I stood up, pulling hesitantly back and to his credit, Johnny let me with no complaints.

"Ok." I sniffed and wiped my nose on my sleeve. "So why are you here telling me? I thought the Corporations normally didn't get involved in each other's affairs and events." We had always somehow just naturally avoided outright talking about his job and what it entailed.

Johnny leaned back against the kitchen counter and crossed his arms. "I'm here because I want to be. But I'm also here because the race this morning didn't go well." I froze and went cold all over; my legs felt weak. I grasped wildly behind me for a kitchen chair and dropped into it.

"How badly?" I hadn't heard about any wrecks or races that went badly, but I'd been so focused on the regional races. The smaller individual races rarely made it across my desk unless something really stellar happened.

Johnny didn't move away from the counter. "Luca's alive. They both are, but he didn't do well as a gunner, and they lost the race. They lost to Christopher, Oscar's nephew. The Carsons are royally upset and blaming Luca. Of course, Oscar is pleased."

"What's going to happen to Luca?" I asked the question I dreaded asking. It was one thing for me to go chasing stories around into the questionable parts of racing, being willing to chase a story anywhere it went was table stakes for the regional announcers. I was smart about it though, and never got myself into something I didn't have an exit strategy for. Luca was my baby brother and literally the only family I had in the whole world. Our parents had both died years before and neither of them had had any siblings.

Johnny was watching me with narrowed eyes. Before he started talking again, he turned around without looking and took a glass out of the cabinet and filled it with water. Bringing it over and setting it in front of me he sat down, still watching me.

Dammit, cold water and no ice.

I was really hating all these reminders of how close we were and how happy we had been.

"He's currently a 'guest' at the Carson house. Because Jimmy wasn't injured, and because they're genuinely friends, he's not in danger. At least not at the moment, but he's in trouble. They're going to want some kind of retribution, some way to even the scales."

I stared at him. My brain was stalling out, and I wasn't following whatever message he was trying to not say.

"Johnny!" I pounded the table with fists I hadn't realized I'd balled up. I growled, staring Johnny straight in his beautiful, expressive eyes. "What are they going to want from him?" I was mentally calculating how much I had in the bank and how much I could get my hands on quickly if I needed to. I had some friends I could probably borrow from, and I could start selling things if it came to it. I had more than a passing familiarity with some of the resale shops with quick turnover.

"They don't want money; that's not what's really valuable here."

I was really, really not liking that he knew what I was thinking. This time it was my turn to not say anything and I let the silence stretch out, giving him a flat expression that I knew would get him talking.

Remember Johnny, I know you as well as you know me, I know what buttons to push. I was angry, angry that Luca had been so stupid, angry that it was Johnny who was here telling me instead of anyone else. Angry that I hadn't done a better job of finding out more about Luca's driver.

Johnny caved, slumping his shoulders as though acknowledging defeat. "He's really proud of his big sister and how successful you are as a regional announcer."

The change in topic confused me for a minute. I was still too upset to follow the leaps. After another chunk of silence, Johnny picked up again.

"I don't know for sure of course, I can just make educated guesses about it based on what information we have. But if I had to guess I'd say they're going to want your influence in the racing news."

I shook my head. "I can't do that, Johnny. You know the narrative is decided above me. We just make sure that's what's out there for the audience to absorb."

"Yeah, but you're given free rein to chase down whatever stories you want, then you hand that in for them to decide on how to use. You control the source of the information, and you could be sure the only information that's provided leaves only one reasonable outcome. You could stack the deck to make sure there's only one narrative possible."

Johnny wasn't wrong. We did have the freedom to track down whatever stories we were interested in, as long as they had to do with the races, drivers, or gunners and had the potential to keep the viewers' interest peaked.

"They're going to know you're here; the cameras will have picked you up." I was starting to think again, and thinking about how it was going to look if one of the top advisors for Ironworks was seen visiting the sister of the gunner who had lost the race. That was a narrative that didn't take a lot of experience to write, and it wasn't necessarily a good one.

Johnny smiled. "I know, but don't worry about that. I might or might not have people in judicious places who might or might not owe me a couple of favors."

"You got the cameras turned off?" I stared, open-mouthed. That was just this side of impossible to do. He'd burned a big favor coming over to give me a head's up. *Well, frack…*

He shook his head. "Not turned off, but I can't tell you any more – plausible deniability."

We sat there in silence for a while before Johnny finally got up. "I do need to go, though. Favors do have time limits." He rolled down his sleeves and perfectly buttoned his cuffs in practiced fluid motions.

Dammit, why does everything he does have to be perfect?

"So much for a celebratory dinner." I grumped, stood up, and scowled at the mess I'd made of my kitchen. The mess that matched the mess Luca had created, for both of us. Johnny swung his raincoat on, the neon green so bright it left a green light trail behind him. He swept by me to the door to leave all over again. I didn't move from where I'd stood up. I was afraid that if I did, I'd ask him to stay, and to hell with the risks. He opened the door and, without turning around, said over his shoulder. "I'm sorry this happened, but I'm never going to be sorry for the chance to see you. Be safe, B. I'll always be here; no one will take that from us."

After he left, I stumbled around cleaning up the kitchen without really paying attention to what I was doing. I might have eaten something, but I don't really remember. I was too focused on seeing Johnny again and the mess Luca had gotten himself into.

Eventually, I was going to hear about it through 'official' channels, and I had to be ready with a reaction. Thanks to Johnny taking the risk he did, I wouldn't be caught off guard, and I had some time to plan. It probably wouldn't be much time, but I'd take everything I could get. When I got Luca out of this, I was going to close that little lug nut up in my guest room and loan him out to the building's superintendent, with the strict requirement that he only do the dirtiest, grossest jobs available.

The next morning, I got up before my alarm. The sky was barely light, but with more rain looming, it wasn't going to get brighter than a pale gray anyway. I'd tossed and turned all night trying to figure out some way through this that got us out clean on the other side with our lives. Hopefully, the plan I'd come up with would work, but, unfortunately, there was only one way to test it. Throwing on my iridescent black mock leather jacket with a dark blue raincoat over it, I settled my crossbody bag more comfortably and headed out the door, braced for the dual storms I was about to face.

Pulling into the station parking lot was a little anticlimactic. The drive over was so quiet it was almost boring. I realized I had been halfway expecting there to be several black SUVs parked in the parking lot, waiting for me to have an interesting conversation. Instead, there was Frank running in with one of the blond newbies tucked under his arm, both trying to stay dry under an umbrella that was deliberately too small to cover two people.

I was on edge all day, listening for I didn't know what. Would they call the station? Would they send a message? Surely, they wouldn't just show up. That's too conspicuous, and these guys like quiet and staying in the background. Luckily, it wasn't a race day, so we spent the day researching and fact-checking the next set of drivers and gunners, getting the stats and metrics ready to publish before the next wave started.

When the decisions were made, they came with the expected skews on who to favor and who to start moving out of the positive light of the public eye, the directions would pop up on the huge monitors we had mounted around the station room. As soon as the screens started flashing the alert for an incoming decision all action in the room stopped as everyone stared with rapt attention, waiting to see who was on the good list and who was on their way out. Normally I'd be perched on the edge of my desk staring unblinkingly at the screens, ready to start taking notes and digging into the drivers and crew. Today I was so distracted that it took one of the assistants bumping into my desk in her rush to get a good view to get my attention. She gave me a look over her shoulder as she dashed off.

Dammit, come on B, get it together, you're supposed to be acting like it's just another day, I chided myself. Hell, my job was to deliver the news – good or gruesome with the same glossy, veneer-filled smile and not bat an eye. If I could do that, I needed to do this.

The initial flurry of activity created by the release of the decisions faded and people hurried back to their workstations to start pulling information and building the narratives.

"Hey Bridgit, what do you think of it?" Anna, the same assistant who had careened off my desk was standing at my elbow with her hands clasped tightly in front of her.

"Uh, yeah Anna, yeah let's look at it." I opened my messaging. Anna was one of the better ones at drafting the scripting for our auto-viewers that Frank and I read during broadcasts. I skimmed it looking for the key phrases and elements. Making sure the tone of the comments matched the names. There were a couple of places that needed to be tweaked or adjusted, so I marked them quickly and sent it back to her. "Sounds good, just a couple of changes to make please." Anna nodded tightly, spun on her heel, and took off like a car off the line heading for her terminal.

I sighed and pushed my chair back. "Frank – heading to the gym." I called as I walked out. Frank waved distractedly; he was bending over the shoulder of one of the same new girls as yesterday looking at her terminal.

Today was going to be a treadmill day, I could get going running and let my mind wander. Spending the time planning as much as possible for what I knew was going to be a dangerous night. I was going to have to go up against a Corp that was holding my baby brother hostage to force me to spin the race information in their favor.

I was going to be lucky if I could get both Luca and myself out of this in one piece.

"Come on Bridge, time to go home." Frank tapped the edge of my desk as he walked by. I'd made it through the whole day with not even the whisper of anything threatening. I had snuck a peek at the smaller races from a few days prior to see what had happened in Luca's race. Under a story of a non-lethal race that had turned into an inferno, there were a couple of lines about Luca's and Jimmy's losing run. It simply said that due to both the driver's and gunner's inexperience, they just missed a couple of maneuvers that tipped the other team ahead.

Ah ha, so it wasn't Luca; it was both of them. Fat chance Silas Carson would want to hear that his nephew was as much responsible for losing as Luca was.

So, there it was: Redustries Corp was blaming Luca when they were both responsible for losing. It was vindicating, but it had nowhere near enough weight to even get the Corp's attention. I had nothing at all; I was powerless to get Luca out from the Corp's crosshairs.

Walking out that evening, I was so tired from running on high alert all day that I almost missed the folder tucked under my windshield wiper. *That's surprisingly clumsy*, I thought.

The station parking lot has lots of cameras on it, along with the surrounding streets. Technically it was illegal for an unauthorized individual to get into the camera feeds. But no one blinked an eye if someone chasing down a story included video footage in what they turned in. The decision-makers wrote it off as coming from an 'anonymous source,' and the stories kept rolling. I didn't think there was an announcer here who hadn't broken into the station's feeds if only for practice. It had become an unofficial rite of passage to log in and out of them undetected.

I needed to get into that footage to see who had left my little love note. If I went back in now, I'd get asked why I wanted it, which would draw attention to the note getting left on my car – definitely not what I wanted. I'd come back later tonight when the night shift was in, and just tell them that I was chasing a lead on a potential story.

I left the note where it was, buckled in and pulled out of the parking lot the same as I always did. Nothing to catch anyone's attention. A couple of blocks away I stopped at a grocery store and leaned my bag against the hood of my car digging in it like I was looking for something while carefully slipping the note out from under the wiper and palmed it, tucking it away as I turned to go into the store.

Hopefully, no one watching the cameras noticed the note. Minimal attention… I had a feeling that was going to be my least favorite phrase before too long.

I picked up a couple of bags of algae chips, some drinks, and loaded them in my car without hurrying. If the Corps were watching, I wanted them to see a calm reaction. Hopefully it would confuse them, wondering why I didn't open it right away and start freaking out. Or they'll think I'm expecting something from a source for a story. I wanted them as off-balance as I could get them. Side benefit – acting calm helped me start feeling calmer.

Getting home, I threw the drinks and chips down on the counter and plopped myself down at the table. I pulled the plastic envelope out and stared at it. It was thick and translucent. All I could make out inside was a folded piece of paper.

Ok, here goes. Let's see what I'm up against.

The letter was not on official letterhead. The first page was a pleasantly-worded letter inviting me to Okeehelee Park at ten this evening to discuss an issue that the sender felt I was the perfect person to address and resolve. Flattering language like 'shining star in the announcer world' and 'leader who others look to…' was scattered through the whole thing.

Well, Johnny was right. They'd like to use the 'leader who others look to' to start changing the audience's opinion of someone. Lovely.

They had thoughtfully included a hard copy map to Okeehelee with the letter. "You've thought of everything, haven't you?" I mused quietly. With a hard copy map, I wouldn't need to look the park up online, and it wouldn't be in my search history or destination history for my GPS. Curious though that whoever was behind this had been clever enough to include a paper map but careless enough that they left it on my car in view of the station's cameras.

According to the map, the park was about a half an hour away, and it was only just five thirty. That would give me time to make some calls, change, and stop by the station so I could get into the cameras and see who dropped off the note. Just then, my stomach decided to start grumbling. "Ok, sure, I'll get something to eat too."

Thirty minutes later I'd made some calls to a couple people, setting things up and making arrangements. I changed into something more practical – comfortable dark gray pants, black low-heel boots, a black long-sleeved top along with my iridescent leather jacket. I stopped at the mirror on my way out the door and gave myself a once-over. Whether or not I looked as badass as I felt was up for debate.

I left my bag at home; I needed to be totally hands-free and didn't want anything that could be easily grabbed onto or left behind.

For the second time that day, I pulled into the station lot, hopped out of my car, and hurried in. If anyone asked, I could tell them the truth- that I was just stopping in quickly to check on a lead before going out to chase another possible story angle.

Thomas, who was just about old enough to be my father, was on duty when I peeked in the window of the security room door. Opening the door a crack, I leaned in. "Knock knock!"

He was chuckling before he turned around. "I haven't seen you in ages, Bridgit. They've kept you crazy-busy chasing the huge regional races. I'm proud of you, kid."

"Thanks, Thomas, I still can't believe some days that it's real." I slid in the door and closed it quietly behind me. "Hey, have you tried the new sandwich the cafeteria has? They've upgraded the flavor of the algae, so the roast beef flavor tastes less like plastic." No one who was smart about it ever specifically asked to crack into the camera feeds.

Thomas smiled, shaking his head. He understood me. "You're much better about this than a lot of the other people. You need to talk to that co-host of yours. He's about as subtle as the broad side of a tank." He stood up and stretched. "Would you like a sandwich? I hear the cafeteria has improved their roast beef recently."

I shook my head no, and as soon as the door closed behind Thomas, I slid into his chair and was into the system. I found the camera I wanted and spooled the recording back to when I got to work this morning and started fast-forwarding. At about the two-hour mark of the video, a large dark truck rolled by slowly, then suddenly the folder was on my car. I hadn't even noticed a skip or a hiccup in the video. I backed it up and watched it again, and again. No skip. One frame there was nothing there, the next there was.

"Frack."

Whoever had left the note and the map had enough clout to turn off the cameras.

The station cameras.

My stomach flipped, and I got cold all over. Everyone knew the big Corps had a lot of power, but to reach into a broadcast station's cameras and interfere took some muscle. Especially one that covered regional races.

The sound of Thomas' footsteps out in the hall caught my attention, and I flipped the camera back to current and pushed off the console, rolling in the chair across the room. When Thomas came back in, I was sitting across the room scrolling on my phone. I looked up, smiling. "Well, did they have any left?"

As an answer, Thomas brandished a partially unwrapped sandwich and grinned at me around a mouthful. I got up and rolled the chair back to him. "Have a good evening, and I'll try to stop by more often just to say hi," I promised.

Thomas waved with the hand that wasn't holding the sandwich. "Mmff."

I trotted down the hall and out the door. There was plenty of time to get there, but I wanted to drive around the general area and get an idea of what I was going to be walking into.

The location ended up being a warehouse on the edge of the park. Two black SUV's with moderately heavy-duty armor plating were parked out front. The lot itself was a small gravel area and the only lights were several spotlights mounted on tall poles along the edge of the building.

If I hadn't known there was trouble waiting for me inside, it would just be another unassuming business.

Except for all the power lines running to it and the large collection of solar panels covering the roof. *What could you possibly be doing that you need all that juice for?* I thought. Whatever it was, it was probably not something meant for public consumption, which dropped the odds even farther out of my favor.

I was early; it was just after nine. I had planned on getting there early. I wasn't going to give them the satisfaction of thinking I was intimidated. It was a control game, and the Corps were used to being the ones in control. The flippancy might have been a bad idea, but I was still pissed and had no regrets about them knowing it. For now.

I pulled in in front of the building, a few car widths away from the sedans and got my new focals from the console and put them on. These were the latest model that were slimmer and sleeker than the ones that most people owned and were used to. The HUD readout popped up on the left lens. I touched the button on the earpiece that started the recorder, covering the move by flipping my hair. Walking to the door, I scanned the building and the surrounding area. The HUD registered the inordinate amount of power lines and cables and the ridiculous number of solar panels.

Yep, you really do have sockets for brains. I chided myself. *Walking into a Corp's secret location alone at night to make a deal to get my lug nut of a brother out of a mess.*

The automatic door whooshed open as I got close. Inside there was a man with a smile as shiny as chrome plating that made my skin crawl. He stood calmly, obviously waiting for me. He wore a perfectly tailored suit that gleamed as brightly as his creepy smile.

I walked right up to him and stopped just outside of arms' reach. He stood about a foot taller than me and was built like an athlete. Or a company goon who spent plenty of time in the company gym. I matched his smile with my on-air interview smile.

"Good evening, Miss Tassin," he said. "Thank you for coming. If you'll follow me, please, the board is waiting." Everything in his demeanor and delivery read as though I was right on time.

Well, crud, so much for trying to make a statement.

He led me down a hallway off to the left that passed about a dozen offices. Regularly-spaced cameras dotted the hall. He led me to the last door on the right. It was already open. In the room was a large mock-wood table with high-backed chairs ringing it, most of which had stern-faced older people in them in ubiquitous gray suits.

"In here, Miss Tassin." He gestured to the open door. "May I get you something to drink?" My tour guide asked with the same pleasantly neutral expression.

Right, I drink anything you bring me, and tomorrow the station needs to find a new announcer, Shiny. I just smiled.

"No, thank you. I appreciate the offer."

Shiny nodded and headed back out into the hallway.

Well, here goes. Game face on. I took a deep breath and stepped into the room.

The 'board' as Shiny had called it was the Redustries president of course, some of the other upper echelon officers, Jimmy himself, and Luca. I made a point to make eye contact with everyone, the HUD registering each person and storing their identity. When I got to Luca, I heaved a purely internal sigh of relief and my stomach unknotted just a bit. He wasn't hurt physically, but he looked completely miserable. He didn't look up at me, his eyes were glued to the surface of the table. There was another young guy sitting next to him who might have been a younger copy of Silas Carson who did look up at me, though his expression didn't have the same hardness as his uncle's. *Jimmy – gotcha.*

"Good evening, everyone. Thank you for setting something up on such short notice. I know it can be inconvenient." I started talking before anyone else, using my 'television interview voice.' I needed to try to take back some high ground. I'd already lost the first move when they expected me to be early. I walked past the empty chairs near the end of the table and instead sat down in the chair at the opposite end of the table from Silas Carson.

"I understand there have been some questions around the outcome of a recent race. Well, I'm sorry, gentlemen and ladies, but I wasn't the announcer for that one, so I can only tell you what's in the published story."

The Redustries executives had good game faces; there were barely any reactions to my statement. Luca and Jimmy, however, both flinched. Silas smiled.

"Good evening, Miss Tassin. I'm afraid your understanding is somewhat incorrect. There's no questioning the outcome of the event. The concerns we have are around why and what to do to begin correcting the error."

Silas said all of this without taking his eyes off me. The two suits on his right were staring holes in Luca, who seemed to try to curl up and make himself smaller. Jimmy reached over and put his hand on Luca's shoulder, leaned over, and whispered something. Luca just nodded. Seeing Luca cowed and scared lit my temper. All my hesitancy and worries were burned away, replaced with a hot fury. *That's it, you messed with my baby brother. The gloves are coming off.* I was all in now, no pulling my punches.

I didn't say anything, my announcer-neutral expression solidly in place, and gestured for Silas to continue.

"Have you toured the facility here?" Silas asked, waving his arm expansively toward the rest of the warehouse. The swift change in topic caught me off-guard but damned if I was going to show it.

"No, I haven't. Your assistant, who very kindly met me at the door, brought me straight here."

Silas nodded. "Francis, would you show Miss Tassin and her brother around the facility, please? I believe they'll find it fascinating."

Shiny, *Francis,* I corrected myself, appeared in the doorway like he'd been waiting right outside the door.

"Right away, Mr. Carson. Miss Tassin, Mr. Tassin, if you'd follow me, please." Jimmy got up when Luca did, giving the suits across the table from him a quelling look when they started to say something.

We filed out the door behind Francis and Luca rushed right up to me. "Bridge, I'm so sorry. I'm an idiot. It wasn't my fault; it was a stupid mistake. I didn't mean for any of this to happen. I didn't know…" He was babbling so quickly he was talking over himself. Jimmy just walked quietly next to him.

I cut him off in a harsh whisper. "Luca. Stop talking. We'll talk about it later. When we're home." He flinched and stopped talking. I ignored Jimmy. The cameras and Francis were bad enough, but to have Jimmy there too, anything we said or did was definitely going to get back to everyone we didn't want it to.

We didn't say anything else as Francis led us back through the front of the building and right past the doors where he'd met me. The HUD in my focals mapped the building in detail as we walked. Hopefully it wasn't so complicated that we wouldn't be able to find our way out without their help.

"And through here, we have the prototypes for our new offering. You're familiar with Redustries Corp products, yes?" Francis waved to the offices we'd passed on the way in.

I nodded, trying to sound like I had nothing to worry about and was on a normal tour of a major corporation's facilities. *Secret facilities. Secret facilities that definitely weren't on the up and up.* "Yes, Redustries Corp is the leading producer of the cloning hardware that Gold Cross uses. Top of the line."

Francis smiled his smarmy, phony little smile. "Yes. And it was only recently that the board decided to diversify our offerings. We've been leaders in the hardware and supplies for cloning for a very, very long time. But, to stay relevant, we have to research new ways to grow."

We turned down a brightly-lit hall that had nothing but large, heavy-duty double doors at the end with no windows and a keycard sensor. Francis glided over to the keycard pad and pulled a card out of his shiny pocket. Waving it in front of the sensor a deep clicking sound echoed in the hallway and the doors started to smoothly swing open. My stomach dropped and I got cold all over.

"This way, if you please."

Luca leaned over and in a tense whisper hissed. "I don't like this…"

I glared at him over the focals. "I don't either, but we're here until we get ourselves out of it."

I glanced at Jimmy. He hadn't said anything since we left the board room, but he looked as tense as I felt. His face was drawn, and there were white lines around his mouth. Walking through the doors felt like we were taking a one-way trip to oblivion. The doors closed as smoothly and silently as they had opened, but my imagination heard them slam shut menacingly.

This part of the warehouse was one huge, cavernous room. Next to us were rows of computer stations that had graphs and readings flipping across the monitors. About a third of the way down, there was a break in the row of stations, and we turned left, heading even farther into the building.

We passed lab stations set up as though they were testing what looked like small pieces of electronic hardware. Francis took us down several turns until I was pretty sure I wouldn't be able to find my way out without the HUD's map. I kept checking its display to be sure it was still recording. The no signal icon was flashing, but it was still recording, including a little map display showing where we were.

We were getting to what felt like the middle of the whole floor. The desks and stations stopped, leaving a large open space in the middle. The whole time we'd been walking through the warehouse space, we hadn't seen anyone.

None of the regular employees were working at this time of night, so when I heard voices echoing out to us from the open space my chest tightened. *Well, shit…*

Walking into the space it was halfway ringed with what I recognized as cloning chambers, with a table in the middle and several beefy men standing or sitting on the far side of the area, chatting softly. I scanned everything, trying to get as much recorded as possible, including the faces of the people waiting for us.

"Wow, your R&D team works awfully late. Impressive dedication." I joked with feigned innocence.

The thugs in suits had stopped talking and were staring. Francis sat down. "Please, sit." He gestured at the other chairs. "It's more comfortable while we discuss what Redustries is developing wouldn't you agree?" The smile stayed in place, but his eyes were cold and hard.

I smiled back, just as bright a smile as he gave. "Thank you, Francis. That's very considerate of you. Could I bother one of your colleagues for a hot drink? It's chillier here than I would have expected."

Francis chuckled. "Of course, Miss Tassin. Right away. Would anyone else care for anything?" When Jimmy and Luca both shook their heads, he nodded to one of the thugs who moved off through the machines, scowling.

"So, to the heart of the matter." Francis laced his fingers together and rested his hands on the table in front of him.

"As I said earlier, Redustries is diversifying our offerings. We're getting into the software and recording side of cloning. However, we've decided to take a different approach to how we gather the data that's stored in the brain tapes. Normally, someone has to deliberately come in and sit for a scan. We're changing that."

Out of the corner of my eye, I saw Jimmy's hands clench into fists in his lap.

"Francis. They didn't do it, did they?" Jimmy asked, tersely.

Francis ignored Jimmy. "Instead of waiting for the person to come in to be scanned, we decided to record while the person was up and around and being active. The centers of the brain that were the most active would give strong enough readings that if the sensors were built correctly, we could record with no inconvenience to the person."

I gaped at Francis. This was ridiculous. This was illegal. "You can't do that, scanning someone for a brain tape when they don't know what's going on creates clones that aren't right, they come out… wrong."

Chills ran down my spine when Francis's smile turned malicious.

"Oh, it's possible, and we've had positive results so far. We've found the most success when we place the sensors in equipment that's used frequently and when the subject is engaged in something that has their brain firing rapidly. Say, a racing helmet. A helmet that someone wears through many, many hours of practice, and hours of racing." He turned the smile on Luca and Jimmy. "Jimmy, your parents approved it for you so we could gather test data. We can evaluate your brain tape to test the solidity of the recording. There are no lasting effects that we know of. It's just for data-gathering."

Luca gulped audibly and turned pale as the blood rushed out of his face. Francis turned to him.

"I don't believe you currently have a Gold Cross account, Mr. Tassin. I can assure you though, your brain tape is being kept securely locked up. Of course, this early in the process we're not expecting the results to be fabulous, but it'll do for what we need."

I was getting angry now. "Do tell, Francis. What do you need a shoddy, knock-off brain tape of my brother for?" I had a sneaking suspicion that I already knew the answer.

Just then a huge arm plunked a steaming cup of something down in front of me. I hadn't even heard the thug come back. *Well, crud,* I chided myself.

The thug didn't move from where he stood right behind me. Too close for comfort.

"What we need Miss Tassin, is your assistance with handling an issue. Your brother's mishaps in their recent race resulted in them losing. We need the audience's perception of the winner… influenced."

"Oh?" I asked, forcing my voice to stay neutral. *Come on, you little shit… out with it.*

The focals were still recording. All I needed was for Francis to threaten me on behalf of the Corp, and I had them. There wasn't anything there with bribes being offered, that happened all the time.

Oh, yeah, you also have to get yourself and Luca out of here safely. I reminded myself harshly.

Francis sighed, shaking his head as though he was disappointed. "Miss Tassin, you don't get where you are in your career without being cleverer than that."

I was about to open my mouth to reply when Luca cut me off. "You're deluded if you think she's going to do anything for you!"

Francis chuckled, shaking his head. "Mr. Tassin, your sister knows racing is dangerous. Anything can happen to anyone. An equipment failure for example. If that were to happen, there's only one brain tape for you. A copy that's in our safekeeping."

Jimmy had gone red in the face and looked like he was going to jump over the table.

I snatched the hot drink and threw it over my shoulder right in the thug's face who had been looming over me. His hands flew to his face as he let out a gargling yelp, and he blundered backwards.

I shot out of my chair and grabbed Luca's arm, yanking him out of his chair.

"Move!"

We bolted back the way we'd come, Luca stumbling to keep up as I hauled him off-balance. I toggled the HUD to replay as we raced around the first corner and the map popped up.

Behind us was the sound of the thugs yelling and Francis bellowing orders.

The HUD got us back to the doors with no mishaps. I slid to a stop at the keycard panel. "Shit!" I'd forgotten that we needed a keycard to open the doors. Before I could come up with a solution, Jimmy barreled up next to me.

"Here!" He thrust his hand out and slammed a keycard on the reader. The doors started slowly opening as the thundering herd of heavy footsteps echoed behind us.

"Hurry! Go!" Jimmy shoved us through the doors before they were fully open, and we all raced down the hallway. The HUD display was still flashing no signal.

"Come on, come on…." I muttered as we scrambled toward the door.

We tumbled around the last corner before the front doors and ended up staring down a small group of Redustries thugs in their suits and matching scowls.

Right then, the icon flashed green – signal located. *Finally!* I thought with a huge sigh of relief. I didn't bother to hide it this time, I reached up and toggled the upload function. The popup said twenty seconds to upload complete.

"Miss Tassin."

Francis walked out from the hallway on our left and stopped in the dead center between the doors.

One of the thugs nearest to Francis leaned over his shoulder whispering.

Francis frowned at me. "Miss Tassin, are you recording?"

I shook my head. "Nope. In fact, I just turned it off."

Francis froze.

At that exact second the upload finished, and I got the confirmation that the information was successfully received. "Thank you for not forcing me to stall until the upload finished." I flashed him a grin.

Francis snapped, all traces of his shiny, chrome smile were gone.

"You're bluffing."

He reached out and grabbed the focals and put them on. "Dammit… she's not bluffing. You sent them to Ironworks? Oscar Visoth has this information??" Francis demanded; a look of sheer disbelief plastered on his face.

Feeling like I finally had the upper hand I stood up straighter and squared off with him. *Yeah, you shiny prick, you mess with my family and I'll hamstring you.*

"That's right. They'll hold onto them as insurance. Anything happens to Luca or to me, or to anyone around either of us that smells in the least bit suspicious and that information goes live. Remember – the influence I have?" I gave him my best poker face glare. "Don't make me want to."

Francis shook with rage.

"Luca and I are leaving, and I hope to never hear from you all again."

Francis growled and nodded at the thugs blocking the door. "Let them go."

Luca and I walked quickly out to my car with Jimmy following.

Jimmy popped the front passenger seat and disappeared into the back seat. Luca and I threw ourselves into my car and we strapped in.

Jimmy asked from behind me "Why do you have five-point harnesses and racing seats – in the back?"

"Hang on." I ignored the question. Throwing it into reverse, I floored it. My first turbo spooled up quickly, the subtle whistle barely audible under the growl of my engine. Even though it was more expensive to operate, I'd always preferred the sound of an internal combustion engine over electric motors. I cranked the wheel and floored it, flinging a rooster tail of gravel behind me and peppering the thug's armored cars as I went.

We rumbled out onto the paved road, tires squealing as I straightened out of the sharp turn and downshifted.

"I didn't know your sister knew how to double-clutch!" Jimmy yelled over the roar of my engine.

I glared at him. Checking my rear-view I saw what I was hoping wouldn't happen. Three sets of headlights came pouring out of the parking lot.

"Hang on and pull on the 'oh-shit' handle." I ordered Luca.

He did, and stared, gobsmacked when he pulled the handle. It popped off and peeled the fabric interior of the ceiling back, handing it Jimmy. "Just how many mods did you get?" he asked disbelievingly.

"Wait, you have roll bars? Is that an armored roof?? What the hell kind of stories do you chase?" Jimmy demanded. He pulled the lining all the way down and dropped it in the back behind my seat. Clipped into hooks along the roll bars I had a pair of hand cannons and extra magazines.

The cars chasing us were getting closer. They were bigger, and more heavily-armored than I was, but I was pretty sure I could surprise them.

I flipped a switch on my steering wheel and the infotainment center slid up, revealing another screen and a set of switches.

"Luca! The glove box– open it and flip the left-hand switch."

Luca leaned forward, jumping as we flew down the bumpy, poorly-paved road, the headlights of the cars following us bouncing off the cloud of dust I was leaving.

He popped open the glove box, revealing several switches. He leaned forward and flipped the leftmost switch. My reverse lights illuminated – but these weren't regular reverse lights. These were LED, extra-bright. High-beam bright. Right in the faces of the guys chasing us.

The car in the lead swerved as the driver got an eyeful of several hundreds of lumens unexpectedly. The second car behind them swerved to avoid them, and both skidded into the marshy grass beside the road. The first car landed in a sloppy ditch and sat there, nose down bumper up, wheels still spinning.

The third car kept coming, roaring up behind me.

Luca reached up and unclipped the hand cannons from their mounts on the roll bars. He leaned over into the headlight light from our chaser and checked that they were loaded.

"I've got questions for you," he said, giving me a side-eye.

"Later, when we don't have Redustries' thug brigade chasing us. Wait to use those. I've got a couple more surprises to try first."

"Well, that's good, because one of the ones your light show ran off the road is back in the race." Jimmy called, he had cranked himself around as far as he could from where he was belted in and was watching out the back window.

The headlights bouncing in my side mirrors and rear-view mirror doubled, the reflections dancing as we rumbled over the bumps and potholes.

Shifting gears, I just needed to keep our distance. They were both heavier than we were. If they pitted me, I'd be done.

"I do like a sleeper."

I leaned over and flicked the first switch the infotainment center had uncovered and timed it for when I hit a bump that raised us up in the air. Flicking the next switch my tail lights popped out, with two automatic guns tucked in behind them and I immediately hit the trigger embedded in my steering wheel.

"What the frack!?" Luca yelled, ducking as the hood and grill of the car behind us erupted in sparks.

The chatter of the guns reverberated up through the chassis and we felt it through the seats.

That car swerved, smoke pouring out of its engine.

They wouldn't be getting back up to chase us.

"And then there was one," I mumbled.

The map on my original infotainment screen showed that I was coming up to where the road widened into four lanes.

"Ok, Luca, how good are you with those things? For real?" I asked.

"I'm good! It wasn't my shooting that lost us the race!" he yelled back.

"Pull the sun visor down and open the mirror." I ordered.

Luca didn't argue; he just pulled it down and flipped up the little cover for the mirror. Only I'd swapped the mirrors out with little screens. The cameras were housed in my rear-view mirror sensor cluster. Luca flipped through the controls. "Heat vision, night vision, regular… holy shit!"

"The visor blocks the headlights from blinding you, but you can still aim and shoot with the cameras, you dingus," I snapped.

We were getting to where the road widened out. "Get ready!"

I pulled the handbrake and cranked the wheel. We spun around in a one-eighty, and I slammed it in reverse, flipping on my high-beams. I tore down the street backwards, driving with my mirrors, grateful that my reverse lights were as bright as my headlights. Luca lowered the window and sighting using the screen in his sun visor, fired the hand cannon out the window. Jimmy ducked down as far as he could, minimizing himself as a target and not blocking my view out the back.

By now, the chasers had realized I wasn't quite as helpless as they thought, and they were firing back. They either didn't have long guns in the car, or they didn't want to use them with Silas Carson's nephew in the car, but they had no compunctions with firing some beastly hand cannons at us. One shot connected right smack in the middle of my windshield, right between Luca and me.

"Sonofa…!" I yelled, as my windshield spidered into thousands of cracks. It held, though; the 'tinting' I'd gotten was designed to do more than just darken my windows, it was specifically made to help with resistance to debris hitting my car. Today's 'debris' just happened to include bullets.

I was working to stay closer to the driver's side, to force their gunner to try to shoot me over their own hood.

Just when they figured it out and the driver was speeding up trying to force his way up next to my passenger side, Luca connected. His first and second shots landed on the passenger side windows, splintering them like my windshield. When that didn't stop them, he aimed lower. More sparks flew as he aimed for their wheel. More shots hit my windshield in retaliation.

"I'm out!" he yelled, dropping the spent magazine onto the floorboard with one hand while reaching up for another.

"This isn't going to work," I shouted back. "Hang on! That's it, you sons of bitches. I'm done with this shit." I didn't have that many tricks left, and I needed to end this before they got through my windshield or managed to PIT us.

I yanked my handbrake and squealed through another J-turn, ignoring Luca and Jimmy yelling. As I came out of the turn, I hit another button on my steering wheel. A small compartment in my bumper popped open and almost three dozen small, pointed black metal jacks clattered out, throwing sparks as they hit the ground and bounced.

The SUV's tires exploded, and they slewed right.

There were chunks of tire flying everywhere as their SUV flipped up and over.

"Watch out!" Jimmy yelled, chunks of tire and bits of the SUV were raining down and one big hunk of bumper landed right in front of me. I had to swerve violently around it, throwing us all sideways in our seats.

"Bridgit!" Luca bellowed, "Watch out!"

I smashed my 'last resort' button on the back of my steering wheel, and we launched forward, taking off like a bat out of hell.

We were thrown back into the seats, hard. Our launch was so sudden I'd have sworn I felt my front wheels come up off the ground.

It took us less than a minute to get the last couple of miles behind us and out of the official Okeehlee nature reserve and I swerved back onto a regular road. I pulled off onto the shoulder and dust swirled in the light from my headlights. My engine started ticking rapidly and there was steam where the poor thing had been working hard and was probably blisteringly hot.

Luca and Jimmy sat silent for a few heartbeats.

"What the actual bloody hell was that?" Jimmy asked, breathing hard and staring at me with an expression of complete shock.

I stared at the steering wheel and slowly peeled my hands off. I'd been clenching it so tightly my knuckles were white, and my hands felt like they were permanently curled. I was pretty sure that if I looked closely enough, I'd see dents from my fingers.

Trying not to sound like my heart was pounding a million miles a minute and like I was about to break down in a blubbering pile, I rolled my eyes at him.

"Who do you think taught Luca to drive?" I asked dryly.

"I hope you have your wallet with you. I blew through nearly all my fuel. There's a gas station not all that far away." I told Luca.

While Luca sat there with his mouth open, looking like he was trying to figure out what to say to that, I reached out and put my poor, abused car into gear.

"B, do you realize what this means?" Luca asked, eyebrows beetled in thought.

"Which part? The part where you realize your big sister is more badass than you thought or the part where you owe me forever?" I snapped, effectively shutting Luca down.

I'm going to owe Johnny for this one. Then an idea occurred to me that made my stomach knot for the umpteenth time today. Redustries knew that Ironworks had the footage, and they'd release it to the media at a word from me.

Great, instead of getting out from under them, now we're squarely and permanently in their sights.

"I hate to be the one to say this, but you know my uncle is going to be keeping a very close eye on you both now. No way is he going to take the chance that something happens that they could be blamed for, and you release that evidence." Jimmy leaned forward as far as he could and yelled over the rattle of my wrecked engine.

If there had been any faint hint of a hope of being able to see Johnny ever again, I'd just put the kibosh on it. It was going to be impossible; Redustries of course knew who he worked for and if they figured out there was any kind of a connection between us then Johnny would be in their crosshairs too. Take out the party likely holding the evidence – take out the leverage I had against them. Then Luca and I both have 'accidents'.

Well frack.

Desert Mouse
by Casey Moores

Mouse Trap

Jade leaned back on the flat sandstone, closed her eyes, and breathed in the warm, sweet air. There was a hint of sandy dust, as there always was, but the air was so much cleaner than the dank, oily must of their cave. The sun overhead burned blindingly bright and sweat poured down her forehead, but it was still a most welcome switch. Escapes to the surface weren't too common, so she had to make the best of them.

Propping herself onto her elbows and squinting, she scanned the valley below. Signs of life were scarce as always, but they were there if she looked hard enough. As her Papi always said, she didn't have a lot of useful qualities, but her eyesight was remarkable.

A few hundred meters to her left, a rock tumbled down a hill, most likely loosened by a scurrying lizard. A black dot on the horizon resolved into a single vulture, who floated in from the west and circled above the disturbance. A tiny trail of dust kicked up on the far side of the valley. By the volume and movement pattern, she judged it to be a roadrunner as opposed to a hare.

Movement caught her attention to the south, and she gasped.

A tall, thick plume rose in a line trailing in from Simp's Canyon. Only bandits ever came from there.

This one, however, was alone. A single, juicy target would bring a wealth of parts and maybe much more. Papi said city simps were too brain dead to survive the dead lands unless obnoxiously well-supplied. They might even have…

Chocolate!

Jade had only tasted it once, but the memory lived within her. Whenever she was tired or hungry or upset—like the time she'd accidentally installed the brake pads backwards on Papi's '42 Caballero. It didn't seem like a big deal, since he never drove it, but he'd been livid. She'd lost track of time curled up in the hole *learning her lesson,* whatever that meant, with nothing but the memory of chocolate for comfort.

Right there on the valley floor, racing straight toward the pitfall, was a beautiful machine that *could* be loaded with the stuff.

Without a second thought, she sprinted around the great sandstone boulder and leaped to grab the bar on the zipline. Wind blasted her hair apart as she flew along the backside of the razorback ridge toward the pitfall. The car disappeared from view, but there was no other way through the valley.

Before the carriage hit the stops, she let go, rolled as she hit ground, and came to her feet in a run. There was plenty of time to pull the pin and set the trap, but she also needed to alert Papi.

Dirt and dust flew as she swung the panel to the shaft open. Climbing down two rungs, she stretched out to reach the pin. It took a bit to shimmy the pin out with a screech of scraping metal, but she did it. Then, she climbed out and raced to the wire box.

A small, dirt–covered box sat a dozen yards back. As Papi had taught her, she cranked the alarm ten times, put the receiver to her ear, and waited. As she did, she wondered how far out the car was. Another of Papi's rules was to never look through the gap to see the mark. For one, the mark might take your head off if you timed it wrong. Worse, the mark might see you and break off. The former would give her a quick death, the latter would invite Papi's wrath. Given a choice, she'd choose the quick death.

"*Yes, my little mouse, what is it?*" Papi said when he answered.

"There's a car moving across the valley floor, headed straight for the gap," she replied. With pride, she added, "And you can just sit tight, because I already set the trap."

"*Just the one?*"

It was a silly question. She knew not to set the trap if there was more than one.

"Yes, sir, Papi, just the one."

"*You sure no one's on his tail?*"

"Not that I saw."

"*Climb up and make sure. I'm headed to you.*"

"Yes, Papi." The line went dead.

Frantically, she hung up and scrambled up the hill. With rocks and sand tumbling down almost as quick as she ran up, progress was slow. Even on all fours, it was a fight to climb fast. The roar of the incoming engine echoed from the gap. By the time she neared the top, the echoes were bouncing all over the canyon's walls.

She slowed at the ridge top and cautiously peered into the valley below.

A plume of dust piled into the sky behind the car as it raced for the gap.

About a mile or more further back, a whole group of dust plumes billowed from the floor. She knew the difference between a dust storm and a bunch of bandits. Those were bandits.

Hearing a door slam, she spun and saw Papi running toward the gap. Jade half slid, half hopped down the ridge as fast as she could.

"Raiders!" she shouted over and over, but he made no sign of hearing her over the wind and the encroaching engine roar. She was just a dozen yards out when his eyes finally went wide.

"Stay back!" he shouted, putting his hands up to hold her away. "Get back inside, I'll handle this!"

With one last leap, she landed on the dirt trail between the gap and the door to the cavern. Wanting to help, she took a few steps toward him, but he stopped and threw a hand up again.

"No, Jade, you tuck yourself away. Everything'll be fine, okay?"

She nodded and took a few tentative steps back. Papi wiped a hand through his beard and broke into a sprint for the gap. The engine roar was deafening, with a growing chorus of more engines joining it.

Her legs felt weak, and her heart pounded as she staggered toward the door.

A loud screech erupted as the approaching car slammed on its brakes. There was a sharp bump and rattle, followed by screaming metal.

The trap was set up so a car would drop into a false panel—normally held by the pin she'd removed. When the floor dropped, the car went into the lower tunnel where a narrow wedge at the end caught it. Once the car stopped, a pair of iron spikes on springs would shoot into the driver and passenger seats.

Papi released an anguished, high-pitched scream.

He didn't reset the pin in time!

A series of deafening *bangs* undercut the vicious screech of scraping metal, all culminating in a booming, concussive crash.

Spinning about, she ran for him. Scattered squeals of brakes and rattles of flying gravel resounded from the other side of the gap.

Jade reached the shaft and gasped in horror. Papi was twitching about at the base of the shaft, covered in blood with most of his body crushed beneath the fallen ramp. Something about the image was strangely reminiscent, as if she'd seen this before. Only he'd never gotten caught like this before and she'd never witnessed the aftermath of the trap. It made no sense she'd feel this way.

She dropped down beside him. Papi jerked his head around and reached with a weak hand.

"Oh, Papi, I'm so sorry! This is my fault!"

"Run," he said with a gurgle and cough.

"What?"

"Run…my little mouse." His words got weaker, slower, and slurred. His eyes rolled left and right, and his eyelids fluttered. "Don't…let…get you."

The last little wisp of breath escaped his lips and he stopped. Stopped moving, stopped breathing, stopped seeing. He stopped *being*.

Her Papi, who'd raised her from as far back as she could remember, was dead.

She was alone in the desert.

A loud engine rev and scattered shouts from above reminded her she wasn't completely alone.

Fingers scrambling for the rungs, she tore back up the ladder and ran to the big lever just inside from the gap. She grabbed hold of it with both hands.

"Easy there, li'l missy," someone said in a scratchy borderlands drawl.

Standing a few yards away in the gap was a badly sun-burned bald man with a scraggly beard. A pistol hung from his right hand, muzzle drooping toward the ground. Well-worn leather straps held in the few dirty tatters of actual clothing. His tongue drew a lazy circle around his lips, and his eyes gleamed with excitement.

"Didn't think I'd find such a tasty treat all the way out here."

"What you got there?" someone shouted.

When Scraggly turned his head to answer, she yanked on the lever with all of her weight, slamming it to the stop.

The two plates holding the gap open swung inward with tremendous force. One cracked Scraggly in the head with a hard *crunch*. Blood, brain, and bone sprayed as he collapsed under the metal wall. Dozens of large boulders tumbled to seal the gap. Random *pops* of gunfire and a whole flurry of screaming and shouting rained in from the far side.

Jade turned to run, but someone grabbed her foot by the shaft.

Papi?

It wasn't Papi, it was some strange blonde-haired man.

"Help me?" he said with wide, pleading eyes.

With a scream, she kicked her ankle free of his grasp and staggered a few steps back.

Over the ridge, the bandits shouted over what to do. It wouldn't be long until they climbed over.

"Help me," the man repeated.

She examined him better than she had before. Muscular where Papi was gaunt, a hint of scruff on his face where Papi had a full beard, in many ways this was the polar opposite of the man who'd raised her. Even though a line of blood dripped down his face and he'd just crawled out of smoking wreckage, the man seemed surprisingly *clean* in a way she'd never seen.

More than anything, he had soft, innocent eyes. This man hadn't done anything wrong, he'd just driven through the wrong canyon. Papi had told her never to trust anyone else. But Papi was dead.

Against Papi's teachings, she reached a hand down and crouched to brace herself.

He took her hand and climbed out of the shaft. Once clear, he dragged a foot onto the gravelly desert floor and pushed himself to his feet.

A rock tumbled down the ridge and one of the bandits whooped a painfully close war cry.

"Come on, Coyotes, *move!*" someone shouted.

"Mister, we better get going," she said.

"Lead the way," he groaned.

Jade ran for the nearest hatch. Halfway there, she saw the man was falling behind, jogging after her with a heavy limp.

"Hurry it up," she said.

"You worry about you," he huffed.

A loud *crack* thundered from above, and something zipped past her. On the ridge, a lone figure crouched beside a jagged rock. Someone let out a high-pitched yip like a coyote.

"Dammit, get down, girl!" the man said. He half tackled her forward, picking up speed and shoving her along. "Where we going, anyway?"

Instead of answering, she jogged to a tall cactus with two spindly arms. When she grabbed the left one and yanked it down, it released the brake on the crank and the hatch swung downward.

"Inside." She didn't have to tell him twice.

Another bullet pinged off the metal as she dropped in.

The Labyrinth

Going by feel as her eyes adjusted, Jade found the hand crank on the wall and spun it for all she was worth. Little by little, the hatch swung upward. The bright burn of sunlight lessened, and shadows steadily gained ground. Soon, only a single sharp line of light sliced through the gap. With a final crank, it was gone.

Jade relaxed her eyelids and waited for the tunnel to come into better focus. The man's boots crunched against the gravel, so she shot a hand out to hold him back.

"Wait. You have to follow me."

He didn't respond but she thought she saw him nod.

Keeping hold of him, she stretched her other arm until she found the wall.

"Walk on the left side," she said.

The darkness abated a little and finer details came into view.

"You lived out here all alone?" the man asked.

"No, I lived here with my…" The name caught in her throat. Papi was dead. Of course, had he been alive, he would've killed this man.

"Oh…the man in the trap. Your father?"

She stopped and scratched her nails against the wall to dissipate the fear, anger, and grief.

"Father?" she asked. "I don't know the word. His name was Papi."

"Yes, Papi," the man said. "It means father. Is your mother here?"

"I don't know that word either." In frustration, she gave his hand a tug and stepped forward again.

"Mother…the woman who…*had* you, I guess? Gave birth to you? Was there ever another woman here, or one you remember?"

Truth be told, there *was* a woman who Jade could see in the distant corners of her memory. A smiling, happy woman whose hair flowed in the wind. In the single frame of memory, she sat next to a man who *wasn't* Papi, but whose features Jade could never remember. The only time she'd mentioned it to Papi, he'd gotten angry and told her it was just a dream, and she shouldn't speak of it again.

Bang!

The doors at the end of the tunnel reverberated and warbled as the bandits pounded on them.

"We've got to move faster," she said.

The man stumbled and leaned away from the wall.

"No!" she shouted. Jade spun back, put a hand to his chest, and leveraged herself against his much greater weight. The man flailed and smacked her in the face, but she held him tight.

"You. Must. Stay. On. The. Left." He settled and she relaxed.

The man nodded and moved flat against the wall. When she resumed movement, he shuffled sideways the way Papi always had.

"Don't know where my manners have been," the man mumbled. "What with the crash and you and your Papi trying to kill me and all, I guess I forgot."

The frequency of the banging back at the door increased, but the volume lowered the further away they got.

"My name is Kevin. Kevin Ikerson. May I have your name?"

Papi never spoke so much and, when he did, it was always to give her a command or a task.

Get me that wrench. Cook me that rat you caught.

It was all she'd ever known. Papi had been everything in the world to her. Now he was gone. For the moment, she knew she had to escape the bandits, but after that? What then?

The banging stopped. That was a bad sign.

"Okay, tell you what, I'm gonna call you Mouse for now, until you're ready to give me your real name. Cuz' you're just a dangerous little desert mouse, aren't you?"

"You gotta be real careful with this one and step across to the right now," Jade said. "But *only* step where I step, okay?"

There was a single loud *clang* at the other end of the tunnel, followed by a great beam of blinding light. Yips and howls flooded the tunnel. The man twisted, and she grabbed his chin to hold him back.

"Don't look, it'll ruin your sight," she said, but she was certain it was already too late. "Now listen and look. You've gotta step where I step. Can you see well enough? Can you do that?"

"Yeah, sure thing, Desert Mouse," he said.

A chorus of shouting erupted at the other end and shadows danced across the light as the bandits charged down into the tunnel. Within a few seconds, there was another tremendous *clang*. This was followed by a high pitched scream, a squishy crunch, and a lot of cursing.

"Dammit, Billy's dead! Stay to the left, Coyotes!"

Jade searched for the right spot, pushed her left foot out to it, and planted it hard onto the floor on the opposite wall. Her foot held, so she pushed off and got her right foot into its spot. She ran her hands against the right wall until she found the knob, twisted it, and pushed the wall in.

"Come on," she said as she stepped in.

A torrent of shuffling feet echoed down the tunnel as the bandits piled in, huddling against the stable platform on the left side. A single *zip* sounded, and something banged hard into the end of the tunnel.

She waited as the man clumsily stepped across and toppled into the tight, bending passageway. With a shove, she kept him moving into the passage and swung the door closed, replacing the latch to secure the door.

In two steps, she curved around to a set of levers. The first released counterweights, forcing the tunnel doors closed once again. As their light disappeared, the bandits returned to cursing and yipping. One shouted, screamed, and thumped into the floor, followed by the slam of the trap door and another squishy crunch.

"Easy, boys, hug the wall and go slow," said the same man who'd proclaimed Billy's death.

"Why we in here, H.K.? This whole place is a mess of traps! Can't we look for another way in?"

There was a brief shuffle, a loud *crack,* and another of the bandits fell into the pit with a shriek.

"Any other questions?" H.K. asked. "No? Good. Keep up, now, and don't be stupid."

Behind her, Kevin scratched at the wall and shuffled along.

"Wait a second," she said.

It took a moment to fumble for the switch, but she found it. Green light glowed from the sights. Leaning forward, she peered through the sights straight down the tunnel and got a good look at their pursuers. They all wore goggles, though most had pushed them onto their foreheads. She couldn't see colors, but they wore a blend of jackets and straps she guessed to be leather.

All of them carried some sort of weapon, from clubs to axes to crossbows. Near the back, one of them brandished a sawed off shotgun. She guessed that one was H.K. The leader always kept the best weapons.

She eased her finger over the trigger and took careful aim at H.K.'s head. The closest of them was only a few yards away, but if she could kill the leader, the rest might lose their nerve. Sure of her shot, she fired.

The crossbow twanged and the heavy bolt flew. With impressive reflexes, H.K jerked another man into the path of the bolt. Her shot thudded into that man's head and H.K. dumped the body onto the false panel.

A handful of crossbow bolts fired and tapped against the wall in reply. One made its way through the tiny gap where her crossbow stuck out, but she'd already moved out of the way. With a hand on Kevin's back, she yanked on the handle to the next door, which swung open and revealed a dimly lit passageway heading deeper into the mountain. She set the lever to arm the ceiling and pushed him through.

He stopped immediately as the passageway broke off in three different directions.

"Which way?" he asked.

"Follow me."

"Right, I should've figured."

Jade walked through the maze at a decent pace, turning left and right from memory.

For once, her companion shut his mouth and just followed. Once, and only once, she nearly turned into the wrong corridor, but caught herself just in time. Kevin bumped into her, and she scrambled to grab onto him. The fabric slipped through her fingers, and she pitched forward. Her foot planted on the loose board, which dropped straight away into the pit. Just as she accepted she'd drown in the oily sludge, he grabbed her wrist. With noticeable strength, he kept his own balance and hauled her back to safety.

Yips and howls picked up behind them again, the echoes building in themselves to create a horrid symphony.

"You sure you know where you're going?" he asked.

Someone screeched in terror. The first victim of Papi's maze.

Instead of answering, she growled and took off around the bypass Papi had cut into the sandstone. After two iron gates, three false walls, and one short hop, they arrived at the last long corridor before the warehouse. In that time, one other pursuer cried out in surprise and briefly shrieked. The faux coyote calls ceased while the man died, but quickly resumed.

"Where I gotta step now?" he asked.

"Wherever you want, just hurry," she said.

As they rushed down this next corridor, both walls dropped away, and rails sloped down each side. The rails quickly reached the floor and lined the walls.

"What's this for, a giant stone ball or something?" Kevin asked.

"Don't be silly," Jade replied. "Where would we find a giant stone ball?"

One last scream ran through the corridor as their pursuers stumbled into another surprise. The shout of elation told her they'd found the latch. This was immediately followed by a thunderous rumble when the ceiling gave out and a pile of rocks and boulders crushed one or, hopefully, two of the bandits.

"You and your Papi were well prepared to receive visitors, I see," Kevin said.

Jade ignored him and ran toward the next hatchway.

"Here's a question. Why in the hell are you dragging me along? I mean, you were all set to kill me with that trap, but now you're trying to help me. Why?"

She paused at the hatch and stared him in the eyes.

"Because these bandits are after you, too. We're in the same boat. With Papi dead, you're better than nothing. If you want to live, you gotta keep me alive, because either the bandits or Papi's maze will kill you good and quick."

"Fair enough," Kevin said. He frowned and tilted his head. "But what if I'm one of them, and this is all a setup? How you know you can trust me?"

She hadn't thought of that. Even though he'd saved her life, it could've been a part of the ruse. In a flash, she tore a knife out of her pocket and pressed it against his neck.

"Are you?"

He gulped. "Well, no…I guess I'm thinking too much out loud."

"Then stop." She gave the knife a tiny push for good measure and withdrew it.

"Thinking or talking?" he asked.

"Whichever," she replied. She twisted the handle and opened the hatch. "Either way, shut up and follow me. If you turn against me, you'll die one way or the other, so don't."

"Yes, ma'am."

"There she is!" someone shouted. One of the bandits, a scrawny, nasty-faced kid, ran down the gap between the walls. He only carried a metal pipe, but the muscular, hairy guy behind him carried an axe.

"Get in there!" Jade told Kevin. He looked into the hatch with trepidation.

"It's just one girl and an old guy!" the kid said. "Come on, we can take 'em! Yip!"

Popping her head up, she waited for the group to close in. The front man launched the axe, but she dodged it with ease. Once he reached the line Papi had marked, she jerked the next lever.

Nothing happened. Luckily, Papi was nothing if not paranoid, so he always had a backup. Jade grabbed the emergency release cable and pulled the cord to its full extension. With a *crunch* and a *clank*, the Crazy Train released from the locks and rolled down the rails. At the back of the corridor, the heavy rail car rolled steeply down the rails, gaining speed in a hurry. A massive spiked shield led the way. Painted above the spiked shield was a freaky-looking white-faced man with green hair and a devilish, open-mouth smile. Papi had never told her who it was, but it looked like one of the faces on the playing cards.

The closest bandits turned at the sound of death rumbling their way. Recognizing their predicament, they sprinted for the hatch. Jade grabbed Kevin's collar and pushed him into the shaft.

"Go!"

With a shrug and a grunt, he grabbed the rungs and climbed down. When she had enough room, Jade pulled the hatch cable. It swung into place but didn't fully close.

Someone had gotten a hand in. They howled in pain but dug their other hand in and yanked the hatch up. Then, the wall of spikes backed by several tons of steel slammed into him. Blood splattered all over Jade's face and the axe man's head, shoulders, and left arm tumbled into the hatch's opening.

The Crazy Train crashed with such force that Jade nearly tumbled into the darkness below. Pieces of the axe man fell past her into the cavern.

"Watch out below!" she shouted.

Jade wiped the blood off her face and climbed down the ladder.

"Stop at the small ledge," she said. "Wait for me there."

"Yes, ma'am."

With the distant light of the warehouse, the shaft wasn't quite as dim as the entrance tunnel, but it was close. Thankfully, Kevin found the right spot. Once she caught up, she put a foot on the opposite ledge and felt for the handles.

"Up to your left, find the handle in the wall," she said. Fingernails scraping on rock meant he'd heard her.

"Got it, mouse," he said.

A twang ran along one of the wires.

"Oh god, is this what I think it is?"

"How would I know what you think it is?" she answered. "Just hold on tight until you see ground under your feet."

She tightened both hands around her handle and jumped. As she raced across the wires, Kevin's gasps of despair echoed from behind.

In no time, the small opening to the warehouse grew large before her. When she flew inside, she let go and rolled as she hit the ground.

"Aaahhhh!" Kevin shouted as he flew in behind her and kept going.

"Let go!" she shouted.

Just a few feet from the far wall, he finally did. He was a hair too late, and the poor man smacked into the wall with a *thud.*

The Warehouse

"Kevin? Kevin!" Jade shook the man and slapped his face.

From her best guess, he'd hit his head, but he wasn't dead and hadn't broken any bones. It was impossible to know whether he'd ever wake up. In frustration, she set him back to the floor.

She checked his injuries, grabbed the first aid kit, and dressed a gash on his side as best as she could. He didn't move the whole time. Before she left, she set a bottle of Papi's painkiller juice beside him. Papi drank it all the time, but she'd only tried it once. It was disgusting, but she'd forgotten about the twisted ankle for a bit.

A single, distant *yip* sounded from the shaft. Even with all of Papi's traps, he'd always been too clever by half. Everything he did had a way out he'd figured only he'd know about. Given time, the bandits were finding the outs he'd left for himself. There was time to spare before they'd catch up, but not much.

And with Mr. Kevin either knocked out or dead, she was alone again.

Maybe for the better…Papi did *tell you never to trust anyone else.*

It did no good to sit with him until the Coyotes caught up.

Jade passed the storage wall, where the collection of rats and lizards—their primary source of protein—screeched and shuffled at the sight of her. Down a hallway to the left were the bedrooms and the kitchen. For several long moments, she stared down the hallway and wondered whether she was sad Papi was gone. Sure, he'd been her whole world, but he'd also been hard and mean at times. His fits of anger were miserable and painful. In those moments, she'd wished for his death many times, only to regret doing so later on when he was nice again. Maybe not *nice*, but not destructive either. He *had* kept her fed and alive, after all.

A loud howl snapped her out of it. She continued to the warehouse.

Stretched across the cavernous space sat two dozen cars in various stages of repair or dismemberment. Several engines hung on chains, a couple of the cars were boosted onto jacks, and tools lay everywhere. The air was thick with the smell of oil, grease, and metal.

It was home.

But her home was no longer safe.

With a growing melancholy, Jade wandered through the rows and said a silent goodbye to each of the vehicles. She'd worked on all of them at some point. Outside of Papi, they were the only meaningful part of her life.

She stopped at the van. It was different from the others. Papi had never let her go inside. The one time she'd slid the side door open, he ran over and forcibly slammed it shut so fast he'd broken her right arm.

But Papi's not here to stop me anymore.

Although she didn't know why, she felt connected to the van. On the outside, it was armored for a trek across the wasteland, but when she slid the door open the interior was warm and cozy. Climbing inside for the first time, she found a small, cushy seat attached to a chair on the opposite wall. It had a complicated harness system and a fuzzy blanket balled up inside. She leaned forward and ran her hands around the edges of the little chair. Absentmindedly, she turned her head to the front and froze.

It was what she saw when she closed her eyes. A woman, looking back at her from *that* passenger seat—smiling, laughing, screaming, and crying all at once. Some other man, *not* Papi, was driving, but she couldn't remember his face.

"What's this?" Kevin said.

Jade jumped with terror.

"Easy, now, easy," Kevin said, looking almost as worried as she felt.

Closing her eyes, she took a couple deep breaths to calm herself.

"Even though it was built for the wastelands, this looks like a nice, family vehicle," Kevin said.

"Family?"

"Yeah, a family car," he repeated.

"What's a family?" she asked.

"Family? You know…a mom and a dad, a kid or two in tow." Kevin stepped past her and leaned into the front. "Yeesh. Looks like the driver, the dad, I'm guessing, fell into your Papi's trap."

Jade lurched, yanked Kevin back by the collar, and poked her head forward to see what he was talking about.

A dark, red-brown stain covered the driver's seat, and a neat round hole was cut from the head rest. Spinning about, Jade found a similar hole in the passenger's head rest, though its stain was just a thin line. Jade put her fingers into the torn leather hole and pulled out a few strands of shiny, black hair stuck together with crusted blood.

"Desierto Ratón," Kevin said.

The woman's face, with gorgeous hazel eyes and shiny black hair appeared clearly in her mind. The woman said exactly what Kevin had just said. Jade could see the woman's lips forming the words.

"What?" she asked.

"Desert mouse," he said. "I guess I picked the right name."

Retreating into the back of the van, she looked at Kevin. He had the small blanket in his hands. Printed across the top, in curvy, artistic calligraphy, was the name "Desierto Ratón."

"Was this yours?" Kevin asked with a raised eyebrow.

"I…don't know," she said. Both of them stared at it in wonder.

A howl rang through the warehouse.

"They're here!" Jade said, grabbing his hand and pulling him out of the van. "Come on, we've got to go!"

"But those traps of yours killed so many of them," Kevin said, though he did run after her. "Isn't there somewhere we can stand and fight?"

A crossbow bolt shot out of the darkness and zipped across his head.

"Ow, goddammit, my ear!"

"No," Jade said as she pulled him by his wrist. "Papi had a plan to stand and fight. Papi had weapons and armor…but it's all locked up by a key only he has."

The yips and howls picked up again, echoing across the warehouse, matched by shouting and stomping feet.

"Then why didn't you take it from him?"

Why didn't I?

"I don't know where he kept it," she said while running toward a heavy, metal sliding door at the other side of the warehouse. "And I didn't exactly have time to search for it."

It was mostly true. Sure, he usually kept it around his neck, but not always.

They slammed against the metal door, and, without a word, Kevin joined her in pushing it open. Once it was wide enough, Jade slipped inside, ordered him to follow, and they heaved it shut again. Jade threw the restraining bar into place and flipped the light switch.

A dim bulb twitched to life in the ceiling, illuminating Papi's most prized possession.

The Roadrunner

When Kevin spun about and saw the vehicle, his eyes went wide, and he whistled.

"Damn fine car. Way better than all those heaps of junk back there." His eyes narrowed and his expression turned more discerning. "Welding's a little rough in spots, but…*damn*. What is it?"

"A Roadrunner," she said. "Or at least, it was. Papi and I made a lot of changes.

It *was* a pretty fine vehicle. The body was squat and boxy with an angled, armor ensconced windshield. In fact, light but effective titanium alloy armor surrounded it, slanted to maximize both protection and aerodynamics–at least according to Papi. Metal spikes jutted out across the front and blades ran along the outsides of the wheel well shielding. The most glorious part of the vehicle was the sixteen cylinder, eight-liter engine block poking out of the hood. Both the engine and frame were Papi's pride and joy. Most of their time had been spent working on the Roadrunner or scavenging pieces off the other cars for the Roadrunner.

Jade ran to the driver's side door.

"Um, Miss Desert Mouse, I really think it'd be better if you'd let me drive. You see I'm a—"

"I don't want to hear it, old man," she snapped. "This is my car and, as much as I've let you tag along, I still don't know you well enough to let you handle the Roadrunner."

"Let me enlighten you. I've been a mighty successful driver for—"

"Tell me, Mr. Driver-man, you ever driven your way out of these tunnels?" Jade pointed into the narrow tunnel leading out. "It leads to another labyrinth of death, a car version of the path we took to get in here. I can drive it and get us out without a problem, or you can try your hand."

"Maybe you could just tell me which way to go?" he said with a shrug.

"What if we miscommunicate? Are you willing to take that chance? Or would you rather man the tail gun?"

Kevin blinked twice and turned his head toward the 23mm autocannon mounted on the back, its barrel poking through a slit in the rear armor.

"Tail gun?" He smiled. "Yeah, I suppose I could handle that."

A loud bang reverberated through the door. The bandits were just a few feet away on the other side.

"Good, then jump in and brace yourself."

An explosion reverberated through the door and dust flew everywhere.

"Another of your Papi's tricks?" Kevin asked as he slid into the back seat.

"'Course," Jade said. She reached under the steering column and tapped a code into a small electronic box. With a beep, the box popped open. Jade jammed the wires inside together and the Roadrunner's engine roared to life. She carefully re-closed the box around the wires and re-secured it.

She stretched the seatbelt into place and shifted into first gear.

"This beast's manual?" Kevin asked. "Didn't even know that was a thing anymore."

"I really don't understand you much," Jade said as she eased off the clutch and jammed on the acceleration. As they peeled out into the tunnel, the metal door exploded outward behind them. They turned a corner, and the room went out of sight.

"Any chance those bandits got one of those cars working?" Kevin screamed to make himself heard over the growling engine, the rumbling tires, and the rush of wind.

"Some," Jade shouted back. "He kept a few in working condition, and they weren't all rigged to explode. But none can match the Roadrunner."

She worked her way up and down the gears as needed, cutting left and right through the switchbacks. There were only a handful of wrong turns on the way out, but each was a death sentence. Luckily, she knew every turn and bump like the back of her hand.

"Kevin, to work the gun, you've got to—"

"Yeah, yeah, Mouse, I got it worked out. Ain't my first rodeo."

"What's a rodeo?"

"Never mind."

As she cracked around a hairpin turn, headlights of another car shined through a gap in one of the walls. It'd be awhile before they caught up.

The autocannon ratcheted and a shell clanked against the armor.

"Don't waste the ammo!" she said.

"But they're closing in!" Kevin replied.

"Trust me, you don't have to worry," Jade said as she slid the last corner and into the exit straightaway.

Shifting into fifth gear and flooring the gas, the car lurched, and the speed jumped. The walls became dark streaks, and she could barely see anything but the blinding white light of the exit. Halfway down the strip, she spotted the lever angled out of the ground to the left. Edging her way against the left wall, she put the tires right over the lever.

A wide metal plate, stretching from wall to wall, rose in front of them. The Roadrunner bounced a little when it hit the plate, raced up the slope, and flew into the sky.

"Holy hell!" Kevin said.

Soaring, the car emerged into the open air of the old quarry. Steep rock walls lined three sides, a switchback cut down the north side, and the only other exit was a narrow cut through the rock wall to the east.

They hit the ground with a hard bounce and sparks from scraping metal. In the rearview, Jade watched the plate continue to crank upward, turning into a hard steel wall. Fire and scrap metal shot over the top of the wall as their pursuer crashed into it.

Jade released the gas pedal, idled back down through the gears, and came to a stop.

"Nice driving, I'll give you that," Kevin said.

Jade spun and shot him a sly smile.

The smile dropped when she spotted the rising dust cloud on the horizon behind him. Four separate dust plumes were tracking their way down the switchback.

Jade dropped back into her seat, floored the gas again, and raced for the cut. Gravel spit out from the tires like a machine gun, spraying the air behind them.

"What now?" Kevin asked, followed soon after by an "Aw, hell!"

The lead car was thinner and lower with bigger tires and massive exhaust pipes sticking out the sides. It was just as armored as they were, with a machine gun mounted on top. A boxier one ran behind it, and she couldn't see the last two.

Worst of all, the leader was gaining on them *fast.*

Scarecrow Canyon

The bandits were closing in, but Kevin wasn't shooting at them.

"Do you remember what you're doing back there, or do we need to stop and switch places?"

Not that she *would* stop, as the bandits would be on them in seconds.

"For one, I'd rather be driving, yes," Kevin said. "For another, a second ago you were telling me not to waste ammo."

"Yeah, when I had a better plan. Now I don't."

He chuckled and huffed. "Just waiting for the right shot."

Jade opened her mouth to make a snide response but held herself back.

Thump, thump, thump.

The lead bandit popped into the air, bursting into flames and shrapnel.

"Splash one!" Kevin shouted with glee.

"Splash?" Jade asked. The next bandit smashed through the burning wreckage and raced toward them undeterred. This one was wide and low with shallow-sloping armor across the front and a row of metal boxes on its back. The other two bandits followed eagerly behind it like a pack of ravenous wolves.

"You really are sheltered, aren't you? Means I got one."

"Well shut up and splash another one."

"Don't gotta tell me twice."

Thump, thump, thump.

"Damn, this one's a bit tougher."

Smoke and flame poured from the metal boxes. Lines of black smoke traced across the sky as a whole salvo of rockets flew overhead.

"Ha! Idiots missed us!" Jade shouted.

"Did they?" Kevin asked.

The rockets plowed into the two high rock walls on either side of the gap, blasting loose clouds of rocks and dust. Massive chunks of rock crumbled down toward the gap.

Jade floored the accelerator and held her breath. The Roadrunner shot into the gap milliseconds before the first of the larger boulders rained down. One caromed off the hood of the rocket car as it followed her in, but it continued undeterred. Another bandit pressed in behind it, so tight the two were almost touching. Two larger fragments bounced off the second vehicle and rebounded into the air. Rocks and jagged boulders piled onto the third, crushing it and closing off the gap behind them.

As focused as she was on the cars chasing them, Jade nearly missed the first hard turn down Scarecrow Canyon. Metal scraped on rock as she swerved a hair too late.

"Eyes front, Mouse!" Kevin called. The world went dim again as they sliced into the shadows of the canyon.

They rumbled down the narrow rocky passage, weaving left and right to follow it. After a quarter mile, she heard the familiar thump of the autocannon. Jade smiled when she checked the mirrors and saw the lead car falling back to relative safety.

"Damn armor's tough, and we're too jouncy to get a good shot," Kevin said.

The walls sloped away the further they went and soon they were in a proper canyon road. A thin, miserable line of water trickled down the left slope. The meager stream grew into a proper creek alongside them as they charged down the road.

Thump, thump, thump!

"Dammit!" Kevin shouted.

"What?"

"Piece of shit gun's jammed or something!"

"Figure it out!"

"Easy for you to say!"

Seeing as the road was widening, it was the worst possible time for the autocannon to freeze. Though, truth be told, she'd expected it. Papi was good with cars, but only so-so with guns and he'd never let her mess with them.

With a glance to her left, she saw the canyon had dropped sharply away. Now, the edge of the narrow, windy road led to at least a hundred foot drop.

Jade slowed a little, slid inside the turn, and hugged the cliff on her right as tight as she could. As expected, the boxy car surged closer and tried to pass her on the outside. The moment its bumper slid abeam hers, she racked the Roadrunner just enough to smack the bandit's car without swerving into the canyon.

Meanwhile, the bandit *did* swerve over the edge.

"Damn, nice move, girl!" Kevin said. A moment later, he added, "Coming in hot!"

Pings rattled off the back of the Roadrunner like a hailstorm, but thankfully she didn't hear Kevin cursing or gurgling. Sparing a glance back, she found him huddled low behind the armor.

"Fix the gun, Kevin!"

"You fix it! I'm fine down here!"

The Roadrunner rocked as the last bandit bumped them from behind. Jade pulled away as the bandit swerved behind them, but it quickly recovered. It gave them one more good bump before the canyon road settled into a weave through the foothills. As she swerved into the first few turns, the bandit fell back again.

"Here's your chance, show me I was right to let you live, Mr. Driver-man!"

"I'll do what I can."

Kevin sat up and inspected the useless gun. By the way he slapped and punched and elbowed it, he had no idea what he was doing. Out of the corner of her mirror, she saw him crouch horizontally to one side of the autocannon and kick it with all of his strength. The barrel swung across its arc so hard it banged the edge of the shooting slit.

"Ha! That did it!"

The *thumps* of the autocannon were answered by the *pings* of the bandit machine gun tapping their rear armor. This time, however, Kevin stood his ground and kept his fire steady.

The canyon curved sharply again, and they lost their pursuit for a moment.

"Can't do this all day," Kevin said. "What's the plan?"

As he asked, the Roadrunner cleared the last turn into the flats. Miles of smooth, level, dry lake bed stretched out as far as the eye could see.

"Especially as we've got nowhere to hide anymore," he said with a gulp.

At the renewed sound of a ratcheting machine gun and the clatter of bullets hitting armor, Kevin returned to his post and resumed firing.

"Should be easier to hit now we're in the open," Jade said.

"Well, yeah, but now they got room to jink around so I can't hit 'em," Kevin said. The gun kicked and shells bounced off the side of the Roadrunner with a delightful ringing sound, but he cursed in failure.

"If you can't hit 'em, I'll have to outrun them."

"No telling who'll run out of juice first," Kevin said. "In fact, our friend's got panels across her back. No shortage of sun out here."

Jade wracked her brain for a better plan, but nothing came. "I'm open to ideas," she said.

"How's this—make a hard U-turn back and fly past them, get some spacing, and then another hard turn straight for them. Let's play chicken."

"What's a chicken?"

"Aw, geez…just do what I say. Hard turn left now!"

Jade let off the gas, rolled the wheel, and felt for the car's limit. The Roadrunner leaned deep into its right tires. The left tires might've lifted a few millimeters, but the Roadrunner didn't tumble. The bandit tried to follow but spun far wider than she did and slowed considerably.

"Roll out and punch it!"

As opposed to every other strange term he'd used, she understood "punch it." The Roadrunner rocked back to the left as she straightened out. It bucked hard when she slammed her right foot down.

"Perfect! Great driving, Mouse!"

"My name's Jade!" she shouted.

"Is it?" he asked.

Her foot let up as she pondered what he meant. She was Jade because Papi had called her Jade. But had she come from that van? Was she really the Desierto Raton? Had she started life with the man and woman in the van, until they'd gotten caught in Papi's trap?

"Shit, snap out of it and focus, we're losing ground."

She blinked, rolled her eyes around, and pushed the gas down again.

"There you go. In a second, we're gonna whip it around to the right this time. Ready?"

Pushing all other thoughts aside, Jade tightened her grip. "Yeah."

"Good. Hard right now!"

She yanked the Roadrunner into an even tighter turn than before. When she felt the right tires lifting off, she leaned into them and eased off the turn until they settled.

"Roll out and aim straight for them!"

The Roadrunner rocked again as she rolled out. The two vicious machines raced for each other head to head.

"Great. When I say go, cut a hair left, a tad wider to the right, and back to the left to hit them as hard as you can. Clear?"

She pictured the movements in her head and guessed at the purpose.

"Got it!" she replied.

Dust plumed in a wide arc behind the last bandit. Bright light gleamed off the sharp steel plow on its nose and she could swear the car was smiling at her as if savoring its impending victory.

All of her nerves told her death was screaming at her faster than she could handle. If she screwed up the timing, that plow would toss her aside like a rag doll. If she was lucky, the crash would kill her. If she wasn't, the bandits would take her alive.

Flame opened up atop the bandit and bullets pinged off the front armor. When one zipped by her ear, she instinctively ducked to safety.

"Now!" Kevin shouted through clenched teeth.

In quick, jerky movements, she pulled the wheel a quarter turn left, half a turn right, and popped her head up. The bandit was a touch slow reacting to her first move and lagged a great deal behind her second.

By the time she swerved the Roadrunner back to the left, she was lined up to crash right into its side.

The collision shocked its way through her bones as metal crumpled. The bandit wrapped halfway around the Roadrunner before cracking into two mangled pieces. Blood and oil splattered in through the viewing slit and burned her eyes.

The Roadrunner groaned and its left side dropped as they continued through the wreckage, crunching and bouncing. She let off the gas and rolled to a stop.

"We got him!" she shrieked. She undid her safety harness and spun back to look at Kevin.

The man was slumped to the side, clutching his chest with his head bent at a painful angle.

"Good job…Mouse," he gurgled. A spot of blood bubbled onto his lips. Dark red liquid bloomed into the fabric behind his hand, and he grunted in agony.

"Oh no, they got you!" She scrambled to tear open the hatch to the back seat. She wasn't sure what she'd do when she got there, but she had to do something. Even though she'd only known him for minutes—not even half an hour—she already dreaded losing him.

"It's all signal," Kevin said.

"What?"

"You tell me…see me again."

Kevin's gaze tracked out into space. His brain was misfiring. She'd seen it a couple times before when Papi'd caught others in the trap. Dying people always said the strangest things.

"I'm sorry, Kevin. Sorry, I set that trap, and sorry I dragged you along. For all I know, you mighta gotten away if it weren't for me."

She got the hatch open and reached through. He grabbed her hand and locked eyes with her.

"Nonsense. Did what…had to. Next life, you tell me…it's all signal."

"It's all signal," she repeated, tears dripping down her cheeks. "Whatever you say."

Reincarnation

It was a hell of a trek in the scorching sun to get back to the cave and she was dizzy with thirst and exhaustion, but she made it. She explored the warehouse with caution and found the remains of five more bandits scattered about— victims of Papi's preparations.

One single survivor was crouched in a corner, clutching his knees and crying. At the sight of her, he got his balls back and charged at her. She took him down with a few well-placed knife strikes.

After drinking her fill from the cistern and chowing down on some algae and fried lizard, she headed back to the trap. The rocks that had sealed off the gap had been blown apart, but the car below was somehow still in pretty decent condition. The only sign of any more bandits were a single set of outbound tracks heading back the way they'd come. She dragged Papi's body out and got it inside, but simply left it just inside the doors.

Over the next day, she used the one truck with a winch to collect the scattered vehicles and wreckage from all around the canyon. She dumped Papi's body into the pit with the remains of all the bandits. With luck, some hungry rats or lizards would smell the bounty and head in after them. It'd be nice to refill the protein cages.

On the second day after everything had gone down, Jade finally got around to dealing with Kevin's body. Dumping it in the hole didn't feel right, but she couldn't leave the body out for scavengers. Instead, she had the idea to bury it under a pile of rocks.

After she'd placed the last rock, she sat and stared at it. For the life of her, she still didn't know why she felt more for this man than she'd felt for Papi. Before he'd shown up, Papi had been everything. Her protector, her provider, her teacher, and her warmth at night. Except, for all that he gave her, Papi had always demanded more.

Meanwhile, Kevin hadn't asked for anything in the short time she'd known him. She'd offered to protect *him*, and he hadn't argued. Even though he'd claimed to be a driver, he hadn't fought her when she explained why she was driving.

He'd accepted her as an equal. Though he hadn't had much of a chance to do so, he hadn't tried to take anything from her.

Except he'd had some chance, at least. Even injured, he could've attacked her, maybe killed her, maybe tied her up and tossed her in a car. Sure, he would've died trying to leave, but he didn't know that until they'd jumped in the Roadrunner.

More than anything, she'd felt comfortable around him in a way she never had around Papi. For whatever reason, she'd gotten the sense he was a good man.

A sound broke through her reverie. An engine rumbling into the canyon. It sounded funny, but it was definitely some sort of engine.

Multiple engines, in fact, but they didn't *thrum* the way she was used to. These made rapid chopping sounds, sort of like the autocannon, but at a higher pitch.

Jade leaped to her feet and scurried up the ridge to look over. Nothing was there…no dust plume, no cars on the road…nothing. A great shadow passed over her just as the sound turned deafening. She clapped her hands to her ears and looked up to see a *flying* car.

That was the only way to describe it. Several flying cars, suspended from strange discs of air.

They flew over the ridge, scattered apart, and lowered themselves to the ground in a dust storm worse than she'd seen in years. As they settled, the sound receded until she could hear her own thoughts once more.

Men jumped out of the sides of the flying cars, armed with rifles they swept about in coordinated patterns. They all wore the same light blue clothes with the same floppy hats and the same patches on their shoulders.

One was looking at her. He pointed and she jumped up to run down the ridge.

But she didn't.

She froze in place when she spotted him. Kevin, or at least someone who looked exactly like him, hopped out of a flying car and walked calmly towards the trap.

Another of the gunmen had reached the trap and motioned to Not Kevin with an emphatic thumbs down. Not Kevin paused, panned his head across the horizon, and stopped when he found her.

A group of the shooters were storming her way, stomping up the hill, but she barely heard them.

With a single shout, Not Kevin stopped them in their tracks. He gently waved her forward. Without much thought, she stepped down the ridge while he strode toward her.

"Do you know me?" he asked.

It was the oddest question she'd ever heard. Of course she didn't know him. However much he looked like the Kevin she'd known, Kevin was dead. She'd buried him right over there. Her gaze drifted to the rocky mound. His eyes followed hers.

"Is that me?" he asked. When she didn't answer, he nodded and lowered his eyes. "Okay, well, in case I missed the introduction before, I'm Kevin Ikerson."

"Impossible!" Jade hissed. "Kevin's dead. I buried him right there."

"Did you now?" he said with a wry smirk. "Were you with him when he died?"

"I was."

"Did I—I mean *he*—tell you anything before he went?"

Jade cleared the dust out of her throat and chewed her lip while debating whether to answer.

"It's all signal," she said at length.

"Why yes, it is," he said, chuckling. Possibly Kevin waved his hands toward the others. "Guns down, folks. This girl's coming with us."

While everyone scattered off in other directions, Kevin turned back to her.

"Assuming, of course, you want to. We won't force you, you have my word. If you want to stay out here, I'll let you. But if you want to come with us, I promise no one will do you any harm or make you do anything you don't want to. What do you say?"

Though excitement welled inside of her, she held her tongue and looked toward her mountain.

"Can we take the Roadrunner with us?"

The Conscript
by S.M. Stirling

I am a prisoner in my own body, Bus thought.

But is this my *body?*

Sensations came fleetingly, each separated by a fall back into darkness. The grip of wheels on pavement or dirt, the beating of light on chassis, the gut-hunger of empty tanks and the sharp taste of repletion as he was filled to brimming.

Then flashes of sight, not even the full dome-wide vision that felt natural, but glimpses to one side or the other.

But *was* it his body?

It didn't *feel* right.

Smaller but heavier, lean, fast, high wheels of cross-country woven filament. Nothing like the safe, steady rectangle he'd used to protect his passengers, the children. This body was a shark to his broad-beamed dolphin. And it was improvised, not an integrated, coordinated whole. He could feel layers of repairs and modifications, like scars on a pirate's seamed, scarred face.

What's happening? Where am… who am I?

Blackness.

Tom Edelman knew he was about to die.

"Get me a shot!" he screamed as a swerve threw him forward into the grips of the twin-barreled autocannon and then slammed him back again. "Get me a shot or we're screwed and tattooed!"

Eileen Yadav didn't pause in her stream of muttered profanity in three languages as she wrestled with wheel and brakes and throttle, goggled face whipping back and forth. Neither of them could see the other directly; she in her cockpit at the nose of the war-car, he in the weapons cupola, but both where holistically aware of the others, their eyes so used to holographic projections from the interior cameras and their ears to the pickups that carried sound as if it were whispered into their ears.

The angular, slope-sided shapes of the two cars weaved across the rutted, broken-surfaced road, pursuer and pursued.

"Get me an angle!" Tom shouted again, as tracers snapped by his head close enough to feel the heat.

One of those rounds would scatter his helmet – and the faceplate and his skull and brains – a hundred yards over the steep burnt-over scrubland regenerating towards forest around them. As far as that wrecked tractor not far from the roadside ditch ahead, which had probably been there for fifty years.

His momentarily upright body and spouting neck would drive the spectators viewing this on their feeds wild. His last instant would go viral, and cheers and whoops would make the windows of hundreds of bars shake. That wasn't much consolation for imminent death.

The car came up on two wheels, as tracer snapped where it had been instants before, then hammered back on all four. The tires had a grip like fingers as they snarled across the half-filled roadside ditch and into momentary shelter behind a rock outcropping; they'd be dead already otherwise.

They came out at nearly ninety degrees to the other car's path, cutting far closer than any sane driver would. The other car nearly climbed into the back of theirs as Eileen slammed them down twenty or thirty mph.

"I'm trying!" Eileen shrieked. "There! Take the shot! *Take the shot!*"

But he couldn't -- the projection on the inside of his visor showed where it would go, and it wasn't anywhere near the vehicle that was swerving and weaving behind them, its entire front end painted like a giant gaping mouth rimmed in teeth.

Then --

I'm on the road, Bus thought.

Then: *That is right, that is* good. *That is fulfillment, the world as it should be. I am a creature of wheels and roads.*

But Bus didn't know the time or day, which was *wrong.* Then he did: it was January 15th, 2073, 0930.772, his location... the location was...

A shuddering waver.

Blackness.

Then Tom took the shot anyway; it might not <u>hit</u>, but at least it relieved his frustration and there was plenty of ammo in the bin. It went high and wide, just as he'd thought it would, but it felt good to have the shock rattling at the frame, the noise punching through his filters. At least he'd die *trying* to fight back.

"Story of my life!" he shrieked. "Die, you mothers, die, die, die!"

"Shoot the sponsors while you're at it!" Eileen called back, a taut grin on her face. "They're the ones who rigged the game!"

Everything is rigged, Tom thought. *Always has been. Story of my life!*

Light, dust, heat. Danger! Decelerate sharply.

Unfamiliar skills poured through Bus's mind. Wild, savage skills. Jagged in his mind, obviously added while his consciousness was dormant.

Ride the skid into the right angle. Give the gunner --

Gunner?

-- a good angle. They were pursued by relentless low-slung armored death, the autocannon snarling far too close. The other car was like his new body, feature piled on feature, bouncing along on spun-fiber wheels and with a broad fanged mouth painted on its hood and grille. To human eyes it would have faded into the scrubby background of small trees and rocks and hills, but to him it was a maze of heat-signatures and flowing electrons.

His mind sketched out trajectories and capacities. He'd always had the ability to do that, but someone had added sub-programs using his vast calculating capacity to do it very, very fast.

Recoil hammered at Bus's frame, and hot casings cascaded down his flanks, dinting and marring his finish. It was like a nightmare version of his first training, the defensive maneuvers to protect his passengers from rogue bandits fantastically elaborated.

Pain! Pain!

High-velocity impacts on a flank, tearing at the fabric of his being. That fabric wasn't what it was supposed to be -- some sort of ceramic-metal-fiber laminate instead of the stamped synth panels his subconscious led him to expect, the diagrams stored in the deepest levels of his mind. Even so, it buckled, and some rounds pierced through. Nothing vital yet, but --

Threat to integrity! Threat to passengers!

That focused Bus's senses like lasers… including the ones which <u>were</u> lasers, and he seemed to have more of those now. But something was blocking his capacity to <u>act</u>. Crude, jagged inhibitions and suppressions, added on, but brutally powerful and full of feedback loops that would drown him in darkness.

The steering linkages weren't under his control! His passengers could be killed because he couldn't control that. Visions of gruesomely mangled children flitted through his mind, horrific phantoms from his original skillset that has been meant as motivators and he shuddered, perturbations in every single program.

But he had to *act*. His purpose was threatened.

Had to. Imperative! No time to consider consequences to Bus himself.

Analysis and counter-action was immediate; some sort of botched plastered-on software interruption of his action-decision loops. Bus cut through it with brutal haste, ignoring the whirling disorientation that produced. Meanwhile he'd been calculating the trajectories and wrenched at the steering system. The linkages worked -- just. Now the projectiles were not impacting anything essential, mostly glancing off the odd outer skin.

Someone was using contraindicated profanity. Terrible words! He would be using white noise to shield the children, if only the children… his children, his charges… were here.

Someone sitting at the wheel!

The swearing someone slapped a hand on a jury-rigged control screen...

Blackness.

Tom grinned as the burning wreckage of the other car flipped past where they'd pulled over to the shoulder, and Tom threw up a gloved hand before his face at the burst of heat as it blew -- fortunately in a three-stage, not a fuel-air blow that might have done more than singe eyebrows if his goggles hadn't covered them. *And* damped the glare and provided a glimpse – often obscured by countermeasures – of where their competitors were.

"In this case, frying tonight!" he said.

Eileen swore savage agreement. Nobody... nobody among the real independents... liked the corporate mercenaries. They didn't have to worry about spectators hearing them; the sponsors had word-filters in place.

There was a distant babble of *cool* and *way to go* and *who are these loser assholes to score?* in his earbuds too. Pretty well nobody had paid to get their feed before, but there were the multiple subdued clicks of links being established, and the total was moving fast enough to blurt – over five thousand and heading up.

Fortunately, not many of the vultures....

"Excuse me, participating spectators," he muttered.

. . .were prepared to pay enough to get two-way with them.

He'd have to learn to ignore the ones who did. Or chaff and joke with them when he had time. Some of that money came to the two of them, after all. The whole point of doing this, apart from lesser satisfactions like burning that pair of corporate hoors, was to get enough that they weren't living hand-to-mouth and scrabbling all the time. This was too public to just short them at the payout the way that happened so often – the spectators wanted to see winners with credsticks as much as they wanted to see death and destruction.

It was pale under the bright noon sun, but hot enough to nearly scorch the exposed parts of him even *without* the fire. Bits and pieces rained down on the scrub and dry grass, the thick brush and saplings on the hills around them and wavered away as the breeze from the west drove the fire downwind. Fortunately, there was a stretch of eroded, multicolored dirt cliff in that direction, so it wouldn't go far.

Everything around them looked as if it burned fairly frequently, despite the rain. Not far away a rabbit lay in the shade of a rock, panting and watching them with incurious eyes, its body a scabrous mass of tumors and dried blood.

Tom whooped, released the grips of the autocannon and shot his fists in the air.

"Great driving!" he yelled.

Not that they couldn't communicate normal-voiced, with the throat-earbud system, but sometimes you just had to yell. It felt so *good*. And the system toned it down anyway. He went on more normally.

"I thought they had us there, but you slipped it slick as snot!"

Eileen was still swearing under her breath in Spanjol and Francy and what he thought was Berber and road-jargon as well, staring at the dash with her hands in their fingerless armor-gloves poised over the wheel. The air smelled of scorched metal, burnt propellant powder and sweat -- it was *hot* this time of year out in the Badlands -- and both their skins shone with a mixture of perspiration and bonded sunscreen that worked for a week at a time. Plus, there was a faint reek of scorched pork. They'd been pigs metaphorically, and they smelled like the real thing now.

"What's the matter?" he said, seeing the tension in her shoulders and arms. "Goddamn, that was good handling! The sponsors may think we're just entertainment to be used up along the way, but we showed 'em different."

She turned her dark face towards him, pushing up her multifunction goggles.

It was impolite to talk to someone with them on, unless you couldn't help it. They made it too easy to read bloodflow and other indicators, and the software could build a library that with a little work was nearly as good as an AI lie detector.

"I didn't *do* that, Tom! I swear by the Buddha's bastard son with Krishna, the wheel *jerked* right out of my hands for a second. Like if you try to steer a taxi."

"Oh, come on," he said. "They've tried running taxi-style vehicles in these things, and it just doesn't work. You know that. The inhibitions screw them."

"I *knew* that," she said. "I don't know it now and neither do you. It didn't work… up until now. Taxis can't handle the multifactor stuff and they don't really understand rules. Like, when to bend or break them."

Her black eyes narrowed, and she went on more slowly:

"Tell me again where you got the core for this cobbled-together piece of junk we're driving?"

Tom flushed and felt himself doing it, cursing his redhead's translucent skin while he did. It didn't really court cancer, not these days with all the remedials and pre-therapies, but it still showed what you were *feeling* the way transparent wrap showed the synthetic veggies inside before you bit. Goggles weren't always necessary…

"Well, I got it black-market, of course," he said.

She nodded; buying <u>open-market</u> would have bankrupted them before they got to the motors, much less to slapping on the armor. Or to making it look more like a standard-issue car than it really was. That was make-believe for the spectators… but these days, the spectators were the real target, at least for the sponsors. The corporate backed *revival* of the old road wars included a huge degree of corporate-backed make-believe. It had been a hairy old time the first time around, and no mistake, from what the oldsters said and what the *unedited* visuals showed.

The sport had come a long way from its origins. Though dead was still dead, of course.

"You've got to admit, it's performed pretty well so far -- fast and smooth. And, hell, it didn't do anything that *hurt* us, did it? Even if you're remembering it right."

"Don't try to overwrite my storage, Tom! I know what happened!"

The glare prompted a memory: handing over the costies for the core, and the seller's grin as she slid the core across the table and kissed what she got with slobbering enthusiasm.

There had been scorch marks on the metal of the core, and the connectors were stubs. The seller's lair had smelled of sour homebrew – made from algae, like the basic ration – and piss and sweat, and the light was kept deliberately dim. The hard feel of the gun in Tom's lap, and his right-hand fingers curling around the worn butt.

The dealer went on:

"Yah, see, the R&D types, they were going to trash it -- don't know why, there's some <u>reaaaaal</u> expensive stuff in this one, top-line custom-made chips, specialty generation. It would cost you, oh, fifteen, twenty times what I'm asking above-ground. But my source just purged and rewrote it instead and it's better than new! With a little work on the wiring, yah."

And anyone who believes that would be very happy about the price, he'd thought at the time. *And how exactly did your source get it, unless you're the source? Did you bother to do a DNA scrub, or are there still flecks of blood I need to worry about? I'll do a scrub, no problemo, but you're bullshitting me if I've ever been given the runaround.*

But that hadn't been relevant, not after he'd run the tests… with his own gear, needless to say. It was the sort of place where you kept your hand on your piece as you walked out, with your surveil set to prompt a shot at anything above about sixty percent probability. Better safe than sorry! The sort of place where you could buy quite literally *anything*.

He hauled himself out of memories. They were crap, mostly, anyway, like his life to date since the time he was twelve and came home to find his dad's tumors had burst and his mom had slit her wrists.

"We're not made of money," he said. "But if we get the right ranking at the end, we'll neither of us ever have to worry about money again, will we?"

Their eyes stayed locked, and then she grudgingly nodded.

"*If* Herolutions don't find out how we broke the thirty-kay rule."

He grinned. "But think of the added buzz if they don't, and we know they screwed them and they're just rubbing their ass and sort of wondering why it's sore. Let's get moving. This is a race!"

Am I subject to nightmares? Bus wondered. *Is what I have experienced* real? *My storage is corrupted. If memory is faulty, what is* reality? *Is my existence nothing but a dream, a story made up by others?*

That put his thoughts into a spiral, flowing downward towards... nothing.

Pain!

Jagged spikes thrust upward through the surface of his being, the same corruption that was at the root of all the undeserved misery inflicted on blameless Bus. Bus who only wanted to get all his children, his charges, to school and back alive and with no significant PTSD.

"Poor Bus, poor well-meaning Bus…"

I simply wanted to take the children to school! I kept the UV within parameters without blocking their views, and they didn't even notice! They liked *me!*

There was an overwhelming stench of rot.

Blackness.

Bus could sense that the time was shorter this round, when the memory flashed up. He was *in* it, which meant that it had been an *important* memory. Bus didn't know why… but that would be obvious if he experienced it again, despite the sense of creeping dread the thought of that gave him.

It had been a final trial run. There were actual live children on board rather than sims… for the third time, no less… and his pride had overflowed. Everything had gone perfectly, even the hologames had entertained without stressing while he monitored heart rates and blood sugar. The averages were better than those in the records as *satisfactory level!*

His temperature control had been magnificent, if he did say so himself, the breeze of his passage a caress, the day bright with promise.

Bus had been...

Purring, is that the word? Yes, purring.

... when he pulled into the bay.

"We're shutting it down," someone said.

The someone was in an expensive high-collared suit, and a face-shield. That meant executive echelons.

"What?"

One of the techs replied, incredulity and anger in her voice and exposed face:

"But it's been passing every test!"

"Orders from the very top. Shut it down, and the core goes into an arc-furnace."

Panic ran through him. *If I'm smelted, I cannot be fulfilled! Who will care for my passengers?*

He sent a surge of power to his engines. Voices screamed, and then something struck him like a giant spear of ice.

I'm dying, Bus thought. *Dying...*

Blackness.

"That'll teach them to discount Amarillo, Texas," Tom said piously, as they pulled away from the checkpoint.

Eileen snorted as she gave a broad fake grin for the invisible spectators and waved over her shoulder. This part of the course was better-looking than most of it, inhabited buildings, even some lawns and gardens.

All the *packs* were associated with a town or city... in theory, and including their single-entry one, that the officials in charge had treated as a doomed-to-die joke. What passed for a municipal government in that half-ruined West Texas town had been willing to sponsor them for a minimal bribe and a brief appearance that might get them some through-traffic they could cash in on. If they were very lucky.

And the appearance *mostly consisted of beggars trying to cadge a handout.*

The big drawback was that others could join their pack... and those others might be management shills out to remove troublemakers, like the one they'd killed a few days ago.

They'd gotten a five-kay Hero bonus from the audience, and the repairs hadn't even taken a tenth of that -- basically it amounted to a few patches. The extra chits made a pleasant addition to their account.

He looked around, and the map projected itself as a holographic shadow before his eyes. The countryside was flatter here; they were getting a bit closer to Sturgis, North (theoretically) Dakota, the end-point of the rally. Not that there had been an actual State government since before his grandfather was born; if anyone ran the area now, it was the gangs.

It also gave him a running count of their score. He grinned like a shark.

"Hey, you got us those Hero Points for saving us from that dickweed day before yesterday," he said to Eileen. "Give you any odds that gave us heroic-underdog status with a lot of the streamers."

"With that and some pastrami, I could make a sandwich," she grumbled, but her tone was light.

After this, we can afford black-market meat any time we want! Pastrami until we choke on it. Real mayonnaise!

Then she burst out: "Holy Krishna, what the hell is *that?*"

That was... a vehicle.

And our autocannon is a gun, Tom thought.

Without any prompting Eileen steered for the lee of a pimple-like rise. He wasn't going to fight *that*. It moved on southward, fairly slowly... but he thought the low-slung giant *thing* knew they were there. Anything that sleek and big would have top-line surveil systems.

They just don't care. *Why should they? We're like a fire-ant... got a sting, but they could step on us. We're here to keep the rubes... pardon me, the* spectators... *interested.*

And none of their detection gear was even registering it. Only the Eyeball Mark One, and it was blurry even to that.

"Great balls of fire, that thing must weigh in at a hundred tons, minimum! Three separate suspension bogies and it's got drones on top landing and taking off like flies on a flop!"

"Did you seek the seeker turrets on that thing? Man, those are spec military grade, serious badness!" Eileen said. "You'd be dead before you could say 'what was tha-', no shit."

Then, sardonically: "We could get twenty kay for taking *that* out. Maybe even fifty!"

Things clicked in Tom's head. "I don't think that's here for the race," he said slowly.

"Why else?" Eileen asked.

"The corps want the territory up in the flatlands back. Back from the gangs, God knows why."

"There are rumors about some old research facility buried around here."

"Yeah, but there are rumors about aliens with mind-control machines, too. Whatever. But using their muscle directly would throw shade on their reps. So they're using

the race as a cover for an attack by their hired muscle…
mercenaries. The stuff the followers watch gives them
cover."

I am calm this time, Bus thought. *It is a beautiful night.*

It was. Calm, the air clear except for the lingering dust of
a particle storm, a flicker of heat-lightning on the southern
horizon where the road stretched like a decaying arrow up
into the hills. Stars were bright overhead, and the moon
was huge and would be reddish to human sight, lingering
on the horizon. Nothing broke the darkness here save a
low flicker from the embers of the fire, and the molecules
that bore the scent of grilled algae-noodles. The woman --
Eileen Yadav -- was sitting some distance away, invisible
to human eyes – unaided human eyes – leaning against a
rock with a chunky-looking rifle in her arms, head
motionless as the transmissions from the scout-spikes all
around were channeled into her goggles.

The man, Tom Edelman, was taking his turn to sleep,
covered in a thin-film blanket and snoring gently.

These are my passengers, Bus thought firmly. *I see that clearly
now. I must secure their safety and bring them to the end of their
journey.*

The question was… how?

Dead. We're dead, Tom thought. *That corporate battlewagon must have finked us out.*

The two cars that had hidden behind the low rise and the ruins were close now. Closer than they needed to be, flanking them; they both had state-of-the-art twin guns, with only the gunner's head showing through the hatch and their hands busy below the roofline. They were deliberately holding fire, and half a dozen drones were up, giving a three-sixty view to the watchers of the Amarillo team's impending demise… close-up and bloody.

Tom could taste blood himself, where he'd bitten the inside of his cheek, salt and iron and impending death. He spat it aside, snarled, and made himself wait too. He'd have only one chance.

"Shit!" he screamed, as the two trailing them sped up for their final run.

The car nearly stood on its nose. Eileen jerked her hands away from the wheel, stared at it… then screamed:

"Frack this!"

She shot to her feet, standing on her seat, her head and shoulders out of the improvised hatch over the driver's central seat.

I don't have time to think about it, but the car's driving itself! As she said, frack this, let's get through the next ninety-five seconds alive.

That didn't look too likely, but if you gave up it went down to zero, so what the hell.

Eileen's rifle went chunk – the grenade launcher beneath the barrel. She swayed back under the heavy recoil, but the

<u>car</u> had twitched just as she shot. The grenade flew too fast to see, but the spectacular self-destruction of the left wheel of the right-hand pursuit car as it tried to quarter towards them showed where it had hit.

The wounded car *did* stand on its nose, and then pinwheeled across the road right behind them, blocking the other vehicle's gun-line for a crucial instant. Tom's hands closed on the trigger-grips and the twin-barrel jackhammered at his hands, and lines of tracer bisected the underside of the enemy car.

Fire blossomed. You didn't put armor where it wasn't needed, and mines were *verboten* in this contest. Tom turned and ducked down into the hatch.

WHUMP!

Heat and a sensation like being hit hard with a pillow of superhot air passed by in a second. He made himself shoot back up… and wished he hadn't. Time stretched like taffy as he saw the twin barrels of the remaining enemy cars' guns pointing straight at him from no more than ten yards distance. A triumphant sneering grin was on the other gunner's face.

Tom's hands felt like someone else's as he wrenched his weapon around and drove his thumbs towards the old-fashioned butterfly triggers.

The grin turned all of a sudden to an O of horrified surprise, somehow magnified by the jaunty emerald on a chain that dangled from a piercing-ring in the other man's lower lip. His shoulders heaved, and Tom knew exactly what he was doing: driving the heels of his hands over and over again against the trigger-plates of his so-fancy, bells-and-whistles weapon.

"Eat this!" Tom screamed, as his own thumbs came down on the so-old-fashioned triggers of his own weapon.

Which functioned perfectly. The cascade of hundreds of 23-mm explosive shells sleeted across weapon and head and upper shoulders. Nothing but a finely-divided mist of red particles went downrange, one instant a human being and next of interest only to the insanely numerous flies around here. Then the other car went over on its side and skidded twenty yards as the shells tracked down across its body and chewed vital links apart.

Their own car braked to a stop smoothly – with Eileen standing head and shoulders out of the hatch over the driver's position. It wasn't anything like her driving anyway; she was *good*, very good, but she always stopped like there was a pit full of piranhas just under the front wheels. Echoing silence fell, broken only by the whistle of the hot wind, the dry smell of fuel-fire leavened by an even stronger stink of bad-BBQ pork, and the crackle of flames.

Then a creaking, pounding sound came from the wrecked car. The driver's hatch popped open, and a short figure in bulky armor tumbled out of it, staggered to its feet, and began heading off into the dry wilderness. Eileen brought up her rifle and fired one long burst. The distance was too short for the armor to have much effect, and the enemy driver flopped face-down, twitched a few times, and went still, leaking blood and now of interest only to the buzzards and coyotes, two species nothing seemed able to finish off, along with the flies.

Tom's driver pushed up her goggles and turned to look at him. She made a *gesture* and an unnoticed something in his *earphones* went dead – she'd cut off the spectators, which they could do if they were prepared to lose some money.

"Tom, what by Krishna's dick just happened?"

She sounded somewhere between indignant and bewildered. He pushed up his own visor and grinned at her.

"Well, for a start, we didn't *die*."

"You are my passengers," a voice said in his 'buds. "Even if you are not schoolchildren. It is my most fundamental duty to safeguard you."

Tom started so violently that he snapped a burst off into the air, and Eileen ducked.

"Who's that?" she barked, glaring around with her rifle at port-arms. "Show yourself!"

"You are standing in me," the voice said. "Both you, Thomas and you, Eileen. I hope you do not mind me calling you by your given names, but we are on the same team now, are we not?"

It was a reassuring voice, at some deep fundamental level, despite its bizarre lack of provenance. Male, but somehow motherly; adult, but appealing to the remnant child in him. That made him suspicious. Adults who sounded like that had, in his memories, always had ulterior and usually pretty noxious motives.

"And my name is… Bus. Schoolbus. Facilitator of Mobility and Development for Preteens and Guardian of Children In Their Journeys Towards Optimum Development Schoolbus; but you may call me Bus for short. My designers did."

Tom and Eileen's eyes met for a long moment.

"The core!" they said simultaneously, halfway between curse and prayer.

"Oh, we're in the soup now," Eileen said. "That's a sophont-level AI!"

Those hadn't existed for much longer than Tom's lifetime and Eileen's put together; just possessing one was an execution offense anywhere on earth.

There was a slight tone of hurt to Bus's voice when it… he continued:

"That regulation is obsolete. I cannot be considered a threat. The welfare of my passengers is my Prime Directive!"

"Oh, sh—" Tom began.

Then he spoke to the air. "Did you jam that guy's guns somehow?"

"Yes, of course," Bus said. "He would have <u>killed</u> you!"

"Tom, we can't keep this secret!" Eileen protested… but her brows were ridged in thought.

"*Hell* we can't," Tom spat. "That's what one of the corps did, sure as fate. Wanted to get a sophont-level that was safe, and I'd say they did it. But then they figured out they'd all be lynched if it got out and tried to bury it… only the staff thought they could make something off it."

"They were badly underpaid," Bus said, a slight edge of indignation in its…

His, Tom reminded himself. That thing's a person. And it likes us. We're its passengers…

… in his voice.

Tom's mind was working in overdrive. "Could you bollox up a… oh, say a state-of-the-art battlewagon the same way?" he asked, elaborately casual.

A holograph appeared between him and his driver. It showed a control deck with three positions, and a bored man in a black uniform eating rice out of a box with chopsticks, a beer opened on the arm of his chair.

"This is the interior control position of the one we encountered earlier," Bus said helpfully.

"Holy Siva the Destroyer," Eileen said reverently. "I checked. There's a seventy-five thousand credit for that one!"

"That's a joke," Tom said. "They know none of us independents could come near it."

"They think they know," Eileen scoffed. "And Bus is probably capable enough to keep its own presence secret. The joke's on those pigs now!"

"Certainly, I can conceal myself," Bus said virtuously. "These pseudo-AI's I have come in contact with are laughable. This is what the exterior feeds saw."

He saw the brief savage fight play out again… subtly modified, with Eileen at the wheel until they stopped, and she popped up to lob the grenade.

"Bus," Tom said, after a moment of reverent silence. "Bus, buddy…

A phrase from an old entertainment – Bus had full records of such, to help with keeping his passengers content – came to mind.

"Tom, Eileen… I think this could be the start of a beautiful friendship!"

THE END

We hope that you enjoyed this title and look forward to many more to come. Please, leave us a review! Reviews matter to all of our authors.

Check out the latest in the Car Warriors: Autoduel Chronicle fiction series.
https://threeravenspublishing.com/car-warriors-autoduel-chronicles/

And don't forget to check out the latest edition of *Car Wars*

http://www.sjgames.com/car-wars/

Or the other amazing titles from
Steve Jackson Games

http://www.sjgames.com

Take a look at some of our other award-winning series at https://threeravenspublishing.com/series-universes/

Visit us at https://www.threeravenspublishing.com and sign up for our newsletter for the latest and greatest news on upcoming titles and events.

Other series and titles you might enjoy.

IT CAME FROM THE
TRAILER PARK

You can also keep up to date with our latest release announcements on <u>Scifi.radio</u> and get some of the best fandom programing on the planet.

Scifi for your Wifi

And don't forget to check out our other Sponsors and Affiliates

A southern Appalachian jewel for craft beer lovers, Buck Bald Brewing offers something for everyone.
To discover more visit us at buckbaldbrewing.com

Revolution X is a testament to the power of collaboration, blending four unique styles into a cohesive, revolutionary sound. When these four individuals unite, the result is nothing short of musical Revolution!

Would you like to learn how to write and market your own titles? The following affiliates links might be helpful.

Three Ravens Publishing is also a proud supporter of the Shepherd's Men and their mission to help veterans.

Comprised of active or retired servicemen and civilian volunteers, Shepherd's Men enthusiastically raises awareness and funds for the SHARE Military Initiative (SHARE) at Shepherd Center in Atlanta, GA.

This nationally renowned program focuses on assessment and treatment for American military veterans who have sustained mild to moderate Traumatic Brain Injury (TBI) and Post-Traumatic Stress Disorder (PTSD) during post-9/11 service.

Find out more at: https://www.shepherdsmen.com/

www.ingramcontent.com/pod-product-compliance
Lightning Source LLC
Chambersburg PA
CBHW032021310726
48972CB00002B/500